Praise for Rainbow Rowell

'Reminded me not just what it's like to be young and in love with a girl, but also what it's like to be young and in love with a book' John Green, author of *The Fault in Our Stars*

'Best for a romantic break . . . Rom-com fans will lap it up' *Grazia*

'Ms. Rowell is talented enough to be uncategorizable. So *Landline* belongs to a genre of its very own' *New York Times*

'Rowell's way with dialogue is amazing . . . great on the complexities of adult relationships too, showing how a search for balance can be what love is made of and how a thousand tiny compromises mean more than the grandest romantic gesture' *Emerald Street*

'A funny, touching portrayal of friendship, loneliness and love in the digital age' *Daily Telegraph*

'Heartwarming, romantic and great fun' *Closer*

'An original, quirky but enjoyable book with many likeable characters and a plot that keeps you guessing all the way through' *South Wales Argus*

'Cracking, laugh-out-loud dialogue, characters that feel painfully real, and a sweet premise about love in the information age. If *Attachments* were an e-mail, I'd be forwarding it to my entire list of contacts' Jodi Picoult

'Perfectly mixing sweet romance with deliciously tart wit . . . a complete charmer' *Chicago Tribune*

'Witty, original and easy to relate to, *Attachments* is an absolute pleasure t

Rainbow Rowell lives in Omaha, Nebraska with her husband and two sons.

By Rainbow Rowell

Attachments
Eleanor & Park
Fangirl
Landline

Landline

RAINBOW ROWELL

An Orion paperback

First published in Great Britain in 2014
by Orion Books
This paperback edition published in 2015
by Orion Books,
an imprint of The Orion Publishing Group Ltd,
Carmelite House, 50 Victoria Embankment,
London EC4Y 0DZ

An Hachette UK Company

1 3 5 7 9 10 8 6 4 2

A CIP catalogue record for this book
is available from the British Library.

ISBN 978-1-4091-5212-5

Printed and bound in Great Britain by
Clays Ltd, St Ives plc

The Orion Publishing Group's policy is to use papers that
are natural, renewable and recyclable products and
made from wood grown in sustainable forests. The logging
and manufacturing processes are expected to conform to
the environmental regulations of the country of origin.

www.orionbooks.co.uk

This book is for Kai.

(Everything that matters is.)

ACKNOWLEDGMENTS

If I had a magic phone that called into the past, the first person I'd call would be my dear friend Sue Moon. . . .

And I'd tell her everything I didn't know I needed to tell her until she was gone.

I'd say *thank you*, mostly. For helping me break out of myself—and for showing me that there's no true solace in fear. Every time I finish a book, I remember that Sue promised I would.

Thank you to the many people who help me write books:

My editor, Sara Goodman, who always knows what I'm trying to say. And who understands the power of "Leather and Lace."

And the team at St. Martin's Press, especially Olga Grlic, Jessica Preeg, Stephanie Davis, and Eileen Rothschild—who are so smart and sharp and compassionate that I kind of wish there was a legal way to make sure they never leave me.

Nicola Barr, who writes the best "I just finished your book" letters.

Lynn Safranek, Bethany Gronberg, Lance Koenig and Margaret Willison, my safe houses.

Christopher Schelling, who knows when to demand some sort of pug emergency.

And Rosey and Laddie, whom I love so much it hurts. Literally.

TUESDAY
DECEMBER 17, 2013

CHAPTER 1

Georgie pulled into the driveway, swerving to miss a bike.

Neal never made Alice put it away.

Apparently bicycles never got stolen back in Nebraska —and people never tried to break in to your house. Neal didn't even lock the front door most nights until after Georgie came home, though she'd told him that was like putting a sign in the yard that said PLEASE ROB US AT GUNPOINT. "No," he'd said. "That would be different, I think."

She hauled the bike up onto the porch and opened the (unlocked) door.

The lights were off in the living room, but the TV was still on. Alice had fallen asleep on the couch watching Pink Panther cartoons. Georgie went to turn it off and stumbled over a bowl of milk sitting on the floor. There was a stack of laundry folded on the coffee table—she grabbed whatever was on the top to wipe it up.

When Neal stepped into the archway between the living room and the dining room, Georgie was crouched on the floor, sopping up milk with a pair of her own underwear.

"Sorry," he said. "Alice wanted to put milk out for Noomi."

"It's okay, I wasn't paying attention." Georgie stood up, wadding the wet underwear in her fist. She nodded at Alice. "Is she feeling okay?"

Neal reached out and took the underwear, then picked up the bowl. "She's fine. I told her she could wait up for you. It was this whole *negotiation* over eating her kale and not using the word 'literally' anymore because it's *literally* driving me crazy." He looked back at Georgie on his way to the kitchen. "You hungry?"

"Yeah," she said, following him.

Neal was in a good mood tonight. Usually when Georgie got home this late ... Well, usually when Georgie got home this late, he *wasn't*.

She sat at the breakfast bar, clearing a space for her elbows among the bills and library books and second-grade worksheets.

Neal walked to the stove and turned on a burner. He was wearing pajama pants and a white T-shirt, and he looked like he'd just gotten a haircut—probably for their trip. If Georgie touched the back of his head now, it'd feel like velvet one way and needles the other.

"I wasn't sure what you wanted to pack," he said. "But I washed everything in your hamper. Don't forget that's it's cold there—you always forget that it's cold."

She always ended up stealing Neal's sweaters.

He was in such a good mood tonight. . . .

He smiled as he made up her plate. Stir-fry. Salmon. Kale. Other green things. He crushed a handful of cashews in his fist and sprinkled them on top, then set the plate in front of her.

When Neal smiled, he had dimples like parentheses—stubbly parentheses. Georgie wanted to pull him over the breakfast bar and nose at his cheeks. (That was her standard response to Neal smiling.) (Though Neal probably wouldn't know that.)

"I think I washed all your jeans . . . ," he said, pouring her a glass of wine.

Georgie took a deep breath. She just had to get this over with. "I got good news today."

He leaned back against the counter and raised an eyebrow. "Yeah?"

"Yeah. So . . . Maher Jafari wants our show."

"What's a Maher Jafari?"

"He's the network guy we've been talking to. The one who green-lit *The Lobby* and that new reality show about tobacco farmers."

"Right." Neal nodded. "The network guy. I thought he was giving you the cold shoulder."

"We *thought* he was giving us the cold shoulder," Georgie said. "Apparently he just has cold shoulders."

"Huh. Wow. That is good news. So—" He cocked his head to the side. "—why don't you seem happy?"

"I'm *thrilled,*" Georgie said. Shrilly. *God.* She was probably sweating. "He wants a pilot, scripts. We've got a big meeting to talk casting. . . ."

"That's great," Neal said, waiting. He knew she was burying the lead.

Georgie closed her eyes. ". . . on the twenty-seventh."

The kitchen was quiet. She opened them. Ah, there was the Neal she knew and loved. (Truly. On both counts.) The folded arms, the narrowed eyes, the knots of muscle in both corners of his jaw.

"We're going to be in Omaha on the twenty-seventh," he said.

"I know," she said. "Neal, I *know.*"

"So? Are you planning to fly back to L.A. early?"

"No, I . . . we have to get the scripts ready before then. Seth thought—"

"Seth."

"All we've got done is the pilot," Georgie said. "We've got nine days to write four episodes and get ready for the meeting—it's really lucky that we have some time off from *Jeff'd Up* this week."

"You have time off because it's *Christmas*."

"I know that it's Christmas, Neal—I'm not skipping Christmas."

"You're not?"

"No. Just skipping . . . Omaha. I thought we could all skip Omaha."

"We already have plane tickets."

"Neal. It's a pilot. A *deal*. With our dream network."

Georgie felt like she was reading from a script. She'd already had this entire conversation, almost verbatim, this afternoon with Seth. . . .

"It's Christmas," she'd argued. They were in their office, and Seth was sitting on Georgie's side of the big L-shaped desk they shared. He'd had her cornered.

"Come on, Georgie, we'll still have Christmas—we'll have the best Christmas ever after *the meeting."*

"Tell that to my kids."

"I will. Your kids love me."

"Seth, it's Christmas. *Can't this meeting wait?"*

"We've already been waiting our whole career. This is happening, Georgie. Now. It's finally happening."

Seth wouldn't stop saying her name.

Neal's nostrils were flaring.

"My mom's expecting us," he said.

"I know," Georgie whispered.

"And the kids . . . Alice sent Santa Claus a change-of-address card, so he'd know she'd be in Omaha."

Georgie tried to smile. It was a weak effort. "I think he'll figure it out."

"That's not—" Neal shoved the corkscrew in a drawer, then slammed it shut. His voice dropped. "That's not the point."

"I know." She leaned over her plate. "But we can go see your mom next month."

"And take Alice out of school?"

"If we have to."

Neal had both hands on the counter, clenching the muscles in his forearms. Like he was retroactively bracing himself for bad news. His head was hanging down, and his hair fell away from his forehead.

"This might be our shot," Georgie said. "Our own show."

Neal nodded without lifting his head. "Right," he said. His voice was soft and flat.

Georgie waited.

Sometimes she lost her place when she was arguing with Neal. The argument would shift into something else—into somewhere more dangerous—and Georgie wouldn't even realize it. Sometimes Neal would end the conversation or abandon it while she was still making her point, and she'd just go on arguing long after he'd checked out.

Georgie wasn't sure whether *this* even qualified as an argument. Yet.

So she waited.

Neal hung his head.

"What does 'right' mean?" she finally asked.

He pushed off the counter, all bare arms and square shoulders. "It means that you're *right*. Obviously." He started clearing the stove. "You have to go to this meeting. It's important."

He said it almost lightly. Maybe everything was going to be fine, after all. Maybe he'd even be excited for her. Eventually.

"So," she said, testing the air between them. "We'll see about visiting your mom next month?"

Neal opened the dishwasher and started gathering up dishes. "No."

Georgie pressed her lips together and bit them. "You don't want to take Alice out of school?"

He shook his head.

She watched him load the dishwasher. "This summer, then?"

His head jerked slightly, like something had brushed his ear. Neal had lovely ears. A little too big, and they poked out at the top like wings. Georgie liked to hold his head by his ears. When he'd let her.

She could imagine his head in her hands now. Could feel her thumbs stroking the tops of his ears, her knuckles brushing against his clippered hair.

"No," he said again, standing up straight and wiping his palms on his pajama pants. "We've already got plane tickets."

"Neal, I'm serious. I can't miss this meeting."

"I know," he said, turning toward her. His jaw was set. Permanently.

Back in college, Neal had thought about joining the military; he would have been really good at the part where you have to deliver terrible news or execute a heartbreaking order without betraying how much it was costing you. Neal's face could fly the *Enola Gay*.

"I don't understand," Georgie said.

"You can't miss this meeting," he said. "And we already have plane tickets. You'll be working all week anyway. So you stay here, focus on your show—and we'll go see my mom."

"But it's Christmas. The kids—"

"They can have Christmas again with you when we get back. They'll love that. Two Christmases."

Georgie wasn't sure how to react. Maybe if Neal had been *smiling* when he said that last thing . . .

He motioned at her plate. "Do you want me to heat that back up for you?"

"It's fine," she said.

He nodded his head, minimally, then brushed past her, leaning over just enough to touch his lips to her cheek. Then he was in the living room, lifting Alice up off the couch. Georgie could hear him shushing her—"It's okay, sweetie, I've got you"—and climbing the stairs.

WEDNESDAY
DECEMBER 18, 2013

CHAPTER 2

Georgie's phone was dead.

It was always dead unless it was plugged in—she probably needed a new battery, but she kept forgetting to deal with it.

She set her coffee down at her desk, then plugged the phone into her laptop, shaking it, like a Polaroid picture, while she waited for it to wake up.

A grape flew between her nose and the screen.

"So?" Seth asked.

Georgie lifted her head, looking at him properly for the first time since she got to work. He was wearing a pink oxford with a green knit vest, and his hair was especially swoopy today. Seth looked like a handsome Kennedy cousin. Like one who didn't inherit the teeth.

"So what?" she said.

"So, how'd it go?"

He meant with Neal. But he wouldn't *say* "with Neal"—because that's how they all got by. There were rules.

Georgie looked back down at her phone. No missed calls. "Fine."

"I told you it'd be fine."

"Well, you were right."

"I'm always right," Seth said.

Georgie could hear him sitting back in his chair. She

could picture him, too—long legs kicked up, resting on the edge of their shared desk.

"You are very occasionally, eventually, partially right," she said, still fiddling with her phone.

Neal and the girls were probably already on their second flight by now. They'd had a short layover in Denver. Georgie thought about sending them a text—*love you guys*—and imagined it landing in Omaha before they did.

But Neal never sent text messages, so he never checked them; it was like texting a void.

She put down the phone and pushed her glasses into her hair, trying to focus on her computer. She had a dozen new e-mails, all from Jeff German, the comedian who was the star of their show.

Georgie would not miss Jeff German if this new deal went through. She wouldn't miss his e-mails. Or his red ball cap. Or the way he made her rewrite entire episodes of *Jeff'd Up* if he thought the actors who played his TV family were getting too many laughs.

"I can't take this." The door swung open, and Scotty slunk in. There was just enough room in Seth and Georgie's office for one other chair—an uncomfortable hammocky thing from IKEA. Scotty fell onto it sideways, holding his head. "I can't. I'm terrible with secrets."

"Good morning," Georgie said.

Scotty peeked through his fingers. "Hey, Georgie. The girl out front said to tell you that your mom's on the phone. Line two."

"Her name is Pamela."

"Okay. My mom's name is Dixie."

"No, the new PA, her name . . ." Georgie shook her head and reached for the black desk phone that sat between her and Seth. "This is Georgie."

Her mom sighed. "I've been on hold so long, I thought that girl forgot about me."

"Nope. What's up?"

"I just called to see how you were doing." Her mom sounded concerned. (Her mom liked to sound concerned.)

"I'm fine," Georgie said.

"Well . . ." Another sigh. A fortified sigh. "I talked to Neal this morning."

"How'd you manage that?"

"I set my alarm. I knew you guys were leaving early—I wanted to say good-bye."

Her mom always made a big deal about plane trips. And minor surgery. And sometimes just getting off the phone. *"You never know when it's going to be the last time you see somebody, and you don't want to miss your chance to say good-bye."*

Georgie propped the phone between her ear and shoulder, so she could type. "That was nice of you. Did you get to talk to the girls?"

"I talked to *Neal,*" her mom said again. For emphasis. "He told me you guys are spending some time apart."

"Mom," Georgie said, bringing her hand back to the receiver. "Only the week."

"He said you were splitting up for Christmas."

"Not like that—why're you making it sound like that? Something just came up for me at work."

"You've never had to work on Christmas before."

"I don't have to work *on* Christmas. I have to work around Christmas. It's complicated." Georgie resisted checking to see if Seth was listening. "It was my decision."

"You *decided* to be alone on Christmas."

"I won't be alone. I'll be with you."

"But, honey, we're spending the day with Kendrick's family—I told you that—and your sister's going to her dad's. I mean, you're welcome to come to San Diego with us. . . ."

"Never mind, I'll figure it out." Georgie glanced around the room. Seth was throwing grapes in the air and catching them in his mouth. Scotty was sprawled out miserably, like he had menstrual cramps. "I have to get back to work."

"Well, come over tonight," her mom said. "I'll make dinner."

"I'm fine, Mom, really."

"Come over, Georgie. You shouldn't be alone right now."

"There's no 'right now,' Mom. I'm fine."

"It's Christmas."

"Not yet."

"I'll make dinner—come." She hung up before Georgie could argue any more.

Georgie sighed and rubbed her eyes. Her eyelids felt greasy. Her hands smelled like coffee.

"I can't do this," Scotty moaned. "Everyone can tell I have a secret."

Seth glanced up at the door—it was closed. "So? As long as they don't know what the secret *is* . . ."

"I don't like it," Scotty said. "I feel like such a traitor. I'm Lando on Cloud City. I'm that guy who kissed Jesus."

Georgie wondered if any of the other writers actually *did* suspect something. Probably not. Georgie and Seth's contract was up soon, but everybody assumed they were staying. Why would they leave *Jeff'd Up* after finally dragging it into the top ten?

If they stayed, they'd get raises. Giant, life-changing raises. The sort of money that made Seth's eyeballs pop out like Scrooge McDuck whenever he talked about it.

But if they left . . .

They'd only leave *Jeff'd Up* now for one reason. To start their own show. The show Georgie and Seth had been dreaming about practically since they met—they'd written the first draft of the pilot together when they were still in college. Their own show, their own characters. No more Jeff German. No more catchphrases. No more laugh track.

They'd take Scotty with them if they left. *(When* they left, Seth would say. *When, when, when.)* Scotty was theirs; Georgie had hired him two shows back, and he was the best gag writer they'd worked with.

Seth and Georgie were better at writing *situations*. Weirdness that twisted into more weirdness, jokes that built and built, and finally paid off big after eight episodes. But sometimes you just needed somebody to slip on a banana peel. Scotty never ran out of banana peels.

"Nobody knows you have a secret," Seth told him. "Nobody cares. They're all just trying to get their shit done so they can get out of here for Christmas."

"So what's the plan, then?" Scotty propped himself up in the chair. He was a smallish Indian guy, with shaggy hair and glasses, and he dressed like almost everybody else on the writing staff—in jeans, a hooded sweatshirt, and stupid-looking flip-flops. Scotty was the only gay person on their staff. Sometimes people thought Seth was gay, but he wasn't. Just pretty.

Seth threw a grape at Scotty. Then another one at Georgie. She ducked.

"The plan," Seth said, "is we come in tomorrow as usual, and we write. And then we write some more."

Scotty picked his grape up off the floor and ate it. "I just hate to abandon everybody. Why do we always move as soon as I make friends?" He shifted to sulk in Georgie's direction. "Hey. Georgie. Are you okay? You look weird."

Georgie realized she was staring. And not at either of them. "Yeah," she said. "Fine."

She picked up her phone again and thumbed out a text.

Maybe . . .

Maybe she should have talked to Neal this morning before he left. *Really* talked to him. Made sure everything was okay.

But by the time Neal's alarm went off at four thirty, he was already out of bed and mostly dressed. Neal still used an old Dream Machine clock radio, and when he came over to the bed to turn it off, he told Georgie to go back to sleep.

"You'll be a wreck later," he said when she sat up anyway.

Like Georgie was going to sleep through telling the girls good-bye. Like they weren't all going to be apart for a week. Like it wasn't Christmas.

She reached for the pair of glasses hooked over their headboard and put them on. "I'm taking you to the airport," she said.

Neal was standing outside his closet with his back to her, pulling a blue sweater down over his shoulders. "I already called for a car."

Maybe Georgie should have argued then. Instead she got up and tried to help with the girls.

There wasn't much to do. Neal had put them to bed in sweatpants and T-shirts, so he could carry them out to the car this morning without waking them.

But Georgie wanted to talk to them, and anyway, Alice woke up while Georgie was trying to slide on her pink Mary Janes.

"Daddy said I could wear my boots," Alice croaked.

"Where are they?" Georgie whispered.

"Daddy knows."

They woke Noomi up, looking for them.

Then Noomi wanted *her* boots.

Then Georgie offered to get them yogurt, but Neal said they'd eat at the airport; he'd packed snacks.

He let Georgie explain why she wasn't getting on the plane with them—"Are you driving instead?" Alice asked—while he ran up and down the stairs, and in and out the front door, double-checking things and rounding up bags.

Georgie tried to tell the girls that they'd be having such a good time, they'd hardly miss her—and that they'd all celebrate together next week. "We'll have two Christmases," Georgie said.

"I don't think that's actually possible," Alice argued.

Noomi started crying because her sock was turned the wrong way around her toes. Georgie couldn't tell if she wanted it seam-on-the-bottom or seam-on-top. Neal came in from the garage and whipped off Noomi's boot to fix it. "Car's here," he said.

It was a minivan. Georgie herded the girls out the door, then knelt down next to the curb in her pajama pants, kissing both their faces all over and trying to act like saying good-bye to them wasn't that big of a deal.

"You're the best mommy in the world," Noomi said. Everything was "the best" and "the worst" with Noomi. Everything was "never" and "always."

"And you are the best four-year-old girl in the world," Georgie said, smashing her nose with a kiss.

"Kitty," Noomi said. She was still tearful from the sock problem.

"You are the best kitty in the world." Georgie tucked Noomi's wispy yellow-brown hair behind her ears and pulled her T-shirt smooth over her belly.

"Green kitty."

"The best green kitty."

"Meow," Noomi said.

"Meow," Georgie answered.

"Mom?" Alice asked.

"Yeah?" Georgie pulled the seven-year-old closer— "Here, give me all your hugs"—but Alice was too busy thinking to hug back.

"If Santa brings your presents to Grandma's house, I'll save them for you. I'll put them in my suitcase."

"Santa doesn't usually bring Mommy presents."

"Well, but *if* he does . . ."

"Meow," Noomi said.

"Okay," Georgie agreed, holding Alice in her left arm and scooping Noomi close with her right, "if he brings me presents, you take care of them for me."

"Mommy, meow!"

"Meow," Georgie said, squeezing them both.

"Mom?"

"Yes, Alice."

"The true meaning of Christmas isn't presents anyway, it's Jesus. But not for us, because we're not religious. The true meaning of Christmas for us is just family."

Georgie kissed her cheek. "That's true."

"I know."

"Okay. I love you. I love you both so much."

"To the moon and back?" Alice asked.

"Oh my God," Georgie said, "so much farther."

"To the moon and back infinity?"

"Meow!"

"Meow," Georgie said. "Infinity times infinity. I love you so much, it hurts."

Noomi's face fell. "It hurts?"

"She doesn't mean it *literally*," Alice said. "Right, Mom? Not *literally*?"

"No. Well. Sometimes."

Neal stepped forward. "Okay. Time to catch a plane."

Georgie stole half a dozen more kisses while she buckled the girls into their car seats, then stood by the side of the van with her arms folded nervously across her chest.

Neal stepped up to her and looked over her shoulder, like he was thinking. "We land at five," he said, "Central time. So it'll be around three here. . . . I'll call you when we get to my mom's."

Georgie nodded, but he still wasn't looking at her.

"Be safe," she said.

He checked his watch. "We'll be fine—don't worry about us. Just do what you have to do. Rock your meeting." And then he was hugging her, sort of, an arm around her shoulder, his mouth bumping against hers. By the time he said, "Love you," he was already pulling away.

Georgie wanted to catch him by the shoulders.

She wanted to hug him until her feet left the ground.

She wanted to tuck her head into his neck and feel his arms a little too hard around her ribs.

"Love you," she said. She wasn't sure if he heard her.

"I love you!" she shouted at the girls, knocking on the backseat window and kissing it because she knew it made them laugh; the back windows of their Prius were covered in kiss smears.

They were waving at her like crazy. Georgie stepped away from the van, waving with both hands. Neal was in the front seat talking to the driver.

She thought he might have looked back at her once, before the van turned the corner—her hands froze in the air.

And then they were gone.

CHAPTER 3

"Do you need some help?"

Georgie blinked.

Seth was standing beside her. Tapping the top of her head with a folder. Jeff German wanted an episode rewritten before the writers all left for the holidays—and it was mostly Georgie's job to finish it. (Because she didn't trust anyone else to help.) (Which was her own issue. And not something she should be irritated about.)

The whole afternoon had been a blur of noise and food and Christmas carols. For some reason—well, for alcoholic reasons—everyone had decided to sing Christmas songs from two to three thirty. Then somebody, maybe Scotty, had tried to slide a shrimp tray under her office door. Now it was six, and quiet, and Georgie was finally making progress on the script change.

"No," she told Seth. "I've got it."

"You sure?"

She didn't look up from her screen. "Yep."

He settled against the desk, her side of the desk, next to her keyboard. "So . . ."

"So what?"

"So," he said, "they went to Omaha."

Georgie shook her head, even though the answer was yes. "It made sense. We already had the plane tickets, and I'm going to be working all week anyway."

"Yeah, but . . ." Seth nudged her arm with his leg. Georgie looked up. "What're you gonna do on Christmas?"

"I'll go to my mom's." It was only sort of a lie. She could still go. Even if her mom wasn't home.

"You could come to *my* mom's."

"I would," Georgie said. "If I didn't have my own."

"Maybe I'll go to your mom's, too." Seth grinned. "She loves me."

"That's not much of a character reference."

"You know, she called here three times this morning before you got in. She thinks you let your phone die on purpose. To avoid her."

Georgie turned back to her screen. "I should."

Seth stood up and slung his leather messenger bag over his shoulder. It was going to take Georgie another hour to rewrite this scene. Maybe she should just start over. . . .

"Hey. Georgie."

She kept typing. "Yeah."

"Georgie."

She looked up one more time. He was standing at the door, studying her. "We're so close," he said. "It's finally happening."

Georgie nodded and tried to smile. It was another weak effort.

"Tomorrow," Seth said, then thumped the doorframe with his palm and walked away.

Georgie was on her way home when her sister called.

"We ate without you," Heather said.

"What?"

"It's nine o'clock. We were hungry."

Right. Dinner. "That's okay," Georgie said. "Tell Mom I'll call tomorrow."

"She still wants you to come over tonight. She says your marriage is over, and you need our support."

Georgie wanted to close her eyes, but she was driving. "My marriage isn't over, Heather, and I don't need your support."

"So Neal didn't leave you and take the kids to Nebraska?"

"He took them to see their *grandmother*," Georgie said. "It's not like he's fighting me for custody."

"Neal would totally get custody, don't you think?"

He totally would, Georgie thought.

"You should come over," Heather said. "Mom made tuna mac."

"Did she put peas in it?"

"Nope."

Georgie thought about her empty house in Calabasas. And the empty suitcase sitting next to the closet. Her empty bed.

"Fine," she said.

"Do you have an iPhone charger?" Georgie dropped her keys and her phone on the kitchen counter. She never carried a purse anymore; she kept her driver's license and a credit card out in the car, shoved in the glove compartment.

"I would if you bought me an iPhone." Heather was leaning on the counter, eating tuna mac out of a glass storage container.

"I thought you already ate," Georgie said.

"Don't talk to me like that. You'll give me an eating disorder."

Georgie rolled her eyes. "Nobody in our family gets eating disorders. Stop eating my dinner."

Heather took another giant bite, then handed Georgie the container.

Heather was eighteen, a change-of-life baby—meaning, Georgie's mom had decided to change her life by sleeping with the chiropractor she worked for, and accidentally got pregnant at thirty-nine. Her mom and the chiropractor were married just long enough for Heather to be born.

Georgie was already in college by then, so she and Heather only lived in the same house for a year or two. Sometimes Georgie felt more like Heather's aunt than her big sister.

They looked enough alike to be twins.

Heather had Georgie's wavy, browny-blond hair. And Georgie's washed-out blue eyes. And she was built like Georgie was in high school, like a squashed hourglass. Though Heather was a little taller than Georgie. . . .

That was lucky for her. Maybe someday, when Heather got pregnant, the babies wouldn't beat out her waist like a Caribbean steel drum. *"It's those C-sections,"* Georgie's mom would say. As if Georgie had chosen to have two C-sections, as if she'd ordered them off the menu out of sheer laziness. *"I had you girls the natural way, and my body bounced right back."*

"Why are you staring at my stomach?" Heather asked.

"Still trying to give you an eating disorder," Georgie said.

"Georgie!" Her mom walked into the room, holding a small but very pregnant pug up to her chest. Georgie's stepdad, Kendrick—a tall African-American guy, still in his dusty construction clothes—wasn't far behind. "I didn't hear you come in," her mom said.

"I just got here."

"Let me heat that up for you." Her mom took the tuna casserole and handed Georgie the dog. Georgie held it away from her body; she hated touching it—and she didn't care if that made her the villain in a romantic comedy.

Kendrick leaned over and took the dog from her. "How're you doing, Georgie?" His face was entirely too gentle. It made her want to shout, *"My husband didn't leave me!"*

But Kendrick didn't deserve that. He was the best shockingly young stepdad a girl could ask for. (Kendrick was forty, only three years older than Georgie. Her mom met him when he came to clean their pathetic excuse for a pool.) (These things actually happen.) (In the Valley.)

"I'm fine, Kendrick. Thanks."

Her mom shook her head sadly at the microwave.

"Really," Georgie said to the whole room. "I'm better than fine. I'm staying in town for Christmas because our show is really, really close to getting a green light."

"Your show?" her mom asked. "Is your show in trouble?"

"No. Not *Jeff'd Up. Our* show—*Passing Time.*"

"I can't watch your show," her mom said. "That boy is so disrespectful."

"Trev?" Heather asked. "Everybody loves Trev."

Trev was the middle son on *Jeff'd Up.* He was Georgie's special creation—a slack-faced, twelve-year-old misanthrope, a character who didn't like anything and never did anything likable.

Trev was where Georgie buried all her resentment. For Jeff German, for the network, for Trev himself. For the fact that she was working on a show that was basically

Home Improvement without anything good—without Jonathan Taylor Thomas and Wilson.

Trev was also the breakout star of the show.

Georgie narrowed her eyes at her sister. "You love Trev?"

"God, not me," Heather said. "But everybody. The thugs at school all wear 'This sucks' T-shirts. Like, not the intimidating, cool thugs—the depressing, homely thugs who listen to Insane Clown Posse."

"It's not 'This sucks,'" Kendrick said helpfully. "It's more like *'This suuuuuuucks.'*"

Heather laughed. "Oh my God, Dad, you sound just like him."

"This suuuuuucks," Kendrick said again.

"This sucks" was Trev's catchphrase. Georgie took off her glasses and rubbed her eyes.

Her mom shook her head and set a plate of tuna mac on the table, then took the dog back from Kendrick, rubbing her face into its damp gray muzzle. *"Did you think I forgot about you?"* she cooed. *"I didn't forget about you, little mama."*

"Thanks," Georgie said, sitting down at the table and pulling the plate of tuna mac toward her.

Kendrick patted her shoulder. "I like Trev. Is your new show going to be more like that?"

"Not exactly," she said, frowning.

It still made her uncomfortable when Kendrick tried to be fatherly with her. He was only three years older. *"You're not my dad,"* she sometimes wanted to say. Like she was twelve years old. (When Georgie was twelve, Kendrick was fifteen. She might have flirted with him at the mall.)

"Passing Time," Heather said in a smooth voice, pulling a pizza box out of the refrigerator, "is an hour-long dramedy. It's something plus something plus something else."

Georgie threw her sister an appreciative smile. At least someone listened to her.

"It's *Square Pegs,*" Georgie said, "plus *My So-Called Life,* plus *Arrested Development.*"

If Seth were here, he'd add, *"Plus some show that people actually watched."*

And then Scotty would say, *"Plus* The Cosby Show*!"*

And then Georgie would say, *"Minus the Cosbys,"* and feel bad that their pilot didn't have more diversity. (She'd bring that up with Seth tomorrow. . . .)

Passing Time was a show that captured all the angst of high school life—all the highs and lows, all the absurdities—and then made them higher and lower and more absurd.

That's how they'd pitched it, anyway. That's how Georgie had pitched it to Maher Jafari last month. She'd been on fire in that meeting. She'd hit every note.

She and Seth had gone straight from Jafari's office to the bar across the street, and Seth had stood on his barstool to toast Georgie, flicking Canadian Club down on her head like holy water.

"You are fucking magic, Georgie McCool. That was a Streisandic performance in there. You had him laughing through his fucking tears, did you see that?"

Then Seth had started stomping his feet on the barstool, and Georgie'd grabbed on to his bare ankles—*"Stop, you'll fall."*

"You," he'd said, craning his head down and holding his drink up, *"are my secret weapon."*

Heather leaned against Georgie's chair now, gesturing with a piece of cold pizza. "*Passing Time* is already my favorite show," she said, "and I'm part of a very desirable demographic."

Georgie swallowed the bite of tuna mac that was sitting at the back of her throat. "Thanks, kid."

"Have you talked to the girls today?" her mom asked. She was holding the pug right up against her face, scratching between its ears with her chin. The pug's watery eyes bulged with every pull.

Georgie grimaced and looked away. "No," she said. "I was just about to call."

"What's the time difference?" Kendrick asked. "Isn't it almost midnight there?"

"Oh God." Georgie dropped her fork. "You're right." Her cell phone was dead, so she walked over to the brown Trimline that was still stuck to the kitchen wall.

Heather and Kendrick and her mom and the dog were all watching her. Another dog shuffled into the kitchen, its toenails clicking against the tile, and looked up.

"Is there still a phone in my room?" Georgie asked.

"I think so," her mom said. "Check the closet."

"Great. I'll just . . ." Georgie rushed out of the kitchen and down the hall.

Her mom had turned Georgie's childhood bedroom into the pug trophy room as soon as she graduated from high school—which was irritating because Georgie didn't actually move out of the house until she graduated from college.

"*Where else am I supposed to display their ribbons?*" her mom had said when Georgie objected. "*They're award-*

winning dogs. You've got one foot out the door anyway."

"Not currently. Currently, I have both feet on my bed."

"Take off your shoes, Georgie. This isn't a barn."

Georgie's old bed was still in the room. So was her night table, a lamp, and some books she'd never gotten around to packing up. She opened the closet and dug through a pile of leftover junk until she found an antique, yellow rotary phone; she'd bought it herself at a garage sale back in high school—because she'd been exactly that kind of pretentious.

Christ, it was heavy. She untangled the cord and crawled halfway under the bed to plug it in. (She'd forgotten the way that felt—the way the outlet bit down on the end of the cord with a *click*.) Then she climbed up on the bed and settled the phone in her lap, taking a deep breath before she picked up the receiver.

She tried Neal's cell phone first, but the call didn't go through—their network sucked in Omaha. So she dialed his mom's home number from memory. . . .

Georgie and Neal had spent one summer apart—junior year, right after they started dating. She'd called him in Omaha every night that summer. From this room, actually, on this yellow telephone.

There were fewer dog portraits on the walls back then, but still enough to make Georgie feel like she needed to hide under the blankets when she stayed up late talking dirty to Neal. (You wouldn't expect Neal to be filthy on the phone; normally he didn't even swear. But it'd been a long summer.)

His mom answered after four rings. "Hello?"

"Hey, Margaret, hi. I know it's late, sorry, I always forget about time zones—is Neal still up?"

"Georgie?"

"Oh, sorry. Yeah, it's me—Georgie."

Neal's mom paused. "Just a minute, I'll see."

Georgie waited, feeling nervous for some reason. Like she was calling some guy she liked when she was fourteen. Not the guy she'd been married to for fourteen years.

"Hello?" Neal sounded like he'd been asleep. His voice was rough.

She sat up straighter. "Hey."

"Georgie."

"Yeah . . . *Hey.*"

"It's really late here."

"I know, I always forget, I'm sorry. Time zones."

"I—" He made a frustrated huffing noise. "—I guess I didn't expect you to call."

"Oh. Well. I just wanted to make sure you got in okay."

"I got in fine," he said.

"Good."

"Yeah . . ."

"How's your mom?" she asked.

"She's fine—they're both fine, everybody's fine. Look, Georgie, it's late."

"Right. Neal, I'm sorry—I'll call you tomorrow."

"You will?"

"Yeah. I mean, I'll call *earlier* tomorrow. I just, um . . ."

He huffed again. "Fine." And then he hung up.

Georgie sat there for a second, holding the dead receiver against her ear.

Neal had hung up on her.

She hadn't even had a chance to ask about the girls.

And she hadn't gotten to say "I love you"—Georgie always said "I love you," and Neal always said it back, no matter how perfunctory it was. It was a safety check, proof that they were both still in this thing.

Maybe Neal was upset with her.

Obviously he was upset with her, he was always upset with her—but maybe he was more upset than she thought.

Maybe.

Or maybe he was just tired. He'd been up since four.

Georgie had been up since four thirty. Suddenly she felt tired, too. She thought about getting back in the car and driving out to Calabasas, to an empty house where nobody was waiting up for her. . . .

Then kicked off her shoes and climbed under her old bedspread, clapping twice to turn off the light. She could still see fifty pairs of mournful pug eyes flashing in the dark.

She'd call Neal tomorrow.

She'd start with "I love you."

THURSDAY
DECEMBER 19, 2013

CHAPTER 4

There was a Post-it note from Pamela (the front-desk girl) on Georgie's office door. She must have missed it when she left last night.

Your husband called while you were talking to Mr. German. He said to tell you they landed and to call when you can.

Georgie'd already tried to call Neal twice that morning on the way to work—she wanted something to replace their last stilted conversation in her head—but he hadn't picked up.

Which wasn't that unusual. Neal often left his phone downstairs or in the car, or he forgot to turn his ringer on. He never *purposely* ignored Georgie's calls. Never so far.

She hadn't left him a message—she kept freezing up. But at least Neal would see that she'd called. That was something.

He'd sounded so off last night. . . .

Clearly Georgie had woken him up. But it was more than that. The way that he'd said his mom was fine—*"they're both fine"*—for a second, Georgie thought maybe he was talking about his dad.

Neal's dad had died three years ago. He was a railroad yardman, and he had a heart attack at work. When the call came that day from his mom, Neal had gone into their bedroom without saying a word. It was only the second time Georgie had seen him cry.

Maybe Neal was disoriented last night, waking up in his parents' house, sleeping in his old room. All the memories of his dad . . .

Or maybe he'd just meant Alice and Noomi. *"She's fine. They're both fine. Everybody's fine."*

Georgie set her coffee on her desk and plugged in her phone.

Seth was watching her. "Are you about to start your period?"

That should probably be an offensive workplace question, but it wasn't. You can't work with someone every day of your adult life and never talk to him about your PMS.

Or maybe you could, but Georgie was glad she didn't have to. "No." She shook her head at Seth. "I'm fine."

"You don't look fine," he said. "Are those your clothes from yesterday?"

Jeans. One of Neal's old Metallica concert T-shirts. A cardigan.

"We should work in the big room," she said, "with the whiteboards."

"Those *are* your clothes from yesterday," Seth said, "and they were sad enough yesterday."

Georgie exhaled. "I spent the night at my mom's house, okay? You're lucky I showered." She'd used Heather's shower, and Heather's shampoo. And now she smelled like frosting.

"You spent the night at your mom's house? Were you too drunk to drive?"

"Too tired," she said.

He narrowed his eyes. "You still look tired."

Georgie frowned back at him; Seth looked pristine, of course. Gingham shirt, tan pants cuffed high over his bare ankles, suede saddle shoes. He looked like he'd just stepped out of a Banana Republic. Or what Georgie imagined that might look like—it'd been years since she was actually inside a Banana Republic. She did all her shopping online now, and only when things got desperate.

Seth, however, had never let himself go. If anything, he'd tightened his grip. He looked like he hadn't aged a day since 1994, since the first day he and Georgie met.

The first time she'd seen Seth, he was sitting on a pretty girl's desk, playing with her hair. Georgie had been excited just to see another girl in *The Spoon* offices.

She found out later that the girl only came in on Wednesdays to sell ads. *"Girls aren't usually into comedy,"* Seth explained. Which was better than what a lot of the other guys on staff said: "Girls aren't funny." (After working at the college humor magazine for four years, Georgie eventually convinced a few of them to add, "Present company excluded.")

She'd chosen the University of Los Angeles because of *The Spoon*. Well, and also because of the theater program, and because ULA was close enough to her mom's house that Georgie could still live at home.

But *The Spoon* was the main thing. It was Georgie's thing.

She'd started reading it in the ninth grade; she used to save back issues and stick the front pages up on her bedroom wall. Everyone said *The Spoon* was *The Harvard Lampoon* of the West Coast—lighter, better-looking. Some of her favorite comedy writers had gotten their start there.

Georgie had shown up at *The Spoon* offices, a rumpus room/computer lab in the basement of the student union, the first week of her freshman year, willing to do anything—willing to make coffee or proofread the personal ads—but *wanting,* so badly, to write.

Seth was the first person she met there. He was a sophomore and already an editor, and initially he was the only guy on staff who'd make eye contact with Georgie at editorial meetings.

But that was because he was Seth, and because she was a girl.

Seth's chief pastime back then was paying attention to girls. (Another thing that hadn't changed.) Lucky for him, then and now, girls usually paid attention back.

Seth was shiny and handsome—tall, with brown eyes and thick auburn hair—and he dressed like he belonged on the cover of an early Beach Boys album.

Georgie got used to Seth's madras shirts and khaki pants.

She got used to *Seth*. Always sitting on her desk or falling onto the couch next to her. She got used to always having his attention at *The Spoon*—because she was almost always the only girl in the room.

And because they were a good team.

That was pretty obvious, almost immediately. Georgie and Seth laughed at all the same jokes, and they were funnier together—as soon as one of them walked into a room, the other started putting on a show.

That's when Seth had started calling Georgie his secret weapon. The other guys on staff at *The Spoon* were so busy ignoring her, they mostly missed how funny she was.

"Nobody cares who writes their favorite sitcoms," Seth

would say. *"Nobody cares if it's a cool guy with little wire-rimmed glasses."* (It was the '90s.) *"Or a cute girl with yellow hair."* (That was Georgie.) *"Stick with me, Georgie, and nobody'll see us coming."*

She did.

After graduation, she'd stuck with Seth through five half-hour sitcoms, each one a little less terrible than the last.

And now they finally had a hit, a huge hit—*Jeff'd Up*—and who cared if it was terrible? (Who cared, besides Georgie. And Seth. And the rest of the bitter, disillusioned writing staff.) Because it was a *hit,* and it was theirs.

And it would all be worth it if this deal went through.

Seth had been ecstatic ever since they got the call from Maher Jafari's office. They'd thought, even after their triumphant pitch meeting, that Jafari was going to pass on *Passing Time*. On them. He'd sent them a weird note that seemed like a rejection. But then, two days ago, he'd called to say that the network needed a midseason replacement. Something they could turn pretty quickly. And pretty cheap. "I've got a feeling about this one," Jafari had said. "Can you make it happen in a week?"

Seth had promised to make *everything* happen in a week. "We can make it happen by *last* week," he said.

Then he'd climbed up on his desk chair to dance again. "This is our *Sopranos,* Georgie, it's our *Mad Men.*"

"Get down," she'd said. "Everyone's going to think you're drunk."

"I may as well be," he said, "because I'm *about* to get drunk. And time is an illusion."

"You're a *de*lusion. We can't write four scripts before Christmas."

Seth didn't stop dancing. He pumped his chin and did a little lasso move over his head. "We've got till the twenty-seventh. That's ten whole days."

"Ten days during which I'll be in Omaha, Nebraska, celebrating Christmas."

"Fuck Omaha. Christmas came early."

"Stop dancing, Seth. Talk to me."

He'd stopped dancing and frowned at her. "Are you hearing me? *Maher Jafari wants our show.* Our show, remember? The one we were put on this earth to write?"

"Do you think anybody actually gets put on earth to write TV comedy?"

"Yes," Seth said. "Us."

He'd been irrepressible ever since—even when Georgie was arguing with him, even when she was ignoring him. Seth wouldn't stop smiling. He wouldn't stop *humming,* which should probably annoy her. But Georgie was used to that, too.

She looked back up at him now to ask about a *Jeff'd Up* deadline. . . .

And ended up just looking at him.

He was grinning to himself and typing an e-mail with his index fingers, just to be silly. His eyebrows were dancing.

She sighed.

They were supposed to end up together, Seth and Georgie.

Well, technically, they *had* ended up together. They'd talked every day since that first day they met.

But they were supposed to end up *together*-together. Everyone thought it would happen—Georgie had thought it would happen.

Just as soon as Seth exhausted his other possibilities, as soon as he worked through his queue of admirers. He hadn't been in any hurry, and Georgie didn't have a say in the matter. She'd taken a number. She was waiting patiently.

And then, one day, she wasn't.

After Seth headed down to the writers' room, Georgie decided to try calling Neal again.

He picked up after three rings. "Hello?"

No. It wasn't Neal. "Alice? Is that you?"

"Yes."

"It's Mommy."

"I know. Your song played when the phone rang."

"What's my song?"

Alice started singing "Good Day Sunshine."

Georgie bit her lip. "That's my song?"

"Yep."

"That's a good song."

"Yep."

"Hey," Georgie said, "where's Daddy?"

"Outside."

"Outside?"

"He's shoveling the snow," Alice said. "There's *snow* here. We're gonna have a white Christmas."

"That's lucky. Did you have a good plane trip?"

"Uh-huh."

"What was the best part? . . . Alice?" The girls liked answering the phone—and they loved calling people—but they always lost interest once they were on the line. "*Alice*. Are you watching TV?"

"Uh-huh."

"Pause it and talk to Mommy."

"I can't. Grandma doesn't have pause."

"Then turn it off for a minute."

"I don't know how."

"Okay, just . . ." Georgie tried not to sound irritated. "I really miss you."

"I miss you, too."

"I love you guys . . . Alice?"

"Yeah?"

"Let me talk to Noomi."

There was some shuffling, then a thump like somebody had dropped the phone—then finally, "Meow?"

"Noomi? It's Mommy."

"Meow."

"Meow. What are you doing?"

"We're watching Chip 'n' Dale."

"Was Grandma happy to see you?"

"She said we could watch Chip 'n' Dale."

"Okay. I love you."

"You're the best mommy in the world!"

"Thanks. Hey, Noomi, tell Daddy I called. Okay?"

"Meow."

"Meow. Tell Daddy, okay?"

"Meow!"

"Meow." Georgie ended the call, then fidgeted with her phone for a minute, flipping through a few photos of the girls. She hated talking to them on the phone; it made them feel farther away. And it made her feel helpless. Like, even if she heard something bad happening, there'd be nothing she could do to stop it. One time Georgie had called home from the freeway, and all she could do was listen while Alice dropped the phone in her cereal bowl, then tried to decide whether to pick it up.

Plus . . . the girls' voices were higher on the phone. They sounded younger, and Georgie could hear their every breath. It just always made her realize that she was missing them. Actually missing them. That they kept on growing and changing when she wasn't there.

If Georgie didn't talk to her kids all day, it was easier to pretend like their whole world froze in place while she was at work.

She called them every day. Usually twice.

Georgie and Seth and Scotty worked on *Passing Time* long after dark. They worked until Scotty fell asleep with his head tipped back over the edge of his chair, his mouth hanging open. Seth wanted to leave him like that. "At least we know he'll be here on time tomorrow."

But Georgie took pity on him. She poured three packets of Sweet'N Low into Scotty's mouth, and he woke up sneezing. Then she made him drink half a can of flat Diet Coke to perk him up before he drove home.

She and Seth stayed and stared at the whiteboard for a while after Scotty left. They'd mostly worked on characters today—drawing a sprawled-out family tree showing how everyone on the show was connected, and brainstorming stories that could branch out from each of them.

A lot of what they were doing was just remembering all the ideas they'd come up with over the years, some of which had definitely expired. (*Chloe decides to be emo but never figures out what it means. Adam is overly defensive of Monica Lewinsky.*) They'd been talking about these characters for so long, Georgie could see them in her head—she could do all their voices.

Seth pulled down a few notecards they'd taped to the wall. "It's still good, right? Inherently? The show—it's funny?"

"I think so," Georgie said. "We're not moving as fast as we should be."

"We never are. We'll get there."

"Yeah." She rubbed her eyes. When she looked up again, Seth was smiling his just-for-her smile. It was smaller than the ones he gave everyone else. More eyes. Less teeth.

"Go home," he said. "Get some sleep. You still look exhausted."

She was.

So she did.

CHAPTER 5

When Georgie got home, the front door was locked. She fumbled for a minute with her keys.

She'd left a few of the lights on, so the house wasn't dark—it just felt dark. Georgie realized she was tiptoeing. She cleared her throat. "It's just me," she said out loud, to prove that she could.

She tried to remember the last time she'd come home to an empty house, and couldn't. Not this house.

They'd moved out to Calabasas when Georgie was pregnant with Noomi; their old house, a squat, mint green bungalow in Silver Lake, only had two bedrooms, and there were more tattoo parlors and karaoke bars in their neighborhood than kids.

Georgie missed it. Not the tattoo parlors and the karaoke bars . . . She and Neal never went out much, even before Alice and Noomi. But she missed the house. How small it was. How close. She missed the scrubby excuse for a front yard, and the crooked jacaranda tree that used to drop sticky purple flowers onto her old Jetta every spring.

She and Neal had decorated that house together. They'd gone to the hardware store every weekend for a year to argue about paint. Georgie would always choose the most saturated color on the card.

"You can't always *pick the bottom color,"* Neal would say.

"But the bottom color makes all the other colors look dull."

"You're looking at them wrong."

"How is that possible?"

Neal almost always let Georgie win; their house in Silver Lake looked like Rainbow Brite lived there—and you could tell which walls Georgie had painted, because she was lousy at edges and corners.

They both had jobs then. Neal worked weekends. So there were plenty of days and nights when Georgie had their old house to herself. She'd watch TV shows that Neal would never watch with her. (Everything on The WB.) And then, when he got home, he'd climb over her on the couch and bother her until it was time to make dinner.

That was back when Georgie still pretended to help. When she'd hang out in the kitchen with him and drink wine while she watched him slice vegetables.

"You could do this for a living," she'd say. *"You could cut tomatoes in a tomato-cutting commercial, that's how good you are."*

Then Neal would chop extra loudly and wave the knife over the tomato slices with a flourish.

"I'm serious. You could be an Iron Chef."

"That or work at Applebee's."

Georgie had a regular spot on the kitchen counter, and Neal worked around it. He'd pour her too much wine—and feed her pieces of things before the rest of dinner was ready, blowing on the fork until the bite was cool enough. . . .

How many years ago was that? Eight? Ten?

Georgie dropped her phone and keys onto the coffee table, on a stack of Noomi's picture books, and wandered into the kitchen. The plate of salmon stir-fry that Neal had made two nights ago was still in the refrigerator. She

hadn't felt like eating it then, even though she'd been
starving. She didn't bother to heat it up now, just grabbed
a fork and brought it out to the living room, sitting on the
couch and turning on the TV for light. There were two
new episodes of *Jeff'd Up* on the DVR, a rerun and an
hour-long Christmas special.

The Christmas special had been a pain in the ass to film.
The script had Jeff and Trev both secretly bonding with a
stray dog they were pretending to hate. Jeff would kick
the dog out of the house, then Trev would let the dog in,
then Jeff would go looking for it, trying to sneak it in himself, then he'd get caught and kick it out again. The laugh
track had more "aw"s than laughs, and Georgie could tell
the sound guy had just used the same "aw" over and over.

The dog was a mistake.

Jeff German had insisted they use *his* dog, an ancient
beagle that couldn't take direction and that nobody else
was allowed to touch. Then it turned out that the kid
who played Trev was allergic to dogs, and his mom followed him around with an epinephrine pen the whole
day. He didn't end up needing it, thank God, but his eyes
got all runny and puffy.

"It's fine," Seth said. *"It looks like he's been crying."*

"Let's get rid of the dog," Georgie said. *"Let's make it
something else."*

"You just don't like dogs. What do you want? A cat?"

"I was thinking an orphan."

"Fuck no, Georgie. The network will make us keep it."

Normally, Georgie would text back and forth with
Seth while they watched *Jeff'd Up*. But her phone was
plugged in on the other side of the room, and she didn't
feel like getting up.

She'd get up if Neal called.

Which wasn't likely, not this late—Neal hadn't called her back all day.

Georgie had tried him half a dozen times since lunch, and every time, the call went to voice mail. She'd tried his mom's house, too, but got a busy signal. (It'd been so long since Georgie had heard an actual busy signal, it kind of confused her.)

She set her empty plate on the coffee table and pulled the afghan up over her shoulders.

"Awwwww . . . ," the TV audience said.

Georgie looked up at the ceiling. Neal had painted a spray of flowers there. They started at one corner, then wound down onto the wall. Blue with white starbursts— she forgot what they were called.

Neal had picked out this house. In Calabasas. He liked the porch and the yard. The wide-open kitchen. The fact that it had a real second floor and an attic. (Their house in Silver Lake was one and a half stories, with the bedroom up in the half. Neal hated the way you could hear the rain hitting the roof at night.)

Georgie was five months pregnant when they moved in, so she couldn't help paint. (Fumes.) Also, she and Seth were working as showrunners by then, so her hours were crazy—and also, she felt like garbage.

She felt like garbage that whole pregnancy. She gained more weight with Noomi. She had more pain. Her fingers got so swollen and purple that she'd stare at them while she typed, imagining she was Violet Beauregarde— imagining that Seth was going to have to roll her out of the writers' room when she went into labor.

(She didn't end up going into labor. Georgie was really

good at getting pregnant, but not so good at getting the babies out. She never had a real contraction with either of the girls.)

Georgie had been relieved when Neal started painting the walls without her. At first he chose colors from the bottom of the paint strip—there were a few Georgie-bright rooms. But mostly this house was white. Or pale yellow. Or watery blue.

He'd started painting murals a few years ago, when Noomi grew out of her baby sling and was okay playing with Alice on the floor. Georgie came home one night and found a willow tree curling out of her closet.

Neal painted landscapes and seascapes. Skyscapes. (Was there such a thing?) He painted murals all over the house, never finishing one before starting another. Georgie didn't ask why.

Neal didn't like to be *asked* things. It made his jaw tense. He'd give you a flippant answer. Like, whatever you were asking, it wasn't any of your business.

Like nothing was anyone's business.

Like nobody should ask questions that didn't absolutely need to be answered.

Georgie had gotten really good over the years at not asking questions. Sometimes she didn't even realize she wasn't doing it.

This house really was much nicer than their old house. . . .

Neal was better at picking out paint and arranging furniture than Georgie had ever been. Plus their laundry actually got done now that he did it.

"It never ends," he'd say.

"We could hire someone," Georgie would offer.

"We don't need to hire someone."

Their neighbors had a nanny and a cleaning lady, a lawn guy, a pool guy, and a dog groomer who made house calls. Neal hated them. *"You shouldn't need a staff of people larger than your own family. We don't live in a manor."*

"Like the Malfoys," Alice said. *"With house elves."*

Neal was reading her the Harry Potter books.

Neal mowed their lawn. In worn-out cargo pants and T-shirts that he'd had since high school. He always smelled like sunblock, because without it, he'd immediately burn. Even with the sunblock, the back of his neck was stained red.

Neal trimmed the trees. Neal kept tulip bulbs in the refrigerator and sketched garden plans on the back of Whole Foods receipts. He'd pore over seed catalogs in bed and make Georgie choose which plants she liked best.

"Purple eggplant or white eggplant?" he'd asked her last summer.

"How can you have a white eggplant? That's like . . . purple green beans."

"There are purple green beans. And yellow oranges."

"Stop. You're blowing my mind."

"Oh, I'll blow your mind. Girlie."

"Are you flirting with me?"

He'd turned to her then, pen cap in mouth, and cocked his head. *"Yeah. I think so."*

Georgie looked down at her old sweatshirt. At her threadbare yoga pants. *"This is what does it for you?"*

Neal smiled most of a smile, and the cap fell out of his mouth. *"So far."*

Neal . . .

She'd call him tomorrow morning. She'd get through

to him this time. This was just—this had just been a weird couple of days. Georgie was busy. And Neal was busy. And time zones weren't on their side.

And he was pissed with her.

She'd make it better; she didn't blame him. Everything would be better in the morning.

Morning glories, Georgie thought to herself just before she fell asleep.

FRIDAY
DECEMBER 20, 2013

FRIDAY,
DECEMBER 20, 2013

CHAPTER 6

One missed call.

Fuck, fuck, fuck.

Georgie'd woken up on the couch this morning a half hour after her alarm would have gone off if she'd remembered to set it. She ran upstairs to take a shower, then threw on a new pair of jeans and the Metallica T-shirt. (It still smelled more like Neal than like Georgie.)

When she went to grab her phone on the way out, she saw the text alert:

One missed call
An Emergency Contact

That's what Neal was filed under in Georgie's contacts. (Just in case.) (Of something.) There was a voice mail, too—she hit PLAY but Neal hadn't left anything, just a half second of silence. He must have called while she was in the shower.

Georgie called right back, got Neal's voice mail and started talking as soon she heard the beep. "Hi," she said. "It's me. I just missed your call, but I won't miss it again—call me. Call me whenever. You won't be interrupting anything."

As soon as she hung up, she felt like an idiot. Because of course he'd be interrupting something. That's why Georgie had stayed in L.A., because she couldn't be interrupted.

Fuck.

Georgie wasn't any good that morning.

Seth was pretending not to notice. He was also pretending not to notice her Metallica T-shirt.

"It feels weird to be writing a different show in here," Scotty said, looking around the writers' room. "It's like we're doing it in our parents' bed." He was sitting in his usual spot at the far end of the conference table, even though there were eight empty chairs closer to Seth and Georgie. "I wish the front-desk girl was here to make us coffee. Georgie, do you know how to make coffee?"

"Are you kidding me?"

Scotty rolled his eyes. "I didn't mean that in a sexist way. I just genuinely don't know how to turn on the coffee machine. You'd think they'd make that part obvious."

"Well, I don't know either," she said.

Seth looked up at Scotty over his laptop. "Why don't *you* go get us coffee?" he said. "We won't need any fart jokes for at least a half hour."

"Fuck you," Scotty said. He frowned at the framed *Jeff'd Up* poster on the wall. "It's kind of like we're doing it in *Jeff German's* bed."

"Nobody's doing it," Georgie said. "Go get us coffee."

Scotty stood up. "I hate leaving you guys alone. You forget that I exist."

"I haven't forgotten you," Seth said, picking up his cell phone. "I'm texting you our orders."

As soon as Scotty was gone, Seth wheeled his chair into Georgie's and leaned against her armrest. "I've *seen* you work the coffeemaker."

"It's the principle of the thing," she said.

"Does that mean you won't man the whiteboard either?"

"I'm not your secretary."

"Yeah, but you don't trust Scotty to take notes, and you can't read my handwriting."

Georgie stood up, reluctantly, found a dry-erase marker, and started updating their progress on the whiteboard. She actually really liked being the one who wrote things down. It was like being the decision-maker.

Back in college, Georgie would type while Seth swanned around *The Spoon* offices, thinking out loud. Then he'd be all righteous indignation when the magazine came back from the presses:

"Georgie. Where's my Unabomber joke?"

"Who can be sure? Probably holed up in Montana."

"That was a great joke that you cut."

"It was a joke? See, it'd be a lot easier for me if you made your jokes funny. Then I wouldn't get so confused."

By junior year, Georgie and Seth were writing a weekly column together on page two of *The Spoon*. Georgie was finally starting to feel like she belonged on staff. Like she was good enough.

She shared a desk with Seth then, too; that's when they first got used to it. Seth liked to have Georgie close enough that he could pull her hair, and Georgie liked having Seth close enough to kick.

"Shit, Georgie, that really hurt—you're wearing Doc Martens."

Georgie remembered the Unabomber tantrum because they were in the middle of it the first time she saw Neal down at *The Spoon*. Seth was telling her that he wanted their column to be more political. More "wry" . . .

"I can pull off wry, Georgie, don't tell me I—"

"Who was that?" she interrupted him.

"Who?"

"That guy who just walked into the production room."

Seth leaned back to see past her. "Which one?"

"Blue sweatshirt."

"Oh." He sat up again. "That's the cartoon hobbit. You don't know the cartoon hobbit?"

"No. Why do you call him that?"

"Because he does the thing—you know, the cartoon, at the back of the paper." Seth had a copy of *The Spoon* and was writing his Unabomber joke in the margin of their column. "One down, four thousand ninety-nine copies to go."

"That's who writes *Stop the Sun*? The comic strip?"

"Writes. Draws. Scrawls."

"That's the funniest part of the magazine."

"No, Georgie, we're the funniest part of the magazine."

"That's Neal Grafton?" She was trying to look into the production room without turning her head.

"Indeed."

"Why haven't I seen him down here before?"

Seth looked up at her and lowered an eyebrow suspiciously. "I don't know. He's not much of a people person."

"You've met him?"

"Do you have a crush on *the cartoon hobbit*?"

"I've barely even seen him," she said. "I just think he's crazy talented—I thought *Stop the Sun* was syndicated. Why do you call him the hobbit?"

"Because he's short and fat and hobbity."

"He's not fat."

"You've barely even seen him." Seth reached over Georgie to grab her copy of *The Spoon* and started writing his joke on the inside cover.

Georgie tipped back in her chair and peeked into the

production room. She could just see Neal hunched over a drafting table, half-obscured by a pole.

"*We* are the funniest thing in the magazine," Seth mumbled.

Scotty brought back coffee, but it didn't help.

Georgie had a headache. And a stomachache. And her hair still smelled like Heather's sugary shampoo, even though she'd washed it again.

She told herself she was just tired. But it didn't feel like tired—it felt like *scared*. Which didn't make any sense. Nothing was wrong, nothing was coming. She just . . .

She hadn't talked to Neal for two and a half days.

And they'd never gone this long without talking. Not since they'd met. Well, practically not since they'd met.

It's not that things were always . . . (What word was she looking for? *Hunky-dory? Smooth? Happy?*) It's not that things were always . . . *easy* between Georgie and Neal.

Sometimes, even when they were talking, they weren't really talking. Sometimes they were just negotiating each other. Keeping each other posted.

But it had never been like this before. Radio silence.

There'd always been his voice.

Georgie would feel better if she could hear Neal's voice.

When Seth ran out to get lunch, she holed up in their office to try Neal again. She dialed his cell number and waited, tapping her fingers on her desk.

"Hello?" someone said doubtfully—like the person wasn't actually sure that this was a phone and that she was indeed answering it. Neal's mom.

"Margaret? Hey, it's Georgie."

"Georgie, hi there. I wasn't sure if the phone was

ringing or if this was an iPod. I thought I might be answering an iPod."

"I'm glad you risked it. How are you?"

"You know, Naomi was watching TV on this thing earlier. In the same room as a perfectly good television. We're living in the future, I guess. It's not even really shaped like a phone, is it? More like a deck of cards . . ."

Margaret was the only person who called Noomi by her given name. It always made Georgie wince—even though Georgie was the one who'd named her.

"I guess you're right," Georgie said. "I've never thought about it. How are you, Margaret? Sorry I called so late the other night."

"Georgie, can you hear me?"

"I can hear you fine."

"Because I don't know where the microphone is—this phone is so small."

"It is small, you're right."

"Do I hold it up to my ear or my mouth?"

"Um"—Georgie had to think about that, even though she was talking on the same style of phone—"your ear. I guess."

"My cell phone flips open. It seems more like a real phone."

"*I think your mother has Asperger's,*" Georgie had said to Neal.

"*They didn't get Asperger's in the '50s.*"

"*I'm just saying maybe she's on the spectrum.*"

"*She's just a math teacher.*"

"Margaret"—Georgie forced herself to smile, hoping it would make her sound less impatient—"is Neal around?"

"He is. Did you want to talk to him?"

"That would be *great*. Yes. Thank you."

"He just took the girls over to Dawn's. She's got a cocka-tiel, you know, and she thought the girls might like to see it."

"Dawn," Georgie said.

Dawn, the girl next door. The *literal* girl next door. Dawn, Neal's ex-almost-fiancée. (It shouldn't count if there was never a ring, right? If it was just a summer-vacation verbal agreement?)

God. And country. And fuck.

Why couldn't Neal have a string of ex-girlfriends? Girls that he'd talked to, girls that he'd dated. Girls he'd used for sex, then felt bad about later . . . Why did he just have to have *Dawn*?

Dawn always came by Neal's mom's house to say hi when Georgie and Neal were in town; she lived next door and took care of her parents.

Dawn had pretty brown eyes and smooth brown hair. She was a nurse. She was divorced. She brought the kids stuffed animals that made it back to California and lived on their beds.

Georgie's head hurt. Her hair smelled like poisonous cupcakes.

"Amadeus!" Margaret said, like she was remembering something.

"Sorry?" Georgie asked, clearing her throat.

"Amadeus. That's Dawn's cockatiel. He's quite a bird."

"Maybe you could just tell him that I called."

Margaret was quiet for a few seconds and then—"Oh, you mean Neal."

"I do. Yeah."

"Sure, of course, Georgie. I'll tell him."

"Thanks, Margaret. Tell him to call me back anytime."

"Sure. Oh, wait, before you go—Merry Christmas, Georgie! I hope your new show gets picked up."

Georgie paused. And remembered that she really did like Neal's mom. "Thanks, Margaret. Merry Christmas. Hug those girls for me."

"Georgie, wait, how do I hang up on you?"

"I'll hang up on you. That'll take care of it."

"Okay, thanks."

"I'm hanging up now, Margaret. Merry Christmas."

"That's funny, right?" Seth asked, then repeated a joke for the fourth time. "Is it funny? Or is it just weird?"

Georgie wasn't sure. She was having a hard time staying focused.

"I need a break," Scotty said. "I can't even see straight."

"Push through it," Seth ordered. "This is where the magic happens."

"This is where I go get frozen yogurt."

"All you do is eat. You eat, then you start thinking about the next thing you're going to eat."

"Eating is the only thing that breaks the monotony," Scotty said.

Seth's eyebrows shot up. "This isn't monotony. This is the fucking dream."

"It will be," Scotty said. "When I have some yogurt."

"Georgie. Tell him. No frozen yogurt until he says something funny."

Georgie was slouched down in her chair with her feet up on the table and her eyes closed. "Can't talk. Too much magic happening."

"Do you want frozen yogurt, Georgie?" Scotty asked from the door.

"No, thanks."

She heard the door close. Then felt a pen bounce off her shoulder.

"You should take a nap," Seth said.

"Hmmm."

"We need a napping couch. *Passing Time* is going to have a napping couch. Remember the couch at *The Spoon*? That was a first-rate napping couch."

Georgie remembered. It was gray velvet and worn smooth on the cushions. If Georgie was sitting on it, Seth would sit down right beside her, even if there was plenty of room. Even if there was no room at all. He liked to rest his head in her lap or on her shoulder. If he didn't have a girlfriend, she'd let him. (He almost always had a girlfriend.)

Seth was a relentless flirt. Even with Georgie—maybe *especially* with Georgie.

For the first few months after they met, she found all the attention thrilling. And then—when she realized that Seth flirted with everyone, and that he was usually *actively* chasing another girl—it was heartbreaking.

And then it was just noise. Like his talking. Like his humming. Georgie liked it, even when she wasn't paying attention. Sitting on the napping couch, Seth's head on her shoulder, his wavy cherrywood hair tickling her ear . . .

They were sprawled out on the napping couch the second time Georgie saw Neal. Seth had a girlfriend at the time—leggy, cheekbony, actressy—so he was supporting his own head. Georgie stuck her elbow in his ribs. "There he is again."

"Ow. Who?"

"The cartoonist," she said.

"The hobbit?"

"I'm going to go introduce myself."

"Why?"

"Because we work together," Georgie said. "It's what people do."

"He doesn't work here. He just turns in his cartoons here."

"I'm going to introduce myself. And tell him how much I like his work."

"You'll wish you hadn't," Seth warned. "He's a scowler. He's the least friendly hobbit in the Shire."

"Stop talking Tolkien at me. All I know is 'Frodo lives.'"

Seth laid his head on her shoulder.

Georgie shrugged him off. "I'm going. To introduce myself." She got off the couch.

"Fine," he moped. "I hope you're very happy together. Cute little hobbit couple with lots of roly-poly hobbit babies."

Georgie turned back to him, but didn't stop walking away. "I'm not hobbity."

"You're short, Georgie." He spread out across the couch. "And round, and pleasant-looking. Deal with it."

Georgie turned the corner into the production room and stopped. The writers almost never went back to the production room. The artists hung out back here—and the paste-up people on the nights that *The Spoon* was going to press.

Neal was sitting at a drafting table. He had a penciled comic strip laid out in front of him, and he was opening a bottle of India ink. There was a radio somewhere playing the Foo Fighters.

Georgie thought about going back to the couch.

"Hi," she said instead.

Neal glanced up at her without lifting his head, then looked back at his comic. "Hi."

He was wearing a black T-shirt under blue flannel, and his hair was dark and short, almost military-short.

"You're Neal, right?"

He didn't look up again. "Right."

"I'm Georgie."

"Are you?"

"Sorry?"

"Are you really?" he asked.

"Um, yes?"

He nodded. "I thought it was a pen name. Georgie McCool. Sounds like a pen name."

"You know my name?"

Neal finally looked up at her. With round blue eyes and practically his whole head. "Your photo's in *The Spoon*," he said.

"Oh." Georgie wasn't usually smooth with guys—but she was usually smoother than this. "Right. So are you. I mean, your comic strip. I came back to talk to you about your comic."

Neal was focused on his page again. He was holding an old-fashioned pen; it looked like a fountain pen with a long nib. "Is there a problem?"

"No," she said. "I just . . . like it. I was going to tell you how much I like it."

"Are you still going to?"

"I . . ."

His eyes met hers after a second, and she thought she might see a smile there.

She smiled back. "Yeah. I really like it. I think it's the funniest thing in the magazine."

She was almost sure Neal was smiling now. But it was just a twitch in his lips.

"I don't know," he said. "People seem to like the horoscopes. . . ."

Georgie wrote the horoscopes. (In character, sort of. It was hard to explain.) Neal *knew* she wrote the horoscopes. He knew her name. His hands were small, and they moved with complete surety across the paper, leaving a thick, straight line.

"I didn't know you used real ink," she said.

He nodded.

"Can I watch?"

He nodded again.

CHAPTER 7

Georgie's mother had spectacular cleavage. Tan, freckled, ten miles deep.

"Genetics," her mom said when she caught Georgie looking.

Heather shoved a bowl of green beans into Georgie's arm. "Were you just staring at Mom's breasts?"

"I think so," Georgie said. "I'm really tired—and she's kinda begging for it in that shirt."

"Oh, sure," Heather said. "Blame the victim."

"Not in front of Kendrick," their mom said. "You're making him blush."

Kendrick smiled down at his spaghetti and shook his head.

Her mom had caught Georgie on her cell phone that afternoon while she was waiting for Neal to call. *Let me make you dinner. I'm worried about you.*

"Don't," Georgie had said. *"Don't worry."* But she'd still agreed to come by after work.

Her mom made spaghetti with homemade meatballs, and pineapple upside-down cake for dessert. And they'd all waited for Georgie to get there before they started eating, so she didn't feel like she could excuse herself right away to call Neal. (It was almost seven thirty already, nine thirty in Omaha.)

Georgie had tried Neal's cell phone twice on the way

here. Her calls went straight to voice mail again—which didn't necessarily mean he was still hanging out with Dawn, but also didn't prove that he wasn't.

(It was stupid to worry about Dawn. Neal was a teenager when he was with Dawn.)

(But weren't people constantly leaving their spouses the moment their prom dates friended them on Facebook?)

(Plus Dawn never got old. In any sense of the word. It was always good to see her, and she always looked good. The last time Georgie'd seen Dawn, at Neal's dad's funeral, she looked like she'd never been removed from the package.)

"Did you talk to the girls today?" her mom asked.

"I talked to them yesterday."

"How are they taking everything?"

"Fine." Georgie choked down half a meatball. "There's not actually anything to take, you know."

"Kids are perceptive, Georgie. They're like dogs"—she offered a meatball from her own fork to the pug heaped in her lap—"they know when their people are unhappy."

"I think you may just have reverse-anthropomorphized your own grandchildren."

Her mom waved her empty fork dismissively. "You know what I mean."

Heather leaned into Georgie and sighed. "Sometimes I feel like her daughter. And sometimes I feel like the dog with the least ribbons."

Heather was eating spaghetti, too, but out of a restaurant to-go box. Georgie decided not to ask. She glanced up at the clock—seven forty-five.

"You know, I promised I'd call Neal before it gets too late." She'd promised his voice mail, anyway. "I'm just going to use the phone in my room, if that's okay."

"But you haven't finished eating," her mom protested.

Georgie was already halfway down the hall. "I'll be back!"

Her heart was beating hard when she got to her room. Was she that out of shape? Or just that nervous?

She curled her fingers behind the hooks of the yellow phone and sat on the bed, pulling it into her lap and waiting to catch her breath.

Please answer, she thought, picturing Neal's somber blue eyes and his stern jaw. Picturing his strong pale face. *Please. I just really need to hear your voice right now.*

She started dialing his cell, then hung up and tried the landline—maybe Margaret was a better bet to pick up; their parents' generation still felt morally obligated to answer phones.

Georgie listened to it ring, trying to hold down the butterflies in her stomach. Trying to crush them, actually, into butterfly bits and pieces.

"Hello?"

Neal. Finally.

Neal, Neal, Neal.

The butterflies burst back to life and started fluttering up Georgie's throat. She swallowed. "Hey."

"Georgie." He said it like he was confirming something. Gently confirming.

"Hey," she repeated.

"I didn't think you'd call again."

"I told your mom I would. I told you the last time we talked—why wouldn't I?"

"I don't know, I didn't think you'd call then either."

"I love you," she blurted out.

"What?"

"The last time we—you hung up before I could tell you that I love you."

"So you called to say you love me?"

"I . . ." Georgie felt so confused. "I called to make sure you got in okay. To see how you are. To see how the girls are."

Neal laughed. Not in a good way. It was the sound effect his defenses made when they snapped into place. "The girls," he said. "*The girls* are fine. Are you talking about Dawn? Because I haven't seen her."

"What? Your mom said you were over there today."

"When did you talk to my mom?"

"Today. She said Dawn was showing you her cockatiel. Amadeus."

"Dawn's cockatiel is named Falco."

Georgie tucked in her chin, defensively. "Sorry. I'm not an expert on Dawn's cockatiels."

"Neither am I."

She shook her head and took her glasses off, holding her palm against her eye. "Neal. Look. I'm sorry. This isn't why I called."

"Right. You called to tell me that you love me."

"*Yeah.* Actually. Yes, I did. *I love you.*"

"Well, I love you, too. That isn't the problem, Georgie." His voice was almost a whisper.

Georgie whispered, too: "Neal. I didn't know you were this upset. You should have told me you were this upset before you left. I wouldn't have let you go—I would have come with."

He laughed again, and this time it was even worse. "I should have told you?" he hissed. "I *did* tell you. I said, 'I can't do this anymore.' I said 'I love you, but I'm not sure it's enough, I'm not sure it will *ever* be enough.' I said, 'I don't want to live like this, Georgie'—remember?"

Georgie was speechless. She did remember. But . . .

"Just a second," Neal said quietly. "I don't want to have this conversation in front of my parents. . . ." What he said next was muffled: "Dad, can you hang this up when I get upstairs?"

"Sure, tell your Georgie girl I said hi."

"You can tell her yourself. She's right there."

"Georgie?" someone said into the phone. Someone who was not Neal's dad. Who couldn't be.

"Mr. Grafton?"

"We're sorry you couldn't come for Christmas this year. We made it snow for you and everything."

"I'm sorry I missed it," Georgie said—she must have said it, she heard herself say it.

"Well, maybe next year," he said. *He who was not, who could not be, Neal's dad—who was dead. Who died in a train yard three years ago.*

There was a click, then the hollow sound of another phone on the line. "I've got it, Dad, thanks."

"See ya, Georgie girl," Neal's dad said. "Merry Christmas."

"Merry Christmas," she said. Autonomically.

There was another click.

Georgie sat completely still.

"Georgie?"

"Neal?"

"Are you okay—are you crying?"

She *was* crying. "I . . . I'm really tired. I haven't been sleeping, and *Neal,* oh my God, I just imagined the strangest thing. I imagined your dad telling me Merry Christmas. Isn't that—"

"He did tell you Merry Christmas."

She sucked in a breath.

"Georgie?"

"I don't think I should be talking right now."

"Georgie, wait."

"I can't talk right now, Neal. I just . . . I have to go."

She slammed the phone down onto the cradle, looked at it for a second, maybe two, then shoved it away from her. It fell to the ground with a heavy, clanging thump. The receiver went flying into the bedside table.

Georgie stared at it.

This wasn't right. None of this was right.

Neal's dad was dead. Neal always said I love you. And he knew who "the girls" were.

And also . . . also, especially—especially, *especially*— Neal's dad was *dead*.

Georgie was . . . She must be imagining things.

Exhausted. She was exhausted.

And upset. Too much stress. Not enough sleep.

Also, maybe someone had drugged her—that was possible. That was more possible than Neal's dad *coming back from the dead* to wish her Merry Christmas. Which didn't. Just. Happen.

What else hadn't happened today? Had she even gone to work? Had she spent last night on the couch? Had she ever woken up?

Wake up! Wake the fuck up, Georgie!

Maybe when she woke up, when she really woke up, she'd find Neal lying beside her. Maybe they wouldn't even be fighting. (*Were* they fighting?) Maybe, in the real world, the waking world, Georgie and Neal never fought.

"I had a dream that things were just like they are now," she'd say when she woke up, *"but we weren't happy. And it was Christmas, and you left me. . . ."*

"Georgie?" Her mom was calling from the kitchen. Unless Georgie was dreaming that, too. "Are you okay?" her mom shouted.

"I'm fine!" Georgie yelled back.

Her mom came to her room anyway. "I heard a noise," she said from the doorway. She looked down at the phone, lying stretched out and off the hook on the floor. "Is everything all right?"

Georgie wiped her eyes. "Fine. I'm just"—she shook her head—"I don't know, maybe having a nervous breakdown."

"Of course you are, honey. Your husband left you."

"He didn't leave me," Georgie said. But maybe he had. Maybe that's why Georgie was falling apart. "I think I need to rest."

"That's a good idea."

"Or maybe I need a drink."

Her mom came into the room and picked up the phone, setting it back on the table. "I hardly think you should start drinking."

Had Georgie been drinking already? Had this ever happened before? Was she blacking out?

"Do you remember Neal's dad?" she asked her mom.

"Paul? Sure. Neal looks just like him."

"Looks? Or *looked*?"

"What?"

"What do you know about Neal's dad?" Georgie asked.

"What are you talking about? Didn't he have a heart attack?"

"Yes." Georgie reached out and grabbed her mom's arm. "He had a heart attack."

Her mom looked significantly more concerned. "Do you think you're having a heart attack?"

"No," Georgie said. Was she having a heart attack? A stroke, maybe? She smiled and touched her own cheeks; nothing seemed to be drooping. "No. No, I just need some rest, I think."

"I don't think you should drive home."

"I don't think so either."

"Okay." Her mom studied her. "You'll get through this, Georgie. I thought I'd spend the rest of my life alone after your dad and I split up."

"You left him for another guy."

Her mom shook her head dismissively. "These feelings aren't rational. There's nothing rational about marriage."

"A *fatal* heart attack, right?"

"Why are you fixated on Neal's dad? Poor man. Poor Margaret."

"I don't know," Georgie said. "I just need to rest."

"You rest." Her mom turned off the light on her way out.

Georgie lay in the dark for an hour.

She cried some more.

And talked to herself. "I'm imagining things. I'm tired. I'm just tired."

She closed her eyes and tried to sleep.

She opened them again, and watched the yellow phone.

She thought about going home. She went out and sat in

the car for a while. Eventually, she plugged in her cell phone and tried to call Neal. (He didn't pick up.) (*Because he never fucking picks up*. And maybe he *had* left her, maybe they were so out of synch that Georgie didn't even recognize when he was actually, really leaving her. Maybe he'd already told her he was leaving, and she just hadn't listened.)

She sat in the car and cried.

Then she tried Neal's mom's number, even though it was late. Georgie just needed to talk to him again. Normally. She needed to have a normal conversation to reset everything.

His mom's line was busy. Maybe his dad had some really important ghost phone calls to make at midnight central time.

Georgie thought again about trying to sleep. She thought about how all her freaking out was probably making this situation—whatever this situation was—worse.

Then she went inside and went through the kitchen cabinets until she found a bottle of crème de menthe, probably left over from the last time her mom made grasshopper pie. (Her mom and Kendrick weren't drinkers.) (Potheads? Possibly. Neal suspected.)

Georgie drank it straight. It was like getting drunk on syrup.

At some point she must have fallen asleep.

SATURDAY
DECEMBER 21, 2013

CHAPTER 8

Four missed calls—all from Seth.

It was already noon, and Georgie was just leaving for work. Her phone rang as soon as she plugged it into the car lighter.

"Sorry," she said, answering it. "I overslept."

"Jesus, Georgie," Seth said, "I was ready to call the police."

"You were not."

"Maybe I was. I was just about to drive all the way out to Calabasas looking for you. What the fuck?"

"I stayed at my mom's again. I'm sorry. I forgot to set the alarm."

That was a vast, vast oversimplification. Georgie had woken up on her mom's couch a half hour ago, with one of the pugs licking her face. Then she'd puked for twenty minutes. Then she'd spent another ten trying to find clothes in Heather's room—nothing fit—before ending up in her mom's closet, settling for a pair of velour sweatpants and a low-cut T-shirt with rhinestones. Georgie hadn't even brushed her teeth. (Didn't see the point; her whole body already smelled like mint.) "I'm coming," she told Seth. "I'll bring lunch."

"We already have lunch here. And half a script—it's fucking terrible, hurry up."

"I'm coming." She ended the call and got on the 101.

Four missed calls, all from Seth. None from Neal.

Georgie rubbed her thumb over the phone's touch-screen. She wasn't thinking about last night. Last night was something Georgie was not going to think about right now.

It was a new morning. She'd call Neal and start over from here. She held the phone up over the steering wheel and thumbed through her recent calls, pressing AN EMER-GENCY CONTACT.

It rang. . . .

"Good day, sunshine."

"Hey, Alice. It's Mommy."

"I know, I heard your song. Also, there's a picture of you when you call—from Halloween. You're dressed like the Tin Man."

Neal had been the Cowardly Lion. Alice was Dorothy. Noomi was Toto the cat.

"I need to talk to Daddy," Georgie said.

"Are you in the car?"

"I'm on my way to work."

"You promised not to talk on the phone in the car—I'm telling Daddy."

"I promised to wait until I was done merging. Where *is* Daddy?"

"I don't know."

"He's not there?"

"No."

"Where's Grandma?"

"I don't know."

"Alice."

"Yeah?"

"Please find Grandma."

"But we're watching *The Rescuers*."

"Pause it."

"Grandma doesn't have pause!"

"You're only going to miss a few minutes. I'll tell you what happens."

"Mommy, I don't want you to *spoil* it for me."

"*Alice.* Listen to my voice. Do I sound like I'm in the mood to debate this?"

"No . . ." Alice sounded hurt. "You're using your mean voice."

"Go get Grandma."

The phone fell. A second later someone picked it up.

"Don't use your mean voice, Mommy." It was Noomi. Crying. Undoubtedly fake crying. Noomi almost never truly cried; she'd start fake crying long before she arrived at actual tears.

"I'm not using my mean voice, Noomi. How are you?"

"I'm just so sad."

"Don't be sad."

"But you're using your mean voice, and I don't like it."

"Noomi," Georgie said, in what probably *was* her mean voice. "I wasn't even talking to you. Calm *down,* for Christ's sake."

"Georgie?"

"Margaret!"

"Is everything okay?"

"Yes," Georgie said. "I just . . . Is Neal around? I really, really need to talk to Neal."

"He went to do some last-minute shopping for the girls."

"Oh," Georgie said. "I guess he didn't take his phone."

"I guess not—are you sure everything's okay?"

"Yeah. I just miss him. Them. Everybody." She closed her eyes, then quickly opened them. "You and . . . Paul."

Her mother-in-law was quiet.

Georgie decided to keep going. She wasn't sure what she was fishing for. "I'm sorry the girls didn't get to know him like I did."

Margaret took a breath. "Thank you, Georgie. And thank you for letting Neal bring them to Omaha. Since we lost Paul, well, this is the hardest time of year to be alone."

"Of course," Georgie said, wiping her eyes with the heel of her thumb. "Just tell Neal I called."

She pressed END and dropped the phone on the passenger seat.

That sealed it.

Georgie had lost her mind.

"Jesus Christ," Seth said when she walked into the room. His jaw dropped, probably just for effect. "Jesus H. Christ on a thousand bicycles."

Scotty shot Diet Coke through his nose. "Oh fuck," he said. "Oh God, it burns."

"Can we just—" Georgie tried.

"What happened to you?" Seth was out of his chair and circling her. "You look like Britney Spears, back when she was dating backup dancers and walking around gas stations barefoot."

"I borrowed some of my mom's clothes. I didn't think you'd want me to waste another hour going home to change."

"Or shower," Seth said, looking at her hair.

"Those are your *mom's* clothes?" Scotty asked.

"She's a free spirit," Georgie said. "We're working now,

right? I'm here, and we're working?"

"There's something green on your face," Seth said, touching her chin. "It's sticky." Georgie jerked away, finding her seat at the long conference table.

Scotty went back to his lunch. "Is this what happens when Neal's out of town? No wonder he keeps you on such a short leash."

"I'm not on a leash," Georgie said. "I'm *married*."

Seth shoved a foam container in front of her. Georgie opened it. Soggy Korean tacos. She waited a second to figure out whether she was more sick or more hungry. . . . More hungry.

Seth handed her a fork. "You okay?"

"Fine. Just show me what you have so far."

Not fine. Completely not fine.

"I should have told you? I did tell you. I said, 'I can't do this anymore.' I said 'I love you, but I'm not sure it's enough, I'm not sure it will ever be enough.' I said, 'I don't want to live like this, Georgie'—remember?"

It made sense, really. If Georgie was going to have a delusional, paranoid nervous breakdown about her husband leaving her, it made sense that she'd flash back to the one time Neal actually *had* left her.

Sort of left her.

Before they were married.

It was Christmas break, their senior year. And they'd gone to some party, some TV party that seemed really important at the time. Seth was already working on a Fox sitcom, and he wanted Georgie to meet all the other writers on the show—the star was even supposed to be there. It was just a party in somebody's backyard, with a pool and beer and Christmas lights threaded through the lemon trees.

Neal spent the whole night standing next to the fence and refusing to talk to anybody. Refusing on principle. As if making small talk—as if being *polite*—would be too much of a concession. (A concession to Seth. To California. To the fact that Georgie was going to get a job like *this* with *these* sorts of people, and Neal would be along for the ride.)

So he stood by the fence with the cheapest beer available and dead-bolted his jaw into place.

Georgie was so infuriated by this little sit-in, she made sure she and Neal were some of the last people to leave. She met and talked to all of Seth's new work friends. She played her part in the Seth-and-Georgie show. (It was a good part; Georgie got most of the punch lines.) She made everyone there love her.

And then she got into Neal's worn-out Saturn, and he drove her to her mom's house. And he told her he was done.

"I can't do this anymore," he said.

"I love you," he said, *"but I'm not sure it's enough, I'm not sure it'll ever be enough."*

He said, *"I don't want to live like this, Georgie."*

And the next morning, he'd left for Omaha without her.

Georgie didn't hear from Neal that whole week. She thought they were over.

She thought that maybe he was right, that they *should* be over.

And then, on Christmas morning, in 1998, Neal was there at her front door—down on one knee on the green indoor-outdoor carpeting, holding his great aunt's wedding ring.

He asked Georgie to marry him.

"I love you," he said. "I love you more than I hate everything else."

And Georgie had laughed because only Neal would think that was a romantic thing to say.

Then she said yes.

Georgie plugged her cell phone into her laptop and made sure the ringer volume was turned all the way up.

"What are you doing?" Seth asked. "No cell phones in the writers' room, remember? That's *your* rule."

"We're not even officially here," Georgie said.

"You're not even *un*officially here," he snapped back at her.

"I'm sorry. I have a lot on my mind."

"Right. Me, too. Four scripts, remember?"

She rubbed her eyes. It was just a dream. Last night. Even though it hadn't felt like a dream—that's all it could have been. An episode.

That was something people had. Normal people. *Episodes.* And then they laid cool cloths over their eyes and made plans to spend time near the sea.

Neal had been on her mind, Neal's *dad* had been on her mind—and her brain had done the rest. That's what Georgie's brain was good at. Episodic storytelling.

"Probably the most important week of our career," Seth was mumbling, "and you decide to check out."

"I haven't checked out," Scotty said.

"I'm not talking about you," Seth said to him. "I'm never talking about you."

Scotty folded his arms. "You know, I don't like being the butt of all your mean jokes when no one else is around. I'm not the Cliff Clavin here."

"Oh my God"—Seth pointed at him—"you're totally the Cliff Clavin. I'll never stop seeing you like that now. Did you ever watch *Family Ties*? You're kind of our Skippy, too."

"I'm too young for *Family Ties*," Scotty said.

"You're too young for *Cheers*."

"I watched it on Netflix."

"You even *look* like Skippy—Georgie, is Scotty our Skippy? Or our Cliff?"

Georgie'd never had an episode before.

Though it felt like she might be having another one now. She stuck her glasses in her hair and pinched the top of her nose.

"Georgie." Seth poked her arm with the eraser end of his pencil. "Are you listening? Scotty—Skippy or Cliff?"

She put her glasses back on. "He's our Radar O'Reilly."

"Aw, Georgie." Scotty grinned. "Stop, you'll make me cry."

"You're too young for *M*A*S*H*," Seth grumbled.

Scotty shrugged. "So are you."

They worked on their show.

It was easier when they were working. Easier for Georgie to pretend that nothing was wrong.

Nothing *was* wrong. She'd just talked to Alice and Noomi, just a few hours ago—they were fine. And Neal was just out Christmas shopping.

So he wasn't in any hurry to talk to her—that wasn't unusual. What did they need to talk about? Georgie and Neal had talked every day since they'd met. (Nearly.) It's not like they needed to catch up.

Georgie worked on her show. Their show. She and Seth got in a groove and wrote dialogue for an hour, batting the conversation back and forth between them like a Ping-Pong ball. (This was how they usually got things done. Competitive collaboration.)

Seth blinked first. Georgie caught him with an especially silly "your mom" joke, and he fell back in his chair, giggling.

"I can't believe you guys have been doing this for twenty years," Scotty said, sincerely, when he was done applauding.

"It hasn't been quite that long," Georgie said.

Seth lifted his head. "Nineteen."

She looked at him. "Really?"

"You graduated from high school in '94, right?"

"Yeah."

"It's 2013. That's nineteen years."

"God."

God. Had it really been that long?

It had.

Nineteen years since Georgie stumbled across Seth in *The Spoon* offices.

Seventeen years since she first noticed Neal.

Fourteen since she married him, standing beside a row of lilac trees in his parents' backyard.

Georgie never thought she'd be old enough to talk about life in big decade-long chunks like this.

It's not that she'd thought she was going to die before

now—she just never imagined it would feel this way. The heaviness of the proportions. Twenty years with the same dream. Seventeen with the same man.

Pretty soon she'd have been with Neal longer than she'd been without him. She'd know herself as his wife better than she'd ever known herself as anyone else.

It felt like too much. Not too much to *have*, just too much to contemplate. Commitments like boulders that were too heavy to carry.

Fourteen years since their wedding.

Fifteen years since Neal tried to drive away from her. Fifteen since he drove back.

Seventeen since she first saw him, saw something in him that she couldn't look away from.

Seth was still watching Georgie, one eyebrow raised.

What would he say if she tried to tell him about the last thirty-six hours?

"Jesus, Georgie, you can go crazy next week. Everything can happen next week. Sleep. Christmas. Nervous breakdowns. This week we're making our dreams come true."

"I'm gonna make some coffee," Georgie said.

CHAPTER 9

The three of them kept working through dinner. They started moving even faster, making even more progress. . . .

And then they all realized they were moving so fast because they were turning their script into an episode of *Jeff'd Up*.

"Oh God, oh God, oh God," Seth said. "We're corrupted. We're completely corrupted."

"This suuuuuuucks," Scotty said.

Seth started erasing the whiteboard with both forearms—he'd regret that later when he saw the state of his checked shirt.

They decided to watch a few episodes of *Barney Miller* to wash out their brains. Seth kept the complete series on VHS in their office. They had a VCR in there, too, crammed into the corner with an old TV.

"We could just watch this online," Scotty said, climbing into the IKEA hammock.

Seth knelt in front of the VCR and popped in a tape. "Not the same. The voodoo won't work."

Georgie brought her laptop with her, with her phone plugged into the side, and tried calling Neal from the doorway. (No answer.)

Seth sighed as soon as the *Barney Miller* bass line started. He flashed Georgie a wide white smile. "We're going to get past this," he said.

She smiled back—she couldn't help it—and sat next to him on the floor.

This was how Georgie had spent her first two years of college. Whenever she wasn't working with Seth at *The Spoon,* she was hanging out at his frat house, watching *Barney Miller* and *Taxi* and *M*A*S*H.* His room was lined and carpeted with VHS tapes.

"What are you doing in a fraternity?" she'd asked. *"Comedy writers don't join fraternities."*

"Don't pigeonhole me, Georgie. I'm infinite."

"Yeah, but why?"

"The usual reasons. Backup friends, navy blue jackets— plus someday I might run for office."

They'd written the first draft of the *Passing Time* pilot in Seth's room. And written the second draft down at *The Spoon,* Georgie doing all the typing.

How had she missed Neal until junior year? He'd started working at *The Spoon* as a freshman, same as her. Georgie must have seen him, without really seeing him, dozens of times. Was she that sucked in by Seth? Seth *was* extra sucky—pushy and loud, always demanding Georgie's attention. . . .

But once Georgie noticed Neal, she saw him around the office constantly. She'd try not to stare when he walked past her desk on his way to the production room. Sometimes, if she was lucky, he'd look her way and nod.

"I just don't understand the attraction," Seth said after a month of this.

"What attraction?"

They were sitting at their shared desk, and Seth was eating Georgie's princess chicken. Stabbing at it with one chopstick. "Yours. To that fat little cartoon man."

Georgie didn't quite understand it either—why Neal was suddenly the only thing on her radar. "We're just friends," she said.

"Really," Seth said.

"Friendly acquaintances."

"Yeah, but that's the thing, Georgie—he *isn't* friendly. He growls at people, literally, if they get too close."

"He doesn't growl at me," she said.

"Well, he wouldn't."

"Why wouldn't he?"

"Because you're a pretty girl. You're probably the only pretty girl who's ever talked to him. He's too stunned to growl."

Georgie tried not to watch for Neal. She tried to play it cool when she saw him. But she usually found an excuse to walk back to the production room a few minutes after he got there. Sometimes she'd pretend she had to talk to one of the other artists. Sometimes, she'd walk right up to Neal's drafting table and lean against the wall, waiting for him to acknowledge her.

Seth was an idiot: Neal wasn't fat. Just sort of soft-looking. Small and strong, without any corners.

"You're lurking," Neal said that night. The princess-chicken night.

Georgie had meandered back to the production room and was leaning idly against a pillar near his table. "I'm not lurking," she said. "I just didn't want to startle you."

"Do you think you're startling?"

This week's comic strip was more complicated than usual. One panel with lots of characters. Neal had started inking at one corner.

She craned her head over the table. "I wouldn't want

you to jump and spill ink all over your drawing."

He shook his head. "I wouldn't."

"You might," she said.

"I don't jump."

"Nerves of steel, huh?"

Neal shrugged.

"So," she said, "I could sneak up behind you and, I don't know, *scream,* and you wouldn't even flinch."

"Probably not."

Georgie pulled a wheeled stool over and sat across from him. "But I could be an ax murderer."

"You couldn't."

"I could."

"Georgie McCool, ax murderer . . ." He cocked his head, like he was considering it. "No. You couldn't."

"But you wouldn't know it was *me* sneaking up on you," she said.

"I'd know it was you."

"How?"

He looked up at her for a second, then went back to his work. "You have a very distinct presence."

"Distinct?"

"Palpable," Neal said.

Georgie tried not to smile. "Is that a compliment?"

"I don't know, do you want it to be?"

"Do I want people to know when I walk into a room?"

"Do you want *me* to know?"

"I . . ."

Neal glanced up over her shoulder, then looked back down. "Your boyfriend needs you."

Georgie spun partway around. Seth was standing in the doorway, his smile falsely bright. "Hey. Georgie.

Could I get you to look at something?"

She squinted at him, trying to suss out whether he really needed her help or whether he was just being obstructionist. "Um, sure," she said, "just a minute."

He waited in the doorway.

"Just. A minute," she said again, pointedly raising her eyebrows at him.

Seth nodded, already pouting, and backed away.

Georgie stood up. "He's not my boyfriend."

"Ah," Neal said, inking a smile onto a cartoon rabbit. "Conjoined twin?"

"Writing partner." She reluctantly made for the door.

"Writing partner," Neal murmured, going about his business.

Seth hadn't really needed her help—of course he hadn't. (And he'd eaten everything good out of her dinner.)

"I knew you were crying wolf," she said, pushing the take-out container onto his side of the desk. "Next time I'm going to ignore you."

"I wasn't crying wolf." He scooted his chair closer to hers. "I was crying hobbit."

"What if I did this to you when you were on the make?"

"Oh God, Georgie, take it back. You can't be *on the make* with *the cartoon hobbit*."

"I never pass judgment on any of your girlfriends."

"Because they're all nice and gorgeous. Uniformly. God, they should wear uniforms, isn't that a delicious idea?"

"The point is—I get to do this, Seth. I get to talk to guys. Do you want me to spend the rest of my life alone?"

"*No.* Don't be ridiculous."

"Then back off."

He leaned forward, resting an elbow on her armrest.

"Are you lonely, Georgie? Do you have needs?"

"I said back off."

"Because you could tell me about your needs," he said. "I think our friendship is ready for that."

"I hate you."

"Where 'hate' equals 'love' and also 'can't live without.'"

"I'm ignoring you now."

"Wait, I really do need your help with this." He turned his computer monitor toward her and pointed. "Is this funny? It's a Snoopy/Snoop Dogg thing, and every time Charlie Brown tries to feed him, he's like, 'Thanks, Chizzuck.' . . ."

The next time Seth tried to interrupt her while she was talking to Neal, Georgie really did ignore him. She sent him away with an "I'm sure it can wait."

That made Neal look almost all the way up from his comic strip. He raised an eyebrow, and the side of his lips curved up into a closed-mouth smile.

Neal had nice lips.

Maybe everybody had nice lips, and you only really noticed it when you stared at their mouths all the time.

Georgie stared at Neal's mouth all the time.

It was easy to stare at Neal because he was always looking down at his comic; there was no danger of getting caught. And it was easy to stare at Neal because Neal was easy to stare at.

Maybe not breathtaking. Not the way Seth could be when he was all dressed up and posing and he'd just run his fingers through his hair.

Neal didn't take Georgie's breath away. Maybe the opposite. But that was okay—that was really good, actually, to be near someone who filled your lungs with air.

Georgie just *liked* to look at Neal. She liked his dark-but-not-very-dark hair. She liked his pale skin. Neal was *so* pale, even on his cheeks and the backs of his short, broad hands. Georgie wasn't sure how anyone could stay that pale, walking around campus all day. Maybe Neal carried a parasol. Anyway, it made his lips seem really pink, in comparison.

Neal's lips were first-rate—small and neat and symmetrical. Horizontally symmetrical, the top lip almost exactly the same thickness as the bottom. There were even matching dents, one just above his top lip and one just below his bottom lip. A permanent, 20 percent pucker.

Of course Georgie thought about kissing him.

Probably everybody thought about kissing Neal, once they'd gotten a good look at him. That was probably why he was so loath to make eye contact with anyone—crowd control.

Neal was drawing something now in the margin of his comic strip. A girl. Glasses, heart-shaped face . . . hair coiling in every direction. Then he drew a thought bubble: *"I can't stay back here all day. Comedy needs me!"*

Georgie worried she was blushing. "Am I bothering you?"

Neal shook his head. "This can't be exciting for you."

"It's not exciting, it's . . . mesmerizing. It's like watching somebody do magic."

"I'm drawing a hedgehog wearing a monocle."

"It's like you can make anything you want come out of your hands," she said. "That's magic."

"Maybe if it were an *actual* hedgehog coming out of my hand."

"I'm sorry." She sat up in her chair. "I'll let you work."

"I can work with you here." He didn't look up.

"But—"

"I can even work if you talk."

Georgie settled back in the chair, hesitantly. "Okay."

Neal added another thought bubble to her caricature: *"Now what am I supposed to say?!?!"*

Then he drew a thought bubble coming out of the bottom of the page, pointing back at himself: *"Anything you want, Georgie McCool."*

And then a smaller thought bubble: *"If that is your real name . . ."*

Georgie knew she was blushing. She watched his hand go back to the comic, then cleared her throat. "You're not from around here, are you?"

That got a smile out of Neal, a real smile, with both sides of his mouth. "Nebraska," he said.

"Is that like Kansas?"

"It's more like Kansas than other things, I guess. Do you know a lot about Kansas?"

"I've watched *The Wizard of Oz* many, many times."

"Well then," he said, "Nebraska's like Kansas. But in color."

"What are you doing here?"

"Mesmerizing you."

"You came to California to mesmerize me?"

"I should have," he said. "That beats the real reason."

"Which is . . ."

"I came to California to study oceanography."

"That sounds like a perfectly good reason," she said.

"Well"—he flicked his pen in short strokes around the hedgehog's face—"as it turns out, I don't actually like the ocean."

Georgie laughed. Neal's eyes were laughing with her.

"I'd never seen it before I got here," he said, glancing quickly up at her. "I thought it seemed cool."

"It's not cool?"

"It's really wet," he said. "And also outside."

Georgie kept laughing. Neal kept inking.

"Sunburn . . . ," he said, "seasick . . ."

"So now what are you studying?"

"I am definitely still studying oceanography," he said, nodding at his drawing. "I am definitely here on an oceanography scholarship, still studying oceanography."

"But that's terrible. You can't study oceanography if you don't like the ocean."

"I may as well." He almost smiled again. "I don't like anything else either."

Georgie laughed.

Neal added another thought bubble to the bottom of the page: *Almost anything.*

"You can't leave yet." Seth stood in the doorway with his arms crossed.

"Seth, it's seven o'clock." Nine in Omaha. Or maybe 1998 in Omaha.

"Right," he said, "and you didn't get here until one, and you've been practically useless all day."

"*A,* that isn't true," Georgie argued. "And *B,* if I'm being useless, I may as well go home."

"No," he pleaded, "stay. Maybe you're about to come out of it."

"I'm exhausted," she said. "And possibly still hungover. And you know what? You've also been useless for the last three hours—what's your excuse?"

"I'm useless when you're useless, Georgie"—Seth

swept one hand up helplessly—"that's a long-established fact."

She unplugged her phone. "Then maybe we'll both be in better shape tomorrow."

"You can talk to me about this," he said, his voice low and losing all pretense. "Whatever's going on with you today. This week."

Georgie looked up at him. At his brown eyes and still-not-even-a-little-bit-gray hair. Never removed from the package.

He was her best friend.

"No," she said. "I can't."

CHAPTER 10

Georgie started to call Neal on the way home that night, her phone plugged into the lighter—then she stopped. Neal hadn't picked up any of her calls, all day.

The last time she'd talked to him was still . . . the *last* time she'd talked to him.

Which Georgie still wasn't dealing with.

Which she still couldn't accept.

Georgie thought about her big, dark, empty house—her house that already felt haunted. . . .

And instead of heading back home, she got off the freeway in Reseda.

She didn't have a key to her mom's house, so she had to knock on the front door.

Heather opened it, looking significantly more kempt than usual. She was wearing lip gloss and at least three shades of eye shadow.

"Oh," she said. "It's you." She pulled on Georgie's arm. "Come inside—hurry—and stay away from the windows."

"Why? Is someone casing the house?"

"Just come *in*."

Georgie came in. Her parents—her mom and Kendrick—were watching TV on the couch, cuddling one of the pugs, the lumpy pregnant one, between them, and petting her with all four hands. "Georgie!" her mom said. "We didn't know you were coming."

"I just didn't feel like driving out to Calabasas. You're so much closer to the studio."

"Of course." Her mom made a concerned face. Georgie couldn't tell if it was for her or for the dog. "You feeling better?"

"Yeah, I—" The doorbell rang. Georgie reached back toward the door.

"No!" her mom snapped. The dog barked. Heather pushed Georgie away, motioning frantically for her to get back.

"It's the pizza boy," her mom whispered.

"That isn't an explanation," Georgie whispered back.

Heather peeked out the window, smoothed down her snug T-shirt, then opened the door and stepped onto the stoop, shutting it behind her.

"She has a crush," her mom said, scratching the pug's distended belly. *"You remember what that was like,"* she said to the dog in a baby voice, *"don't you? Don't you, little mama?"*

"I don't think she remembers," Georgie said. "You bred her with some dog in Tarzana she'd never met before."

"Shhh," her mom said, covering the dog's eyes. "Only because her hubby shoots blanks."

"Uhhhhghh." Georgie shuddered.

"You *look* like you're feeling better," her mom said, still in the baby voice, still smiling at the dog.

"I am," Georgie said. She was. Relatively. She wasn't drunk or hungover. And she hadn't talked to any dead people for almost twenty-four hours now, so that was a plus.

"Well, good," her mom said. "There's leftover Swiss steak in the fridge if you're hungry."

"And pizza," Heather offered, walking back into the living room. Aglow. She closed the front door and leaned against it, holding the pizza box against her stomach.

Georgie looked down at the box. "Oh, no. That's very special pizza. I wouldn't dare. Anyway, I ate at work—I think I might just lie down."

She started walking through the living room toward the hall. "Actually . . ." She turned back to her mom. "Could I use your cell phone?"

"Sure, it's in my purse." Her mom pushed the dog onto Kendrick's lap and got off the sofa. "I washed your jeans for you," she said, finding her purse, rifling through it, "but you look so good in those pants. You should wear more loungewear." She handed Georgie her phone, a bejeweled Android something-or-another with a pug screen saver.

Georgie dialed Neal's number and hung up when it went to voice mail. Then she dialed his mom's house, holding her breath. Busy.

"Thanks," she said, handing the phone back. "Kendrick? Could I use your phone?" Georgie felt like she was testing something, but she wasn't sure what.

Kendrick's phone was plain and black and splattered with drywall mud. Voice mail again. Then busy on the landline. "Thanks," Georgie said, handing it back.

Her mom looked down at her phone, probably checking to see whom Georgie had called. "Oh, honey, do you really think Neal's screening his calls?"

"I don't know," Georgie said, honestly. "Thanks. And thanks for letting me stay."

Her mom put an arm around Georgie's shoulder and kissed the side of her head. Georgie slumped into the half hug for a minute, then headed to her room.

It felt so much like coming home from school after a really bad day. Her mom had folded her jeans and Neal's T-shirt, and set them on the pillow as if she'd known Georgie would come back. (As if Neal had left Georgie and also kicked her out of the house.) There were even new sheets on Georgie's old bed.

She thought about taking a shower, then climbed onto the bed and pulled the phone into her lap. There wasn't any reason to call Neal again. She'd just tried; he hadn't picked up.

Was he actually avoiding her calls?

It sure seemed that way. The only time someone answered Neal's phone was when he wasn't there . . . supposedly. Maybe his mom was running interference for him. Maybe she knew something that Georgie didn't.

Margaret wouldn't want this to happen. She liked Georgie, and she'd never want this for the girls. (*This,* Georgie thought, not wanting to find better words for her worst-case scenario.)

Margaret wouldn't wish for it or want it. . . .

But Neal was Margaret's son. And she knew he was unhappy.

That was just a fact.

That wasn't Georgie being melodramatic or paranoid or delusional. That was Georgie being honest.

Neal wasn't happy. Neal hadn't been happy for a long time.

He didn't complain about it. He didn't say, "I'm unhappy." (*God—in a way, that would be a relief.*) He just wore it, breathed it. Held it between them. Rolled away from it in his sleep.

Neal wasn't happy, and Georgie was why.

And not because of anything she'd ever done or said. Just because of who she was.

Georgie was Neal's anchor. (And not the good kind. Not the happy anchor that keeps you safe and grounded, the one you get tattooed across your chest.) Georgie was . . . dead weight.

Okay. *Now* she was being melodramatic.

This was why she never let herself think about *this*. Because her brain would dive and dive and never touch bottom. She didn't let herself think about it. But she still *knew* it. Everyone around them knew it—Margaret must. That Neal wasn't happy. That he hated California, that he felt alternately lost and thwarted here. Trapped.

And everyone knew that Georgie needed Neal far more than he needed her. That the *girls* needed Neal far more than they needed her.

Of course Neal would get custody. Neal already had custody. Neal and Alice and Noomi—they were a closed system, an independent organism.

Neal took them to school, Neal took them to the park, Neal gave them baths.

Georgie came home for dinner.

Most nights.

When Georgie drove Alice to swim lessons, Alice worried that Georgie would get lost on the way there. *"I guess we can call Dad if you can't find it."*

On Saturday mornings when Neal left to run errands, the girls wouldn't ask for breakfast until he came home. When they fell and hurt themselves, they screamed "Daddy!"

Georgie was extra. She was the fourth wheel. (On something that only needed three wheels. The fourth wheel on a tricycle.)

She'd be nothing without them. *Nothing*. But without her? They'd be exactly the same. And Neal . . . maybe Neal would be happier.

She felt sick again.

She picked up the yellow receiver but kept one finger on the phone's plunger, not ready to hear the dial tone. There wasn't any reason to call Neal now—she'd just tried.

Georgie should pick up a wall charger for her cell phone tomorrow on the way to work.

Or just get your battery fixed, her brain yelled at her. *Or just go home, where you have wall chargers stashed all over the house!*

I'm not going home again until Neal is there, Georgie yelled back, realizing for the first time that it was true.

She let the plunger go and listened to the phone hum.

It isn't going to happen again, she told herself. After all, nothing strange had happened all day. Neal was avoiding her, but that wasn't strange; it was just horrible.

It wasn't going to happen again. Georgie's head was clear. She felt firmly rooted in reality. Miserably rooted. She tapped the receiver against her forehead to prove that it hurt. Then she ran her index finger along the phone's plastic face and started dialing Neal's mom's landline.

Because . . .

She wanted to.

Because she'd gotten through landline-to-landline twice so far, never mind what had happened after.

One, she dialed, *four, oh, two . . .*

These rotary dials were like meditation. They forced you to slow down and concentrate. If you pulled the next number too soon, you had to start over from the top.

Four, five, three . . .

It wasn't going to happen again. The weirdness. The delirium. Neal probably wouldn't even pick up.

Four, three, three, one . . .

CHAPTER 11

"Hello?"

Georgie exhaled when she heard Neal's voice, then resisted the urge to ask him who the president was. "Hey," she said.

"Georgie." He sounded relieved. (He sounded like Neal, like heaven.) "You called."

"Yeah."

"I'm sorry I was such a jerk last night," he said quickly.

Last night. She felt a wave of panic. *Last night, last night, last night.* Neal shouldn't remember last night, because last night hadn't happened outside of Georgie's crazy head.

"Georgie? Are you there?"

"I'm here."

"Look, I'm sorry about the way I acted." He sounded determined. "I've been thinking about it all day."

"I'm sorry, too," Georgie choked out.

"You just caught me by surprise," he said. "Hey—are you crying again?"

"I . . ." Was she crying? Or hyperventilating? Maybe a little of both.

Neal's voice dropped. "Hey. Don't cry, sunshine, I'm sorry. Don't cry."

"I'm not crying," Georgie said. "I mean, I won't. I'm sorry, I just . . ."

"Let's start over, okay?"

Georgie sobbed half a hiccuppy, hopeless laugh. "Start over? Can we do that?"

"This conversation," he said. "Let's start this conversation over. And last night's, too. Let's go back to last night, okay?"

"I feel like we have to go back further than that," Georgie said.

"No."

"Why not?"

Neal was whispering. "I don't want to go back any further. I don't want to miss any of the rest."

"Okay," she said, wiping her eyes.

This was crazy. This was weird and crazy. It wasn't real. But it was still *happening*. If Georgie hung up, would it stop?

Or should she keep crazy on the line, so she could trace the call?

"Okay," she said again.

"Okay," Neal said. "So . . . you called to see if I got in all right. I did. It was a long drive, and I only had three CDs, so I listened to this radio show in the middle of the night—it was called *Coast to Coast*—and now I think I believe in aliens."

Georgie decided to play along. She must be having this hallucination for a reason. Maybe if she played along, she'd figure out what it needed, and it would move on. (Or did that just work for ghosts?)

"You've always believed in aliens," she said.

"I have not," Neal said. "I'm a skeptic—I *was* a skeptic. Now I believe in aliens."

"Did you see some?"

"No. But I saw a double rainbow in Colorado."

She laughed. "John Denver wept."

"It was pretty amazing."

"Did you drive straight through, without stopping?"

"Yeah," he said, "I did it in twenty-seven hours."

"That was stupid."

"I know. But I had a lot to think about—I figured the thinking would keep me awake."

"I'm glad you got home okay."

For a hallucination, this conversation was progressing very rationally. (Which made sense; Georgie had always been good at writing dialogue.)

She'd guessed right: She was obviously talking to Neal—or imagining that she was talking to Neal—just after their big Christmas fight, in college.

But they *hadn't* talked after that fight.

Neal didn't call Georgie after he left for Omaha, so Georgie didn't call him either. He'd just shown up at the end of the week, on Christmas morning, with an engagement ring. . . .

"You still sound pretty upset," Neal said. Not-Neal said. Hallucinatory, aural-mirage Neal said.

"I've had a weird day," Georgie replied. "Also—I think you might have broken up with me a few days ago."

"No," he said quickly.

She shook her head. It still reeled. "No? Are you sure?"

"No. I mean . . . I got angry, I said some terrible things— and I meant all of them—but I didn't break up with you."

"We're not broken up?" Her voice broke on "broken."

"No," Neal insisted.

"But I always thought you broke up with me."

"Always?"

"Always . . . since we fought."

"I don't want to break up with you, Georgie."

"But you said you couldn't do this anymore."

"I know," he said.

"And you meant it," she said.

"I did."

"But we're not broken up?"

He growled, but she could tell that it wasn't at her. Usually when Neal growled, he was growling at himself. "I *can't* do this anymore," he said. "But I'm hoping *this* can change because . . . I don't think I can live without you either."

"Sure you can." Georgie wasn't joking.

Neal laughed anyway. (Well, he didn't *laugh*—Neal rarely laughed. But he had a sort of huffy, roof-of-the-mouth breathy thing that counted as a laugh.) "You really think I can live without you? Because I haven't had any luck with that so far."

"Not true," Georgie said. She might as well say it; this conversation wasn't real, it didn't cost her anything. In fact, maybe that's what she was supposed to be doing here—saying everything she could never say to the real Neal. Just getting it out of her chest. "You had twenty years of luck before we met."

"That doesn't count," he said, like he was playing along. *(No, I'm the one playing along,* Georgie thought. *You, sir, are a hallucination.)* "I didn't know what I was missing before I met you."

"Frustration," she said. "Irritation. Douchebag industry parties."

"Not just that."

"Late nights," she continued. "Missed dinners. That

voice I use when I'm trying to impress people . . ." Neal hated that voice.

"Georgie."

" . . . Seth."

Neal made another huffy noise. This one wasn't anything like a laugh. "Why are you trying so hard to push me away?"

"Because," she pushed. "Because of what you said before you left. About how it wasn't working and you weren't happy, and how you didn't think you could go on like this. I keep thinking about what you said—I haven't stopped thinking about it—and I can't think of any way to argue. You were *right,* Neal. I'm not going to change. I'm all caught up in a world that you hate, and I'm just going to pin you here. Maybe you should get out while you still can."

"You think I should break up with you?" he said. "You want that?"

"Those are two different questions."

"You think I'd be better off without you?"

"Probably." *Say it,* she told herself. *Just say it.* "I mean— yes. Look at everything you said after that party. Look at the evidence."

"A lot has happened since I said that."

"You saw a double rainbow," she said, "and now you believe in aliens."

"No. You called three times to tell me that you love me."

Georgie caught her breath and held it. She'd called Neal so many more times than that.

He sounded like he was holding the phone even closer to his mouth now: *"Do* you love me, Georgie?"

"More than anything," she said. Because she was still telling the truth, damn the torpedoes. "More than everything."

Neal huffed, maybe in relief.

"But," she kept pushing, "you said that might not be enough."

"It might not be."

"So . . ."

"So I don't know," Neal said. "But I'm not breaking up with you. I can't right now. Are you breaking up with me?"

"*No.*"

"Let's start over," he said softly.

"How far back?"

"Just to the beginning of this conversation."

Georgie took a deep breath. "How was your trip?"

"Good," he said. "I did it in twenty-seven hours."

"Idiot."

"And I saw a double rainbow."

"Miraculous."

"And when I got here, my mom had made all my favorite Christmas cookies."

"Lucky."

"I wish you were here, Georgie—it snowed for you."

This wasn't happening. This was a hallucination. Or a schizophrenic episode. Or . . . a dream.

Georgie slumped back against her headboard and brought the tightly coiled telephone cord up to her mouth, biting on the rubbery plastic.

She closed her eyes and kept playing along.

CHAPTER 12

"I can't believe you drove straight through."

"It wasn't so bad."

"You drove for twenty-seven hours. I think that's illegal."

"For truckers."

"For a reason."

"It wasn't so bad. I started dropping off a bit in Utah, but I stopped the car and walked around."

"You could have died. Right there. In Utah."

"You make it sound like that's worse than regular dying."

"Promise me you'll never do that again."

"I promise never to almost die in Utah. I'll be extra careful from now on around Mormons."

"Tell me more about the aliens."

"Tell me more about the drive."

"Tell me more about your parents."

"Tell me more about Omaha."

Georgie just wanted to hear his voice, she didn't want it to stop. She didn't want Neal to stop.

There were moments when it started to rise up on her, what was happening. What she had access to, real or not. *Neal. 1998.* The immensity of it—the improbability—kept creeping up the back of Georgie's skull like dizziness, and she kept shaking it off.

It was like getting him back. Her Neal. (Her old Neal.)

He was right there, and she could ask him anything that she wanted.

"Tell me more about the mountains," Georgie said, because she wasn't really sure what to ask. Because *"tell me where I went wrong"* might break the spell.

And because what she wanted more than anything else was just to keep listening.

"I went to see *Saving Private Ryan* without you."

"Good."

"And my dad and I are going to see *Life Is Beautiful.*"

"Good. You should also rent *Schindler's List* without me."

"We've been through this," he said. "You need to watch *Schindler's List.* Every human being needs to watch *Schindler's List.*"

Georgie still hadn't. "You know I can't do anything with Nazis."

"But you like *Hogan's Heroes.* . . ."

"That's where I draw the line."

"The Nazi line?"

"Yes."

"At Colonel Klink."

"Obviously."

She wasn't crying anymore. Neal wasn't growling.

She was burrowed under the comforter, holding the phone lightly against her ear.

He was still there. . . .

"So Christmas with the Pool Man, huh?"

"God," Georgie said. "I forgot I called him that."

"How could you forget? You've been calling him that for six months."

"Kendrick's not so bad."

"He doesn't seem bad—he seems nice. Do you really think they'll get married soon?"

"Yeah. Probably." *Imminently*.

"When did you get so Zen about this?"

"What do you mean?"

"The last time we talked about it, you went on a whole rant about how weird it is. About how you and your mom are now drawing from the same dating pool."

Oh. Right. Georgie laughed. "And you said, 'No, your mom's dating pool is literally a pool.' . . . God. I remember that."

Neal kept going: "And then you said that if your mom proceeds at her current pattern and rate, your next stepdad must currently be in the sixth grade. That was funny."

"You thought that was funny?"

"Yeah," he said.

"You didn't laugh."

"You know I don't laugh, sunshine."

Georgie rolled over and switched the phone to the other side of her head, curling up again under the comforter. "I still can't believe my mom was checking out twenty-something guys at *forty*. That she was looking at college guys and thinking, 'Yep. Fair game. Totally doable.' I don't think I ever appreciated how disturbing that was until *just now*." That would be like Georgie hooking up with Scotty. Or with one of Heather's friends—her pizza boy. "Guys in their early twenties are *babies*," she said. "They don't even have all their facial hair yet. They're literally not done with puberty."

"Hey, now."

"Oh. Sorry. Not you."

"Right. Not me. Unlike many of my peers, I'm plenty mature enough to date your mom."

"Stop! Neal! Don't even joke."

"I knew you weren't suddenly Zen about this."

"God. My mom's a pervert. She's a libertine."

"Maybe she's just in love."

"I'm sorry about the party," she said.

"I don't want to talk about it, Georgie."

"I'm still sorry."

"That it existed? That you were a huge hit?"

"That I made you go."

"You didn't make me go," he said. "You can't *make* me do anything—I'm an adult. And I'm much stronger than you."

"Upper body strength isn't everything; I have wiles."

"Not really."

"Yes, I do. I'm a woman. Women have wiles."

"Some women. It's not like every woman is born wily."

"If I don't have wiles," she said, "how come I can get you to do almost anything I want?"

"You don't *get* me to do anything. I just do things. Because I love you."

"Oh."

"Christ, Georgie, don't sound so disappointed."

"Neal . . . I really am sorry. About the party."

"I don't want to talk about it."

"Okay."

"And it's not just my upper body," he said. "My entire body is stronger than yours. I can pin you in like thirty-five seconds."

"Only because I *let* you," she said. "Because I love you."

"Oh, okay."

"Don't sound so disappointed, Neal."

"I'm pretty sure I don't sound disappointed at all."

Georgie sank deeper into her pillow. She pulled her comforter up to her chin. She closed her eyes.

If this was just a dream, she wished she could have it every night—Neal not-quite-whispering sweet somethings into her ear.

"My parents were disappointed that you didn't come home with me."

"I'll bet your mom was happy to have you to herself."

"My mom likes you."

She didn't. Not in 1998.

"I think that's an exaggeration," Georgie said. "She intentionally frowns whenever I try to be funny—it's like *not laughing* at me isn't a strong enough negative reaction."

"She doesn't know what to do with you—but she likes you."

"She thinks I want to write jokes for a living."

"You do."

"*Knock-knock* jokes."

"My mom likes you," he said. "She likes that you make me happy."

"Now you're putting words in her mouth."

"I am not. She told me so herself, the last time they came to see me in L.A., after we all went to that tamale place."

"She did?"

"She said she hadn't seen me smile so much since I was a kid."

"When were you smiling? No one in your family smiles. You're a dynasty of wasted dimples."

"My dad smiles."

"Yeah . . ."

"They like you, Georgie."

"Did you tell them why I didn't come?"

"I told them your mom wanted you to stay home for Christmas."

"I guess that's true," she said.

"Yeah."

It was one in the morning. Three in the morning in Omaha. Or wherever Neal was.

The hand that was holding the phone to her ear had gone numb, but Georgie didn't roll over.

She should let him go. He was yawning. He might even be falling asleep—she'd had to repeat her last question.

But Georgie didn't want to.

Because . . .

Well, because she couldn't expect this to go on. Whatever this was. This thing that she'd started, just in the last few hours, to think of as a gift.

And because . . . she wasn't sure when she'd hear Neal's voice again.

"Neal. Are you asleep?"

"Hmmm," he answered. "Almost. I'm sorry."

"S'okay. Just—why didn't you want to talk about everything tonight?"

"*Everything*. You mean, why didn't I want to fight?"

"Yeah."

"I—" He sounded like he was moving, maybe sitting up. "—I felt so bad when I left California, and I felt so bad when I yelled at you on the phone last night, and—I don't know, Georgie, maybe it's never going to work with us. When I think about coming back to L.A., all my anger starts to come back. I feel trapped, and frustrated, and I just want to drive as far as I can away from there. Away from you, honestly."

"God, Neal . . ."

"Wait, I'm not done. I feel that way. Until I hear your voice. And then . . . I don't want to break up with you. Not right now. Definitely not tonight. Tonight, I just wanted to pretend that all that other stuff wasn't there. Tonight, I just wanted to be in love with you."

She pressed the phone into her ear. "What about tomorrow?"

"You mean today?"

"Yeah," she said.

"We'll figure it out when we get there."

"Do you want me to call you later? Today?"

Neal yawned. "Yeah."

"Okay. I'll let you go to sleep now."

"Thanks," he said. "Sorry I'm so tired."

"It's okay. Time zones."

"Tell me again."

"What?"

"Why you called."

Georgie squeezed the phone. "To make sure you're okay. To tell you that I love you."

"I love you, too. Never doubt it."

A tear slipped over the bridge of her nose, into the eye below. "I never do," she said. "Never."

"Good night," Neal said.

"Good night," Georgie answered.

"Call me."

"I will."

SUNDAY
DECEMBER 22 , 2013

CHAPTER 13

Georgie stretched and rolled into someone.

Neal?

Maybe this was it. Maybe she was waking up from whatever this was, and Neal would be here . . . and Uncle Henry and Auntie Em.

She was scared to open her eyes.

A phone rang next to her head. Some Beyoncé ringtone.

Georgie rolled over and looked at Heather, who was sitting on top of the comforter, answering her phone.

"Mom," Heather said, "I'm in the same house—this is lazy, even for you. . . . Fine. Be patient, I said I'd ask her." She looked at Georgie. "Do you want waffles?"

Georgie shook her head.

"No," Heather said. "She says no. . . . I don't know, she just woke up. Do you have to work today?" She poked Georgie. "*Hey*. Do you have to work today?"

Georgie nodded and looked at the clock. Not quite nine. Seth wouldn't be calling the police yet.

"Okay," Heather said into the phone, then sighed. "I love you, too. . . . No, Mom, it's not that I mind saying it, but you're right down the hall. . . . Fine. I love you. Good-bye."

She ended the call and flopped down next to Georgie. "Good morning, sleepyhead."

"Good morning."

"How are you?"

Delusional. Possibly certifiable. Weirdly happy. "Fine," Georgie said.

"Really?"

"What do you mean, 'really'?"

"I mean," Heather said, "I know you have to tell *Mom* that you're fine, no matter what, but if you were *really* fine, you wouldn't be here."

"I'm fine, I just don't feel like going home to an empty house."

"Did Neal actually leave you?"

"No," Georgie said, then groaned. "I mean, I don't think so." She reached for her glasses. They were balanced on the headboard. "He was mad when he left, but—I think he'd tell me if he was leaving me. Don't you think he'd tell me?" She was asking it seriously.

Heather made a face. "God, Georgie, I don't know. Neal's not much of a talker. I didn't even know you guys were having problems."

Georgie rubbed her eyes. "We're always having problems."

"Well, it doesn't ever look like it. Every time I talk to you, Neal is bringing you breakfast in bed, or making you a pop-up birthday card."

"Yeah." Georgie didn't want to tell Heather that it wasn't that simple. That Neal made her breakfast even when he was pissed; sometimes he did it *because* he was pissed. As a way to act like he was present in their relationship, even when he was chilled through and barely talking to her.

"When I was a kid," Heather said, "I always thought Neal was your Prince Charming."

Georgie's weirdly happy feelings were rapidly fading. "Why?"

"Because I could remember your wedding. . . . That big white dress you wore and all the flowers, and Neal was so handsome—he totally had Prince Charming hair, he still does, like Snow White's Prince Charming—and he called you 'sunshine.' Does he still call you 'sunshine'?"

"Sometimes," Georgie said, glancing over at the phone.

"I thought he was so romantic. . . ."

"Do me a favor."

Heather looked suspicious. "What?"

"Call the house phone."

"What?"

"The landline," Georgie said. "Call the landline."

Heather frowned, but picked up her cell phone and dialed.

Georgie held her breath and watched the yellow rotary phone. It rang. She exhaled and reached for it. "Hello?" Georgie said, looking at Heather, knowing she must look disturbed.

"Hi," Heather said, "do you feel like waffles?"

"No," Georgie said. "Love you, bye."

Heather smiled. "Love you, bye."

Georgie took a shower in her mom's bathroom. Her mom's shampoo smelled even worse than Heather's. Like marzipan.

She put her jeans back on, and Neal's black T-shirt. Her bra had seen better days, but it was still wearable. She decided her underwear had gone too many days to be mentionable; she shoved them to the bottom of the trash and went without.

Maybe you should get a change of underwear when you go home to get your wall charger, her brain said.

Maybe you should shut up, Georgie thought back at it.

After she was dressed, she sat on her bed and looked at the rotary phone.

Time to deal with this.

She picked up the receiver and steadily dialed Neal's parents' house.

His mom picked up after the third ring.

"Hello?"

"Hi . . . Mrs. Grafton," Georgie said.

"Yes?"

"It's Georgie."

"Oh, hi, Georgie. Neal's still asleep. He must have been up pretty late. Do you want him to call you back?"

"No. I mean, just tell him I'll call later. Actually, I already told him I'd call later. But—I was going to ask him something." She couldn't ask about the president; that would seem mental. . . . "Do you happen to know who the Speaker of the House is?"

Neal's mom hummed. "It's Newt Gingrich, isn't it? Did it change?"

"No," Georgie said. "I think that's right. His name was at the tip of my tongue." She leaned closer to the base of the phone. "Thanks. Um, bye. Thanks." She dropped the receiver onto the hook and stood up suddenly, taking a few steps away.

Then she dropped to her knees and crawled under the bed, reaching for the telephone outlet and unclicking the plug. She pulled the cord away, then backed out from the bed and crawled to the opposite wall, staring at the nightstand.

She had to deal with this.

It was still happening.

She had to deal with it.

Possibilities:

1. *Persistent hallucination.*
2. *Really long dream. (Or maybe normal-length dream, perceived as really long from the inside?)*
3. *Schizophrenic episode.*
4. *Unprovoked* Somewhere in Time *scenario.*
5. *Am already dead? Like on* Lost?
6. *Drug use. Unrecalled.*
7. *Miracle.*
8. *Interdimensional portal.*
9. It's a Wonderful Life? *(Minus angel. Minus suicide. Minus quasi-rational explanation.)*
10. *Magic fucking phone.*

She had to deal with this.

She sat in the car and plugged in her iPhone. No missed calls from Neal. From thirty-seven-year-old, real Neal. *(Why wasn't he calling her? Was he really this pissed? Neal, Neal, Neal!)*

She dialed his cell phone and didn't even flinch when his mom answered.

"Georgie?"

"Margaret."

"I knew it was you this time," his mom said, "because I saw your photo on the phone. Who are you supposed to be? A robot?"

"The Tin Man. Hey, Margaret, who's the Speaker of the House?"

"Oh, I don't know. Isn't it that Republican with the piercing eyes?"

"I don't know," Georgie said, realizing that she really

didn't. *Who came after Nancy Pelosi?* "It's not Newt Gingrich, though, right?"

"Oh, no," Margaret said. "Didn't he just run for president? Are you doing a crossword?"

That would have been an excellent cover; she should have told the other Margaret she was doing a crossword. "Yes," Georgie said, "hey, can I talk to Neal?"

"He just stepped out."

Of course he did.

"Didn't he call you yesterday?" Margaret asked. "I told him you called."

"I must have missed him," Georgie said.

"Here's Alice, do you want to talk to Alice? Alice, come say hi to your mom. . . ."

"Hello?" Alice sounded far away.

"Alice?"

"Talk louder, Mommy, I can't hear you." She sounded like she was sitting across the room from the phone.

"Alice!" Georgie tipped her own phone away from her ear and shouted. "Pick up the phone!"

"I am!" Alice shouted. "But Dawn says you shouldn't put cell phones on your head, or you'll get cancer!"

"That's not true."

"What?"

"That's not true!" Georgie yelled.

"Dawn said! Dawn's a nurse!"

"Meow!"

"Is that Noomi? Let me talk to Noomi!"

"I don't want Noomi to get cancer."

"Put me on speaker phone, Alice."

"I don't know how."

"It's the button that says 'speaker'!"

"Oh . . . like this?"

Georgie put the phone back to her ear. "Can you hear me?"

"Uh-huh."

"Alice, you're not going to get cancer from the cell phone. Especially not from a few minutes on the cell phone."

"Meow."

Alice sighed. "It's not that I don't trust you, Mommy, but you're not a nurse. Or a doctor. Or a scientist."

"A scientist!" Noomi said, giggling. "Scientists make potions."

"How are you guys?" Georgie asked.

"Fine," they both said. Why did Georgie even ask that question? It always made them clam right up. She'd be better off arguing with them about brain cancer.

"Where's Daddy?"

"He's at the grocery store," Alice said. "We're gonna make all Grandma's famous Christmas cookies. Even the ones with Hershey's Kisses that look like mice."

"They have cherries for bottoms," Noomi said.

Alice was still talking: "And we're gonna make peanut butter balls and green Christmas trees, and Grandma already said I could use the mixer. Noomi's gonna help, but she has to stand on the chair, and Dawn says that sounds dangerous, but it won't be, because Daddy will hold her."

Nurse Dawn. "That sounds wonderful," Georgie said. "Will you save me some cookies?"

"Meow!"

"Sure," Alice said. "I'll have to get a box."

"Meow, Mommy!"

"Meow, Noomi."

"We have to go now because we're getting the kitchen ready."

"Alice, wait—will you give Daddy a message?"

"Uh-huh."

"Will you tell him that I called to say I love you?"

"I love you, too," Alice said.

"I love you, honey. But tell Daddy that I love *him*. Tell him that's why I called."

"Okay."

"I love you, Alice. I love you, Noomi."

"Noomi's in the kitchen with Grandma now."

"Okay."

"Bye, Mommy."

Georgie started to say good-bye, but Alice had already hung up.

Someone was knocking on her windshield.

Georgie lifted her head off the steering wheel. It was Kendrick. She couldn't really hear what he was saying. She rolled down the window.

"Are you okay?" he asked.

"I'm fine."

"Okay." Kendrick nodded. "'Cause, the thing is, you look kind of like you're sitting in your car crying."

"I'm done crying," she said. "Now I'm just sitting in the car."

"Oh, well. Okay."

Georgie rolled the window back up and hid her face in the steering wheel.

There was more knocking. She looked up.

"You're blocking me!" Kendrick shouted—so that she could hear him, not because he was angry—and motioned at the open garage where his truck was already running.

"Sorry," Georgie said. "I'll just . . ."

She put the car in reverse and backed out of the driveway.

She'd just go to work.

Options:

1. *Call doctor. (End up on drugs? Possibly institutionalized . . . Would at least earn Neal's pity.)*
2. *Consult psychic. (Pros: Very romantic-comedy. Cons: Sounds time intensive; have always disliked strangers' living rooms.)*
3. *Pretend this never happened. Just have to avoid yellow phone, apparently . . .*
4. *Destroy yellow phone? (Conduit to the past too dangerous to allow. Nightmare scenarios possible, i.e., what if Marty McFly's dad doesn't take his mom to the prom?)*
5. *CHRIST ALMIGHTY. I DO NOT HAVE A CONDUIT TO THE PAST.*
6. *Call doctor?*
7.
7.
7. *Keep playing along?*

"Ma'am?"

"I'm sorry, yes?"

"That was a Venti vanilla latte, right?"

"Right," Georgie said.

"You can go ahead and drive through."

Someone honked, and Georgie checked the rearview

mirror. There were at least five cars behind her.

"Right," she said. "Sorry."

If this were a movie . . .

If there were an angel . . .

Or a machine that told fortunes . . .

Or a magic fountain . . .

If this were a movie, it wouldn't be random. A random call to a random point in the past. It would *mean* something. So what did this mean?

Christmas 1998:

Georgie and Neal went to a party. They fought. Neal dumped her—at least, she thought he was dumping her. And then, a week later, he proposed.

And now she was talking to him during that week, that lost week. . . . *Why?*

Was she supposed to change something? If this were *Quantum Leap,* there'd be something specific she was supposed to change. *(This is not* Quantum Leap, *Georgie—this is your life. You are not Scott Bakula.)*

But *what if . . .*

Christmas 1998. They fought. Neal went home. He came back. He proposed. They lived not-exactly-happily ever after. Wait, was *that* what she was supposed to fix? The not-exactly-happy part?

How was she supposed to fix something like that, *over the phone,* when she wasn't even sure it was fixable?

Christmas 1998. A week without Neal. The worst week of her life. The week he decided to marry her . . .

Was Georgie supposed to make sure that he didn't?

CHAPTER 14

"I don't know what to say," Seth said. He was leaning on the whiteboard, frowning at her Metallica T-shirt. "On the one hand, your hair is wet, so you've obviously showered and changed. I applaud that. On the other, I miss the velvet jogging pants. . . . Georgie? Hello? *Hey*."

Georgie stopped trying to plug her phone into her computer and looked up at him. He'd kicked away from the wall and set his hand on her shoulder.

"I know I've been asking you this all week," he said, "but I'll try one more time—are you okay?"

She wound the USB cord around her fingers. "If you could travel into the past and fix a mistake, would you?"

"Yes," he said, without even thinking about it. "Are you okay?"

"Yes, you would? You'd mess with the past?"

"Absolutely. You said there was a mistake—I'd fix it."

"But what if you messed everything up?" Georgie asked. "Like, what if that one action changed everything?"

"Like in *Back to the Future*?"

"Yes."

Seth shrugged. "Meh. I don't believe it. I'd go back and fix my mistake—everything else would work itself out. World War Three isn't going to happen just because I got a higher SAT score."

"But if you'd gotten a higher SAT score, you might not

have gone to ULA, and then you'd never have met me, and we wouldn't be standing here right now."

"Pfft," he said, lowering an eyebrow. "Do you really think that's all that brought us together? Circumstance? Location?" He shook his head. "I find your perspective on space and time to be very limiting."

Georgie went back to fumbling with her laptop. Seth took the cord out of her hand and plugged it in. "I printed out what we worked on yesterday," he said. "Why don't you take a look?"

Neal had noticed Georgie was different—on the phone last night. He'd mentioned it. Maybe he'd figure out what was happening. . . .

There was no way he'd figure out what was happening.

Why would Neal ever jump to the completely implausible and *correct* conclusion that he was talking to her in the future?

Georgie hadn't said anything to date herself. She hadn't mentioned the Internet. Or the war. Or their kids. She hadn't tried to warn him about the stock market or 9/11.

"You don't sound like yourself tonight," he'd said. It was after they'd been on the phone about half an hour.

"Why not?" Georgie'd asked. God, it was like talking to a ghost. Something weirder than a ghost—a sending.

"I don't know what it is."

"Is my voice lower?" That would make sense. She was fifteen years closer to menopause. "Maybe it's the crying."

"No," he said. "I don't think so. You seem . . . like you're being really careful."

"I *am* being really careful."

"You seem like you're not sure of anything."

"I'm not," she said.

"Yeah, but Georgie, 'sure of everything' is kind of your signature color."

She laughed. "Was that a *Steel Magnolias* reference?"

"You know all about my Sally Field crush," he said. "I'm not apologizing for it now."

She'd forgotten about Neal's Sally Field crush. "I know all your dirty Gidget secrets," she said.

"It was the Flying Nun who really did it for me."

Had Georgie been sure of everything at twenty-two?

She'd had a plan.

She'd always had a plan. It seemed like the smart thing to do—have a plan and follow it, until you have solid reasons to change course.

Neal had the opposite approach. His one big plan, oceanography, had gone sour on him; and then his plan turned into keeping his eyes open until something better came along.

Georgie used to think she could fix that for him. She was really good at making plans, and Neal was really good at everything else; this seemed like a no-brainer.

"You could just do *this* for a living," Georgie said one night at *The Spoon,* before they even started dating.

"Entertain you?" Neal said. "Sounds good. How are the benefits?"

She was sitting across from him (always sitting across from him) leaning on his drafting table. "No. This. *Stop the Sun.* You're good enough—I thought you were already syndicated."

"You are very kind," he said. "Very wrong, but very

kind."

"I'm serious."

"I couldn't do this for a living." He gave the wood-chuck he was drawing a cigar. "It's just messing around— it's just doodling."

"So you wouldn't want to be Matt Groening?"

"With all due respect, no."

"Why not?"

Neal shrugged. "I want to do something real. I want to make a difference."

"Making people laugh is real."

The corner of his mouth twitched. "I'll let you take up that mantle."

"Do you think that comedy is just messing around, too?"

"Honestly?" he asked.

"Of course, honestly."

"Then yes."

Georgie sat up straighter and folded her arms on the table. "You think my dreams are a waste of time?"

"I think your dreams would be a waste of *my* time," he said. "I wouldn't be happy."

"So what *would* make you happy?"

"Well, if I knew that, I'd do it." He'd looked up at her then, his eyes pained and almost too sincere for the cir-cumstances, for the bright lights and the basement of the student union. He held his dip pen over the margin of his comic and let it drip. "I mean it. If I figure out what makes me happy, I'm not going to waste any more time. I'm just going to grab it. I'm just going to *do* it."

Georgie nodded. "I believe you."

Neal smiled and looked down, sheepish now, shaking

his head a bit. "Sorry. I've had too much time in my own head lately."

She waited for him to start inking again. "You could be a doctor . . . ," she said.

"Maybe."

"You have doctorly hands. I can imagine you performing very neat stitches."

"Weird," he said. "But thank you."

"Lawyer?"

Neal shook his head.

"Indian chief?"

"Don't have the connections."

"Well," Georgie said, "that's all I've got—wait. Butcher? Baker? Candlestick maker?"

"None of those sound bad, honestly. The world needs bakers."

"And candlestick makers," she added.

"Actually, I've been thinking about—" Neal glanced up at her, then looked down, licking his lips. "—I've been thinking about the Peace Corps."

"The Peace Corps? Really?"

"Yeah. It'd give me something worthwhile to do while I figure the rest out."

"I didn't know there was still a Peace Corps."

"That or the Air Force," Neal said.

"Aren't those two radically different directions?"

"Not at all." He glanced up over her shoulder, then lowered his eyebrows and looked down.

Georgie knew that expression. She sat up and turned around to see what Seth wanted.

Seth had stepped all the way into the production room—usually he didn't come past the door. But tonight he sat down on a stool near Georgie and leaned onto a desk. "Hey, Neal, what's going on?"

"Not much," Neal muttered without looking up.

Seth nodded and turned to Georgie. "So we're just waiting on that cover story. Mike and Brian are still hammering it out."

Georgie looked down at her watch. *The Spoon* went to press tonight. She and Seth were the managing editors, so they'd have to wait for the story, set it, then send the files to the printer. It'd be a late night.

"There's no reason for both of us to stay," Seth told her. "You should just take off."

"That's okay," Georgie said. "I'll stay. You go home."

Seth wrinkled his nose. She was pretty sure he did it because it was adorable. She was pretty sure Seth had practiced all his facial expressions and gestures in front of a mirror, and worked out which ones made him look like a cross between an Abercrombie model and a kitten. "I don't want to dump it on you," he said. "You might be here all night."

"I really don't mind," she said. "Don't you have a date?"

He nodded slowly. "I do have a date."

"With the lovely Breanna, I've heard."

"With the lovely Breanna," Seth said, still nodding; he pursed his lips and twisted them to the side.

"Go on," she said. "You can owe me."

Seth narrowed his eyes at Georgie, then at Neal, then seemed to make up his mind. "Okay." He stood up. "I owe you."

"Have fun on your date," she said.

He got as far as the door, then spun around. "You know what? I'll call Breanna. I can't just abandon you like this.

It's going to be late, you'll have to walk to your car by yourself—"

"Don't worry about it," Neal said. Georgie looked back at him, surprised to hear his voice. "I'll be here," he said. "I'll make sure she gets to her car."

Seth stared at Neal. Georgie was pretty sure they'd never made eye contact before; she waited for one or both of them to start on fire.

"What a gentleman," Seth said.

"It's nothing," Neal parried.

"Great," Georgie said, trying to signal Seth with her eyes—wishing they had a nonverbal sign for *Leave me alone with this cute guy, you idiot.* "Problem solved. Go ahead, Seth. Go on your date. Get down with your bad self."

"I guess that's settled then. . . ." Seth nodded again. "All right. Well. See you tomorrow, Georgie. You still coming over? To my room?"

"Yep. Give me a call when you sweep out the lovely Breanna and all of her underthings."

"Right," he said, and finally walked away.

Georgie turned back to Neal, feeling fluttery.

"You have terrible taste in sidekicks," he said after a moment.

"Writing partner," she corrected.

"Hmm."

Neal *did* walk her to her car that night. And he *was* a perfect gentleman.

Much to Georgie's disappointment.

*

Neal had sounded different, too, last night on the phone.

His voice was a little higher, his thoughts came out looser. Neal with less clench, less control.

He'd sounded like the boy on the other side of the drafting table.

CHAPTER 15

Seth and Scotty both liked to be laughed at.

As long as Georgie laughed at their jokes, they usually wouldn't notice that she wasn't contributing to the brainstorming, that she was just writing things they said on the whiteboard and underlining them.

But today wasn't usually. Seth was still watching Georgie like he was trying to figure out was going on. . . .

Well, he could keep on trying—he was never going to come up with, *Magic fucking phone!* (Though Georgie was a little worried he'd figure out she wasn't wearing underwear.)

Seth and Scotty brainstormed.

Georgie brain-hurricaned.

What if it *was* happening for a reason? What if she was supposed to fix what was wrong between her and Neal? "What's wrong?" wasn't such an easy question to answer.

Oh, she could answer it broadly:

A lot.

A lot was wrong between them, even on good days. . . .

(The breakfast-in-bed and coming-home-early days. Days when Neal's eyes were bright. When the girls made him smile, and he made them laugh. Easy days. Christmas mornings. Coming-home-late days when Neal would catch Georgie at the door and crowd her against the wall.)

Even on *good* days, Georgie knew that Neal was unhappy.

And that it was her fault.

It wasn't just that she let him down, and put him off, and continually left him waiting—

It was that she'd tied him to her so tight. Because she *wanted* him. Because he was perfect for Georgie, even if she wasn't perfect for him. Because she wanted him more than she wanted him to be happy.

If she loved Neal, if she really loved him . . .

Shouldn't she want more for him than *with me, always with me*?

What if Georgie could give Neal the chance to start over? What would he do?

Would he join the Peace Corps? Would he go back to Omaha? Marry Dawn? Marry somebody even better than Dawn?

Would he be happy?

Would he come home from work every night, smiling? Would Dawn or Better-Than-Dawn already have dinner on the table?

Would Neal crawl into bed and pull her close to him, fall asleep with his nose in the hollow of her neck. . . .

Georgie had gotten that far in her imagining—to Neal spooning with his more-suitable-than-Georgie wife—when she imagined Neal's second-chance *kids* in this second-chance world. Then she slammed the door shut on all his hypothetical happiness.

If the universe thought Georgie was going to erase *her kids* from the timeline, it had another fucking thing coming.

She went to the bathroom and cried for a few minutes.

(That was one good thing about being the only woman on the writing staff—Georgie almost always had the bathroom to herself.)

Then she spent the next hour mentally throwing the yellow rotary phone down a deep well and filling it in with concrete.

She wasn't going to *touch* that thing again.

It wasn't really a conduit to the past. It wasn't magic. There was no such thing as magic. (*I don't believe in fairies. Sorry, Peter Pan.*) But Georgie still wasn't going to risk it. She wasn't a Time Lord, she didn't want a Time-Turner. She felt weird even praying for things—because it didn't seem like she should ask God for something that wasn't already part of the plan.

What if Georgie accidentally erased her marriage with these phone calls? What if she erased her kids? What if she'd already screwed something up—would she even know?

She tried to remind herself that this was all an illusion. That she didn't have to worry about the dangerous implications, because illusions don't have implications.

That's what she tried to remind herself, but she wasn't sure she believed it.

Illusion.

Delusion.

Mirage.

Magic fucking phone.

"Korean tacos again?" Seth asked.

Georgie nodded.

After two months of hanging out in *The Spoon*'s production room, Georgie was 53 percent sure that Neal liked her.

He put up with her; that seemed to mean something. He never asked her to go away. *(Was she really going to put that in the plus column? Not asking her to go away?)*

He talked to her. . . .

But only if Georgie talked to him first. If she sat across from him long enough.

Sometimes it seemed like Neal might be flirting with her. Other times, she couldn't even tell whether he was listening.

She decided to test him.

The next time Neal came down to *The Spoon,* Georgie said hi, but she stayed at her desk, hoping that *he* might come to *her* for once.

He didn't.

She tried it again a few days later. Neal nodded when Georgie said hello, but he didn't stop or walk over.

She told herself to take the hint.

"I notice you seem to be avoiding the hobbit hole," Seth observed.

"I'm not avoiding," Georgie said. "I'm working."

"Oh, right," he said. "You're working. I've noticed your uncrackable work ethic all those nights you barricaded yourself back in the hobbit hole just as soon as Bilbo showed his face."

"Are you complaining about my work ethic now?"

"I'm not complaining, Georgie. I'm *noticing.*"

"Well, stop," she said.

"Did he break it off? Were you too tall for him?"

"We're the same height. Actually."

"Really. That's adorable. Like salt and pepper shakers."

Georgie must have looked 53 percent wrecked because Seth let it drop. Later, when they were working on their column, both of them huddled in front of Georgie's computer, Seth gave her ponytail a solid pull. "You're too good for him."

He said it quietly.

Georgie didn't turn from her screen. "Probably not."

He pulled her hair again. "Too tall. And too pretty. And too good."

Georgie swallowed.

"I'm not worried about you," Seth said. "Someday your prince will come."

"And you'll do your best to scare him off."

"I'm glad that we both understand the terms." He pulled her hair.

"That hurts, you know."

"I'm trying to get your mind off the emotional pain."

"If you do it again, I'm going to slap you."

He immediately tugged on her ponytail. Gently this time. Georgie let it slide.

Seth always had to force Georgie to go to parties. Once she was there, she was fine. Once she was there, she was usually great—if not *the life* of the party, certainly one of its most valuable players. People (new people, strangers) made Georgie nervous. And nervous Georgie was much more extroverted than regular Georgie. Nervous Georgie was practically manic.

"It's like you turn into Robin Williams in nineteen-eighty-two," Seth told her.

"Oh God, don't say that, that's mortifying."

"What? Nineteen eighty-two Robin Williams was hilarious. Everybody loved nineteen-eighty-two Robin Williams."

"I don't want to be Mork at parties."

"I do," Seth said. "Mork kills."

"Cute guys don't want to go home with Mork," Georgie groaned.

"I think you're wrong," he said, "but I take your point."

(It hadn't gotten better over the years; Georgie *still* got nervous at parties and pitches and big meetings. Seth said their careers would be over if Georgie ever realized she was awesome and stopped freaking out about it.)

Not long after Georgie gave up on Neal, Seth talked her into going to the *Spoon* Halloween party. Seth was dressed like Steve Martin. He had a white suit, and he'd spray-painted his hair gray, and there was a gag arrow on his head.

Georgie was going as Hot Lips Houlihan from *M*A*S*H*. Which just meant fatigues, an olive green T-shirt, and dog tags. Plus, she'd blown out her hair. She figured she must look okay because Seth seemed distracted by her breasts.

As soon as they were inside the party, he was distracted by somebody else's breasts. There were a lot of girls here for a *Spoon* party; there must be some cross-pollination—maybe somebody's roommate was a business major.

Georgie grabbed a Zima, then poured it into a cup so she wouldn't look like she was drinking Zima.

She'd already started nervously chattering at some guy dressed like Maggie Simpson when she saw Neal on the other side of the room. He was leaning against a wall between two clusters of people—watching her.

When Georgie didn't look away, he raised his bottle of beer not quite to his chest and nodded his head. She squeezed her cup until it dented, then tried to nod back. It was more of a spasm.

Georgie returned her attention to the guy dressed as Maggie Simpson. (Why would a guy dress like Maggie Simpson?) He was trying to guess who she was. "That chick from *Tomb Raider*?" Georgie looked back at Neal. His head was tilted to the side. Still watching her.

She felt herself blushing and peered down at her drink.

Maybe he'd come over. Maybe Neal would finally walk fifteen steps out of his way to say hello to her. Georgie glanced back at him, just as he was glancing up again from his beer—he wouldn't even lift his entire head to look at her.

Fuck it.

"Sorry, would you . . . excuse me? I just saw my, um, I'm just—my friend's over there. Excuse me." Georgie backed away from Maggie Simpson and squeezed through an extremely pathetic dance circle to get to Neal's wall. There wasn't much room between him and the people next to him; he slid over to make room for her.

"Hey," she said, leaning in sideways.

Neal had his back to the wall, and he was holding his beer with both hands. He didn't look up. "Hey, Hot Lips."

Georgie grinned and rolled her eyes. "How'd you know who I was?"

His lips twitched just enough to give him dimples. "I know about your weird preoccupation with '70s sitcoms." He took a drink of beer. "I'm surprised you didn't come as Detective Wojciehowicz."

"Couldn't find the right tie," Georgie said.

Neal nearly smiled.

She glanced down at his clothes. He was dressed like normal—jeans, a black T-shirt—but there was a silvery white pattern creeping up from his sleeves and down from his collar. He must have painted it himself. It looked almost crystalline.

"Give up?" he asked.

She nodded.

"The first frost." He took another drink.

"It's lovely," Georgie said. Someone had just cranked up the music, so she said it again, louder. *"It's lovely."*

Neal shrugged his eyebrows.

"I have to admit I'm surprised to see you here," she said.

"You shouldn't be."

"You don't seem like Party Guy."

"I hate parties," Neal said.

"Me, too," she agreed.

He quirked an eyebrow at her. "Really."

"Really."

"I could tell by the way you walked in, and everybody shouted, 'Georgie!' and you blew a thousand air kisses, and the stereo started playing 'Gettin' Jiggy wit It' . . ."

"A, you're exaggerating, and *B,* just because I'm *good* at parties doesn't mean I like them."

"You prefer things you're not good at?"

Georgie took a frustrated gulp of Zima and thought about walking away. "Obviously."

Then there was a whoop of laughter behind her, and somebody fell against Georgie's back, pushing her into Neal's shoulder. She held her cup against her chest, so it wouldn't spill on him. Neal quickly turned toward her, making more room on the wall and steadying her for a second, his hand on her arm.

"Sorry," the guy behind her said.

"No worries," Georgie told him. She and Neal were

standing closer now, their shoulders almost touching on the wall.

They really were almost the same height. Georgie was five-five; Neal might be five-six. Maybe. It was nice—having a guy's eyes right there where she could reach them. If he'd just look at her . . .

"So," Neal said, "you came with your not-boyfriend, right?"

"He's *not* my boyfriend."

"Right. I think I saw him come in. He's dressed like The Jerk."

Georgie closed her eyes for a second. When she started talking, her voice was so quiet, she wasn't sure Neal would even be able to hear her: "Sometimes I think the only reason you ever talked to me at all was because you knew it pissed off Seth."

His reply came cold and quick: "Sometimes I think that's the only reason you ever talked to me."

She opened her eyes. "What?"

"Everybody knows." Neal's chin was practically touching his chest—that's how *not* he was looking at her. "Everybody at *The Spoon* says you're crazy about him."

"Not everybody," Georgie said. "*I've* never said that."

Neal shrugged harshly and went to take a drink of his beer, but the bottle was empty.

Georgie pushed away from the wall and took a step backwards. She needed to get out of here before she started crying, but first—"You know what? This is why you're standing alone at a party. Because *you're* a jerk. You're a jerk to people who actually, inexplicably like you." She took another step backwards. Into some other guy.

"Hey, Georgie!" the guy shouted. "Are you Private Benjamin?"

"Hey," she said, trying to get past him.

"Georgie, wait," she heard Neal say. She felt a hand on her wrist. Firm, but not tight—she could still pull away. Neal kept talking, but the music buried it. (*God,* she hated parties.) He stepped in closer. Close. They were standing in a crowd of people who were all trying to decide whether they wanted to dance. Neal's head dipped toward hers. "I'm sorry!" he shouted in her ear. And then something else.

"What?" Georgie yelled.

He seemed frustrated. They looked in each other's eyes for a few seconds—a few overwhelming (to Georgie) seconds—then he started pulling her back toward the wall.

Georgie followed. Neal tightened his grip on her wrist.

He cut through the crowd and led her down a short hallway, stopping in front of the only closed door. There was a piece of caution tape stretched over it and a sign that said:

STAY OUT!!
IF ANYONE GOES IN HERE,
MY ROOMMATE WILL **END** ME.
HAVE MERCY.
—Whit

Whit worked at *The Spoon.*

"We can't go in there," Georgie said.

"It's fine." Neal opened the door and ducked under the tape.

Georgie followed.

He leaned over and turned on a floor lamp without

letting go of her wrist. The door swung mostly closed behind them, and the roar of the music receded.

Neal turned back to her and set his jaw. "You're right," he said in his normal voice. His hand dropped, and he rubbed his palm on his jeans. "I'm sorry. I'm a jerk."

"Seth would agree with you there."

"I don't want to talk about Seth anymore."

"*You're* the one who brought him up."

"I know. I'm sorry." Neal had a way of holding his chin down and looking out the top of his eyes, even when he wasn't sitting at the drafting table. "Can we go back and start over?"

"How far back?" Georgie tried to fold her arms, but she was still holding that stupid Zima.

"Back to the wall," he said. "Back to you walking across the living room toward me. To you saying, 'I'm surprised to see you here.'"

"Are you saying you want to go back to the living room?"

"No. Just go ahead, say it again now."

Georgie rolled her eyes, but she said it: "I'm surprised to see you here."

"You shouldn't be," Neal said. He lifted his chin and looked directly in her eyes. For the second time in five minutes. For the second time ever. "I'm here because I knew you'd be here. Because I hoped you would be."

Georgie felt like a snake was unwinding itself in the back of her neck and along her shoulders. She swayed a little, and her mouth clicked open. "Oh."

Neal looked away, and Georgie took in three gallons of air.

He was shaking his head. "I'm . . . sorry," he said. "I

wanted to see you. But then I got angry. I didn't know what to—*you've been ignoring me.*"

"I haven't been ignoring you," she said.

"You stopped coming back to talk to me."

"I thought I was bothering you. "

"You weren't bothering me," he said, facing her again. "Why would you *think* that?"

"Because *you* never come talk to *me*."

"I never *had* to come talk to you." Neal looked bewildered. "You always came to me."

"I . . ." Georgie finished her drink so she could put down the cup.

Neal took it from her. He set the cup and his bottle on a desk behind him.

"I thought I was bothering you," she said. "I thought you were just humoring me."

"I thought you got tired of me," he said.

She brought her hands up to her forehead. "Maybe we should stop thinking."

Neal huffed and nodded, smoothing down the hair at the back of his head. They were both quiet for a dozen awkward heartbeats; then Neal motioned toward the bed. "Do you want to sit down?"

"Oh," Georgie said, looking at the bed. There was another sign there:

NO, SERIOUSLY. HE WILL **END** ME.
Get out of here, okay?
—*Whit*

"I don't think we should," she said.

"It's *fine*."

They should leave. They were violating someone's

privacy. But . . . Georgie looked up at Neal, with his black T-shirt and his pale skin. He was smoothing down his hair again—ridiculously, it couldn't be even a quarter-inch long in back. His elbow was in the air, his triceps flexed.

Georgie slid against the bed, sitting on the floor.

Neal looked down at her and nodded. "Okay . . . ," he murmured, sitting next to her.

After a few seconds, she nudged her shoulder against his. "So. What have I missed?"

"When?"

"Since I've been sitting at my own desk," she said, "playing hard to get."

Neal smiled a little and looked down; his eyelashes brushed the top of his cheeks. "Oh, you know. Ink. Talking rabbits. Singing turtles. A chipmunk who wishes he was a squirrel."

"Your comic last week was one of my favorites."

"Thanks."

"I put it in my Save Box," she said.

"What's that?"

"It's actually just a box. I, uh . . . I hate that feeling, you know, when you're thinking about something you've read or heard, and you thought it was so smart at the time, but now you can't remember it. I save things I don't want to lose track of."

"Must be a big box."

"Not as big as you'd think," she said. "I started putting your comic strips in there before I knew you were you."

"Before you knew I was me?"

"You know what I mean."

"Thanks." Neal's legs were bent in front of him, and he

was picking at loose threads on his thighs.

He seemed uncomfortable. Georgie had that feeling again, that she was the only one keeping the conversation alive. Maybe she should shut up and see if Neal would say anything. *No. No more games.* "Would it be easier to talk to me if you were holding a pen?"

Neal lowered his eyebrows, and his head bounced. "Huh. I guess so. Too bad I don't smoke."

"What?"

"Oh, you know—something to do with my hands."

"Oh," Georgie said. And then, because she wanted to, she reached out and took his hand. Laid her palm on the back of his hand. Curled her fingers behind his thumb. Neal looked down at their hands, then slowly turned his palm up, bending his fingers around hers. Georgie squeezed.

Neal's magic hand. (This was the left one, so maybe it was slightly less magic.)

Neal's wide, square palm. Neal's short, straight fingers— softer than Georgie expected, smoother than her own.

Neal, Neal, Neal.

"Before I knew you were you . . ." He shook his head. "There is no 'before I knew you were you.'"

Georgie pushed her shoulder into his, and Neal pushed back, still looking at their hands.

"I saw you the first time I came down to *The Spoon,*" he said. "You were sitting on the couch. And Seth was there, and you kept shoving him away. You were wearing that skirt you have, the blue and green plaid one, you know? And your hair was a mess."

She jabbed him with her shoulder, and he smiled a one-sided, one-dimpled smile for a second before he shook it away.

"It looked like spun gold—that's what I remember thinking. That your hair wasn't a real-person color. You're not blond, you know? Your hair isn't yellow. It isn't yellow mixed with white or brown or orange or gray. It defies four-color CMYK processing. It's metallic."

Neal kept shaking his head. "Whit told me your name, and I didn't believe him—*Georgie McCool*—but I started reading everything you wrote in *The Spoon,* and every time I came downstairs, there you were, on the couch or at your desk, always surrounded by half a dozen guys or just . . . him. I thought . . ." He shook his head some more. "When you came back to introduce yourself—Georgie, you didn't have to introduce yourself. I always knew you were you."

She pulled Neal's hand into her lap and turned to face him. And then, because never in her life had Georgie been able to wait for someone to kiss her first, she pressed her mouth into his cheek. Neal clenched his teeth, and she felt the pressure on her lips.

"Georgie," he whispered. He closed his eyes and tilted his head toward her.

She kissed his cheekbone from nose to temple, then rubbed her lips in his cheek again, wishing he'd smile.

He was holding her hand tight. "Georgie . . . ," he whispered again.

"Neal . . ." She kissed his jaw from ear to chin.

He started to turn his body toward her, slightly, and she reached for his shoulder to make it happen faster, to make him come closer. He caught her hand by the wrist, but still let her pull him in.

Georgie thought they'd kiss then. She tried to find his mouth.

But Neal kept rubbing his cheek into hers, and it felt so nice—all the soft and hard parts of their faces catching on each other. Cheekbone on brow. Jawbone on chin. Neal's skin was flushed and warm. His hands were holding firm. He smelled like bar soap and beer and fabric paint. *God* . . .

This was better than kissing.

This was . . .

Georgie arched her neck and felt Neal's chin, then nose, then forehead push down to her collarbone. She dropped her face into his short hair—and closed her eyes.

When Georgie was a kid, this was what she'd pictured whenever she'd heard the word "necking"—two people rubbing their faces and necks together, kissing like giraffes. She'd had a crush on her babysitter's son, and this was what she'd fantasized about doing with him, rubbing her neck into his, burying her face into his Simon Le Bon hair. (She was nine, and he was fifteen, and this fortunately never happened.)

She lifted her chin again, and Neal dragged his face back up to hers, humming almost helplessly in her ear.

Whatever this was—non-kissing, hard-core nuzzling—it felt so good that the next time Neal's lips were over hers, Georgie ghosted right past them, pulling his mouth open with her cheek instead.

Neal hummed again.

Georgie smiled.

The bedroom door opened.

"Are you fucking kidding me?" somebody said. "Can't you people read?"

The music from the living room banged back into the bedroom. "You Oughta Know" by Alanis Morissette. Georgie looked up at the doorway—it was Whit from *The*

Spoon. Whit who lived here and wrote beseeching notes. Neal let go of Georgie's arm, but she caught his hand. She held both his hands now. Fast.

"Oh," Whit said, looking a little dumbfounded. "Neal . . . and Georgie. Sorry, I thought some asshole was using your room. Uh, carry on, I guess."

Whit closed the door—and Georgie started giggling.

"This is your room?"

Neal's head dropped. "Yeah."

"Why didn't you tell me?"

He shrugged. "I don't know. 'Why don't you come back to my room?'—it sounds sleazy."

"It sounds better than 'Let's go make out in this stranger's room.'" She spread her fingers and pushed them through his, squeezing his hands tight again. Then she leaned toward him, mouth-first. Yes, the non-kissing was good. But there were Neal's perfectly formed lips right there—a testament to symmetry and cell division—and surely kissing would be even better.

"Georgie," he said, turning his head away.

She kissed his cheek again. His ear. Neal's ears were perfect, too, even if they did stick out at the top like pot handles. She opened her mouth over his ear, and Neal gripped her hands, using them to push her away.

"Georgie," he said. "I can't."

"You can," she said. "You are."

"No." He let go of her hands and took hold of her shoulders, holding her back. "I want to, but I can't."

"You want to?"

Neal locked his jaw and closed his eyes, then growled. "I can't. Georgie, I . . . I have a girlfriend."

Georgie jerked away from him. Like he was on fire.

(Like he was on fire, and it wasn't her job to put him out.) His hands fell from her shoulders.

"Oh," she said.

"It's not—" He seemed so angry. Probably angry with himself. He licked his lips. "I mean . . ."

"It's okay," she said, putting her hands on the floor and pushing herself to her feet. Of course it wasn't okay. Nothing was okay. "I'll just . . ."

Neal was scrambling up, too. "Georgie, let me explain."

"No." It was her turn to shake her head. "No, it's okay. I'll just . . ." She reached for the doorknob.

"It's not what you think," he said.

Georgie laughed. "No. No, it's not." She stumbled through the door and closed it behind her. God, it was loud out here. It was . . .

God.

Neal.

Of course he had a girlfriend. Because he liked her and wanted to kiss her, and every time they talked, it felt like her brain was fizzing out her ears, so it *only stood to reason* that he had a *girlfriend.*

How could Neal have a girlfriend? Where was he keeping her?

Somewhere other than *The Spoon* offices, clearly. God, God, God—it's not like he'd led Georgie on. He'd never sought her out. It was always Georgie hanging off his drafting table, making eighth-grade eyes at him. Neal hardly even looked at her. (*Spun gold. CMYK. A half a dozen guys.*)

Seth was going to love this.

Georgie wasn't going to tell Seth.

She wasn't going to tell anybody.

God, she'd thought that Neal *liked* her. Better than he liked anyone else, anyway. (He even *said* that he liked her. He said he wanted to kiss her. . . .) (Though apparently not enough to actually do it.)

She should never have tried to kiss him first.

She should never kiss anyone first. . . .

Georgie *always* kissed first.

She always fell for the guy in the room who seemed the least interested in her. The guy who was toxically arrogant or cripplingly shy. Or both. The guy at the party who looked like he'd rather be anywhere else.

"You should try dating nice guys," her friend Ludy used to say in high school. "They're *nice.* I think you'd like them."

"Boring," Georgie'd said. "Pointless."

"Not pointless—*nice.*"

They'd had this conversation in the cafeteria. They were waiting by the door so that Georgie could casually get in line behind Jay Anselmo, who was two years older than they were, really into No Doubt and competitive car stereos, and who would undoubtedly ignore her. "What's the point of making a nice guy like me?" Georgie said. "Nice guys like everybody."

"You shouldn't have to *make* anybody like you, Georgie. You should want to be with somebody who can't help but like you."

"Nothing good is easy."

"Not true," Ludy said. "Sleep. TV. Jell-O Instant Pudding." (Ludy was a riot. Georgie missed her.)

"I don't want to go out with Jell-O Instant Pudding," Georgie said.

"I would *marry* Jell-O Instant Pudding."

Georgie rolled her eyes. "I want to go out with Mikey."

"I thought you wanted to go out with Jay Anselmo."

"Jay Anselmo *is* Mikey," Georgie explained. "He's the guy in the Life cereal commercial who hates everything. If *Mikey* likes you, you know you're good. If Mikey likes you, it means something."

Georgie'd ended up kissing Jay Anselmo one night after a football game, at a party in Ludy's backyard. He'd let her kiss him all through her sophomore year. And then he'd gone off to college, and Georgie'd found a few other guys to kiss.

She'd never really thought of kissing-first as a problem; Georgie tended to hook up with guys who appreciated the clarity.

But tonight, in Neal's room, it was a problem.

She'd read Neal all wrong: She'd thought he was a Mikey. She'd thought he was the grumpiest hobbit in the Shire. But really, he just had a girlfriend.

Georgie was done kissing first. The next person she kissed was going to have to do all the work. Assuming she ever found anybody who thought she was worth it.

Georgie wanted to go home.

She wanted to cry all the way there, thinking about Neal's sideways symmetrical mouth and the way he could freehand a perfectly straight line.

She wanted to find Seth.

CHAPTER 16

Georgie's cell phone chimed. She picked it up.

"Earth to Georgie."

She looked up from the text message to Seth, who was sitting across from her at the writers' table.

He met her eyes, then looked down at his phone and typed something.

Chime. She looked at her phone.

"We're running out of time."

Georgie thought for a second, then thumbed in a reply—

"I know, I'm sorry."

When Seth looked back up at her, his eyebrows were crowded together over his brown eyes.

She felt herself tearing up.

He tilted his head, then scrunched his nose unhappily. Seth hated it when Georgie cried. He went back to the phone again, typing rapidly.

"Talk to me."

"I can't. I wouldn't know where to start."

"I don't care where you start."

She wiped her eyes on her shoulder.

Seth sighed.

"Georgie, whatever it is—we'll get through it."

She stared down at her phone. After a few seconds, AN EMERGENCY CONTACT popped up on the screen, and it started to ring. It was just the standard ring— *Marimba*—

Georgie never had time to figure out special ringtones.

She grabbed her laptop and stood up, answering the call and walking toward the door, careful not to close the computer or unplug the phone. "Hello?"

"Meow!"

Georgie felt a cold surge of disappointment. Then felt guilty about it. You're not supposed to feel a cold surge of disappointment at the sound of your four-year-old daughter's voice.

"Meow," Georgie said, leaning against the wall outside the writers' room.

"Grandma said I could call you," Noomi said.

"You can always call me. How are you, sweetie? Did you make me some cookies?"

"No."

"Oh. That's okay."

"Maybe Grandma did. I made some for Santa and some for me."

"That was smart. I'll bet they're delicious."

"Meow," Noomi said. "I'm a green kitty."

"I know." Georgie tried to focus. "You're the best green kitty in the world. I love you so much, Noomi."

"You're the best mommy in the world, and I love you more than milk and fishbones and . . . what else do kitties like?"

"Yarn," Georgie said.

"Yarn," Noomi giggled. "That's crazy."

Georgie took a calming breath. "Noomi, is Daddy there?"

"Uh-huh."

"Can I talk to him?"

"No."

Georgie knocked her head back against the wall. "Why not?"

"He's sleeping. He said we can't even go upstairs to pee."

Georgie should tell Noomi to do it anyway. Neal was her *husband*. And she hadn't talked to him for *three* days. (Or thirteen hours.) (Or fifteen years.)

Georgie sighed. "Okay. Can I talk to Alice?"

"Alice is playing Monopoly with Grandma."

"Right."

"I have to go. My hot chocolate is cold now."

"Meow," Georgie said. "Meow-meow, love you, green kitty."

"Meow-meow, Mommy, I love you even more than yarn."

Noomi hung up.

There's a magic phone in my childhood bedroom. I can use it to call my husband in the past. (My husband who isn't my husband yet. My husband who maybe shouldn't be my husband at all.)

There's a magic phone in my childhood bedroom. I unplugged it this morning and hid it in the closet.

Maybe all the phones in the house are magic.

Or maybe I'm magic. Temporarily magic. (Ha! Time travel pun!)

Does it count as time travel? If it's just my voice traveling?

There's a magic phone hidden in my closet. And I think it's connected to the past. And I think I'm supposed to fix something. I think I'm supposed to make something right.

When Georgie got back to the writers' room, Seth looked like he was at the end of his rope. He'd unbuttoned his shirt an extra button, and his hair was sticking up around his ears and at the back of his neck.

She stood at the whiteboard and took charge of the outline.

It wasn't that hard—they'd been talking about these characters for years. They just needed to get their ideas into writing. Wrestle them into a few workable scripts. Georgie could do this in her sleep. Sometimes she *did* do it in her sleep. She'd wake up in the middle of the night and hang off the side of her bed, scrounging around for a piece of paper. (She never remembered to put a notebook by the bed when she was lucid.)

Neal would stir in his sleep and reach for her hips, pulling her back onto the bed. *"What're you looking for?"*

"Paper," she'd say, leaning off the bed again. *"I have an idea I don't want to forget."*

She'd feel his mouth at the base of her spine. *"Tell me. I'll remember."*

"You're asleep, too."

He'd bite her. *"Tell me."*

"It's a dance," she'd say. *"There's a dance. And Chloe, the main character, will end up with one of her mom's old prom dresses. And she'll try to fix it to make it cool, like in* Pretty in Pink, *but it won't be cool; it'll be awful. And something embarrassing will happen at the dance to 'Try a Little Tenderness.'"*

"Got it." Then Neal would pull her back into bed, into him, holding her in place. *"Dance. Dress. 'Try a Little Tenderness.' Now go back to sleep."*

And then he'd push up Georgie's pajama shirt, biting her back until neither of them could go back to sleep.

And then, eventually, she'd drift off with his hand on her hip and his forehead pressed into her shoulder.

She'd get out of the shower the next morning, and it would be written in the steam on the mirror:

Dance. Dress. Try a little tenderness.

Georgie shook her head and looked up at the whiteboard and tried to remember where she'd left off.

The night that Neal told her about his girlfriend (fucking *of course* he had a girlfriend), Seth took Georgie home, then went back to the Halloween party. Georgie stayed up listening to her mom's Carole King albums and wrote a really angsty monologue for one of her theater classes.

That was back when she still thought about performing someday. Before she'd decided that she had a better face and brain for the writers' room. *"Why would you want to act, anyway?"* was Seth's take on the subject. *"Stand there and say other people's words, let everybody else tell you what to do . . . Actors are just beautiful puppets."*

"If that's true," Georgie'd said, *"you sure date a lot of puppets."*

Georgie didn't really want to act—she wanted to do stand-up. But she hated bars, that was a problem. Also, she wanted to get married and have a family.

Seth said nothing beat writing for TV. *"It's comedy with health insurance,"* he said. And big houses and cars. And sunshine.

The morning after the Halloween party, Georgie picked up bagels on the way to Seth's frat house. She passed last night's girl—the lovely Breanna again—in the hallway. Breanna looked surprised to see Georgie; Georgie just nodded, as if they were coworkers.

When she got to Seth's room, his hair was wet, and he was changing his sheets.

"Gross," she said.

"What's gross?"

"This."

"You'd rather I *didn't* change my sheets?"

"I'd rather you got all this—girl, sheets, shower—taken care of before I showed up, so that I don't have to think about you having sex."

Seth paused, holding the sheet in the air with both hands, and grinned. "Is that what you're thinking about?"

Georgie sat down at his desk, ignoring him. He was a senior, so he didn't have a roommate. She turned on his computer and watched him make his bed.

He really was gorgeous. Intentionally so.

Most guys just walked around with nothing but raw material. Pretty eyes, bad hair, ill-fitting clothes. Most guys didn't even know what they had to offer. But Seth was like a girl—he was a better girl than Georgie—he knew what his strengths were. He let his coppery brown hair grow long enough to shine and curl. He wore pale colors that made his skin look tan. He *presented* himself to you. To everyone. *Here I am. Look at me.*

Georgie looked. She watched. And nothing stirred in her stomach. She didn't take any special thrill in being here, being the one Seth wanted to see when he was done with the lovely whomever.

Neal had cured her of Seth.

Now what would cure her of Neal?

And why was she only attracted to guys who were *sleeping with somebody else*? If Georgie were a wild animal, she'd be a genetic dead end.

Seth fell onto the bed and turned on the TV. *Animaniacs.* Georgie threw him his bagel.

"So," he said, unwrapping it, "feeling any better this morning?"

She put her feet up on his desk and watched the show. "I'm fine."

When the episode was over, Georgie turned to the computer and opened a file. Aside from their column, and Georgie's horoscopes, and their duties as managing editors—they also wrote a regular movie-review parody for *The Spoon,* "Your Mom Reviews . . ." It ran with a photo of Seth's mom. This week, they were doing *Trainspotting.*

Seth was still watching cartoons.

"He has a girlfriend," Georgie said.

Seth's face jerked toward her; his eyebrows lowered. "This whole time?"

"Apparently."

He turned off the TV and was up off the bed, pulling another chair next to Georgie and sitting on it backwards. "Fuck him," he said, elbowing her. "I'm telling you, it wasn't meant to be."

"Since when do you believe in 'meant to be'?"

"Since fucking ever, Georgie, pay attention. I'm a romantic."

"Just ask the parade of Saturday-morning girls."

"Parades are romantic. Who doesn't love a parade?"

They worked on the movie review until it was time for Seth to go to work (to his other job, at the J. Crew factory store). He tried extra hard to make Georgie laugh; and when he leaned on her shoulder while she typed, she mostly let him.

By the time she walked out of the frat house, she felt better about Neal and his inevitable girlfriend. . . .

No, that wasn't true.

She still felt terrible about that—but she felt better about life. At least Georgie was probably going to be one of those *cool* single women, one with an interesting job and a dashing best friend and good hair. She could probably have halfway decent one-night stands if she loosened up her standards.

She felt utterly terrible again as soon as she saw Neal sitting at the bus stop across the street. A bus pulled up. When it drove away, Neal was still sitting there, staring right at her.

He held up his hand and motioned for her to come over.

Georgie folded her arms and frowned.

Neal stood up.

She should just ignore him. Walk straight to her car. Leave him hanging. What was he doing here, anyway?

Neal beckoned her again.

Georgie frowned, looked both ways, then half ran across the street.

She slowed down when she got close to him. "Fancy meeting you here," she said stupidly.

"Not really," he said. "I've been waiting for you."

"You have?"

"Yeah."

Georgie narrowed her eyes. Neal looked tired. And intent. And surprisingly pink in the daylight.

"I'm trying to figure out if that's weird," she said.

"I don't really care if it is." He took a step toward her. "I knew you'd be here, and I needed to tell you something."

"You could have called," she said.

"Right." Neal tore off the first page of his notebook and

handed it to her. There was a sketch of the cypress tree in front of Seth's frat house. Also a skunk driving an AMC Gremlin. And then, Neal's name—*Neal G.*—and a phone number.

Georgie took the piece of paper with both hands.

"I just needed to tell you—" He swallowed and pushed his bangs out of his face, even though they were too short to be in the way. "—I don't have a girlfriend anymore."

Georgie swallowed, too. "You don't?"

He shook his head.

"That was fast," she said.

Neal huffed out half a breath and just barely shook his head again. "It really, *really* wasn't."

"Okay . . . ," Georgie said.

"So." Neal looked determined. "I wanted you to know. That. And, also, I thought maybe . . . we could try again. Or just *try*. You know, go out or something. Someday. Now that I . . . don't have a girlfriend."

A smile snuck out of Georgie's mouth. She tried to catch it.

Neal didn't have a girlfriend.

This may even be a direct result of Georgie herself. And even though she didn't consider herself a homewrecker—even though she didn't particularly want to date a guy who kissed other girls, then ran home to break up with his girlfriend—Georgie *did* want to date Neal. Or maybe she just wanted to rub faces again.

"I'd like that," she said.

Neal's head tipped forward—in relief, she thought. He bit his bottom lip and exhaled. "Good."

"Good," Georgie repeated.

She took a step away. Past him, actually. Her car was

just there, not even half a block up. "Okay," she said, waving his number awkwardly at him.

He waved back, then pushed his hands into his jeans pockets.

Georgie took a few more steps, then turned around. "Yeah, okay—how about now?"

"What?"

"How about we try again now?"

"Now."

She started walking back to him. "Yeah, I mean . . . I could pretend that I need to think about this and that I don't want to rush in to anything. But I'm *really* not good at all that—I'm much better at rushing in. And it's not like you just left your wife."

"We *were* engaged," Neal said. Like he was duty-bound to say it.

Georgie stopped. "Oh God, you *were*?"

"Not recently," he said, pained. "We *were* engaged. Then we were just dating. Then we were spending some time apart."

"What were you last night?"

"Spending some time apart."

"So, last night, you actually *didn't* have a girlfriend."

Neal winced. "That seemed like a technicality at the time."

"When did you break up?"

"This morning."

"You woke up this morning and immediately went to break up with your girlfriend?"

"I called her."

"No." Georgie covered one eye. "Don't tell me you did it over the phone." She really didn't want to go out with a guy who might break up with her someday over the phone.

Neal pushed his hair out of his face. "I had to. She's in Nebraska."

"Nebraska?"

He nodded, biting his lip again.

"How long have you been together?"

"*Had* been together," Neal said. "Since high school."

"Jesus," Georgie said. "You broke up with your high-school-sweetheart-slash-fiancée for me?"

"Not my fiancée," he said. "Anymore. And not just for you."

Georgie frowned. Now that she wasn't the reason, she kinda wanted to be.

"We were going to break up anyway," he said.

She frowned some more.

"I mean," Neal said, "we'd been talking about trying again. But then I met you. And I figured that if I felt the way I feel about you, maybe that was pretty solid evidence that she and I should break up."

"I don't think I've ever heard you say so many words in a row," Georgie said.

"I'm a bit off my game."

She smiled. A bit. "I throw you off your game?"

"Christ," he muttered, "yes. Welcome to me staying up all night, then breaking up with my high school girlfriend for you."

She stepped closer to him. "Not *just* for me." Georgie really was terrible at playing hard to get. Or even playing reasonable to get. She had zero game.

"You're one hundred percent of the reason I did it this morning," Neal said.

That shouldn't make Georgie happy. How terrible would it be to be that poor girl in Nebraska—to know that your boyfriend broke up with you first thing in the morning, so he could rush off to be with somebody else? Georgie pictured a blond girl with tearstained cheeks, standing in the middle of a lonely prairie.

"Are you sad?" she asked him. Sincerely. "Do you need to go home and listen to all your mixed tapes and think about this chapter of your life closing?"

"Maybe," he said. "I think I just need some sleep."

"Okay. Just . . ." How was she supposed to avoid kissing Neal when his mouth was right there at mouth-level all the time? She didn't even have to stand on tiptoe. Georgie took hold of the front of his sweatshirt and leaned in.

She kissed him on the cheek.

"Thank you," she said before she pulled back again. "For telling me."

"Call me," Neal whispered.

"I will."

"Call me before you think you should."

"I'll call you tonight."

Georgie grinned all the way to her car.

Neal didn't have a girlfriend.

For, like, the next three hours, at least.

She called him that night. Then she took him to Versailles down on Venice Boulevard for garlic chicken and fried plantains. Neal didn't know about anything cool in Los Angeles—he spent all his time at his apartment or on campus, or on the water, which he hated.

Which he hated, in practice.

Neal loved the *concept* of the ocean. He was practically

animated once you got him talking about sea life and coral.

Nobody would ever describe Neal as *fully* animated. Or expressive. His thoughts didn't play across his face like light on water. Which meant Georgie cataloged every flinch, every flick of his eyes, and tried to figure out what they meant. This seemed like a great way to spend the rest of her life.

Neal wasn't sure how to spend the rest of his life.

He joked about being tragically bad with big decisions. He'd decided to study oceanography because nothing else appealed to him, and then he'd ended up stuck in California for four years. When he and his high school girlfriend— her name was Dawn (Prairie Dawn!)—drifted apart freshman year, Neal's solution was to propose to her.

"I'm not good at knowing what I want," he said at the end of the night, at the beginning of the morning. They were sitting on the beach, and Neal was holding Georgie's hand. "I'm not usually good at *wanting* things."

The sand was damp, and there was a cool breeze. Georgie was using it as an excuse to sit too close to him. She was wearing her blue and green plaid skirt and her red Doc Martens boots, and she was pushing her knee into his thigh because the reality of Neal—Neal without a girlfriend, Neal who said he liked her—was too much to leave be.

"Then we'll get along fine," she said, "because I'm *extra* good at wanting things. I want things until I feel sort of sick about them. I want enough for two normal people, at least."

"Really," Neal said. That's what he always said when he didn't have anything to say and he just wanted her to keep talking. There was a smile that went with it, sort of a mocking smile that would have seemed mean if his eyes weren't shining.

"Really," she said.

"What do you want?" he asked.

It would've been too easy—and too cheesy—to say "you," even if it was top-of-mind right at the moment.

"I want to write," Georgie said. "I want to make people laugh. I want to create a show. And then another show. And then another show. I want to be James L. Brooks."

"I have no idea who that is."

"Philistine."

"He's a philistine?"

"And I want to write a book of essays. And I want to join The Kids in the Hall."

"You'll have to pretend you're a man," Neal said.

"And a Canadian," she agreed.

"And you'll have to do lots of sketches where you're in drag as a man, in drag as a woman—it'll be very confusing."

"I'm up for it."

Neal laughed. (Almost. He smiled, and his shoulders and chest twitched.)

"And I want a Crayola Caddy," Georgie said.

"What's a Crayola Caddy?"

"It's this thing they made when we were kids, kind of a lazy Susan with crayons and markers and paints."

"I think I had one of those."

Georgie yanked on his hand. "You had a Crayola Caddy?"

"I think so. It was yellow, right? And it came with poster paints? I think it's still in our basement."

"I've wanted a Crayola Caddy since 1981," Georgie

said. "It's all I asked Santa Claus for, three years in a row."

"Why didn't your parents just buy it for you?"

She rolled her eyes. "My mom thought it was stupid. She bought me crayons and paint instead."

"Well"—he lowered his eyebrows thoughtfully—"you could probably have mine."

Georgie punched his chest with their clasped hands. "Shut. Up." She knew it was stupid, but she was genuinely thrilled about this. "Neal Grafton, you have just made my oldest dream come true."

Neal held her hand to his heart. His face was neutral, but his eyes were *dancing*. He whispered: "What else do you want, Georgie?"

"Two kids," she said. "A boy and a girl. But not until my TV empire is under way."

His eyes got big. "Christ."

"Also a house with a big front porch. And a husband who likes to take driving vacations. And a car, obviously, with a roomy backseat."

"You really are spectacular at this."

"And I want a Disneyland annual pass. And a chance to work with Bernadette Peters. And I want to be happy. Like, seventy to eighty percent of the time. I want to be actively, thoughtfully happy."

Neal was rubbing their hands into his blue sweatshirt. It said NORTH HIGH WRESTLING. TAKE 'EM DOWN, VIKES! His jaw was tight, and his blue eyes were almost black.

"And I want to fly over the ocean," she said.

He swallowed and reached out to touch her face with his free hand. It was cold, and sand fell from it onto Georgie's neck. "I think I want you," he said.

Georgie squeezed the hand he was holding to his chest,

and used it as an anchor to pull herself closer. "You *think* . . ."

Neal licked his bottom lip and nodded. "I think . . ." The closer she was, the more he looked away. "I think I just want you," he said.

"Okay," Georgie agreed.

Neal looked surprised—he almost laughed. "Okay?"

She nodded, close enough to bump her nose up against his. "Okay. You can have me."

He pushed his forehead into her, pulling his chin and mouth back. "Just like that."

"Yeah."

"Really," he said.

"Really," she promised.

She reached her mouth toward his, and he twisted his head up and away, looking at her. He was breathing hard through his nose. He was still holding her cheek.

Georgie tried to make her face as plain as possible:

Really. You can have me. Because I'm good at wanting things and good at getting what I want, and I can't think of anything I want more than you. Really, really, really.

Neal nodded. Like he'd just been given an order. Then he let go of Georgie's hand and pushed her (pinned her) gently (firmly) back into the sand.

He leaned over her, his hands on either side of her shoulders, and shook his head. "Georgie," he said. Then he kissed her.

That was it, really.

That was when she added Neal to the list of things she wanted and needed and was bound to have someday. That's when she decided that Neal was the person who was going to drive on those overnight road trips. And

Neal was the one who was going to sit next to her at the Emmys.

He kissed her like he was drawing a perfectly straight line.

He kissed her in India ink.

That's when Georgie decided, during that cocksure kiss, that Neal was what she needed to be happy.

They were all tired.

Seth had finger-combed all the curl out his hair. It was looking less JFK Jr., more Joe Piscopo. "We're not adding a gay Indian character," he said. "That's final."

Scotty leaned over the table. "But Georgie said she wanted to add some diversity."

"She didn't say she wanted to add *you*."

"Rahul isn't me. He's tall, and he doesn't wear glasses."

"He's worse than you," Seth said. "He's fantasy-you."

"Well, all these white guys are just fantasy-yous."

Seth abused his hair some more. "Fantasy-me would never show up on this show. Fantasy-me was already on *Gossip Girl*."

"Georgie," they both said at once.

"Rahul can stay," Georgie said. "But this is a misfit comedy; he has to be short and wear glasses."

"Why would you do that to Rahul?" Scotty folded his arms. "Now he'll never find love."

Seth rolled his eyes. "Jesus, Scotty, you'll find love."

"One, I'm talking about Rahul. And two, I don't think you mean that."

Georgie put her hand on Scotty's shoulder. "He'll find love, Scotty. I'll write him a dreamy boyfriend."

"You'd do that for me, Georgie?"

"I'll do it for Rahul."

"That episode better be fucking hilarious," Seth said.

Scotty stood up and shoved his laptop in his backpack. "Rahul stays," he told Seth. "I just made some Indian kid a star."

Scotty walked out, head high.

Seth was still frowning. "Does this mean we have to go back and write Rahul into the pilot?"

"He can start in the third episode," Georgie said. "You were just saying we needed a couple gay characters. You said our 1995 was showing."

"I know."

Georgie closed her laptop. "I know we said we'd take home scripts, but I don't know how much I'm going to get done tonight. . . ."

"Stay," Seth said. "We'll get dinner and work on it together."

"I can't. I have to call Neal." It was already eight o'clock in Omaha. Georgie wanted to call him by ten.

Seth studied her for a minute. Like the one thing she wasn't telling him was the only thing he didn't know about her.

What would happen if she called *Seth* tonight from the yellow phone? Would she get the Sig Ep house in 1998? Would one of his Saturday-morning girls answer?

Seth never talked about the Saturday-morning girls now, but Georgie assumed the parade marched on.

"Thanks," he said. "For pushing through today. I know that something is seriously fucked up with you."

Georgie unplugged her phone.

"And it's killing me that you won't talk about it," he said.

"I'm sorry."

"I don't want you to be sorry, Georgie—I want you to be funny."

CHAPTER 17

By the time Georgie pulled into her mom's driveway, she was 100 percent sure that if she called Neal tonight from the yellow rotary phone, he'd pick it up in the past.

Or that it would seem that way—that the grand illusion was going to hold.

And she was 1,000 percent sure she was going to call him. Even though that might be dangerous. (If it were real.) (Georgie needed to pick a side—real or not real—and stick with it.)

She had to call. You can't just ignore a phone that calls into the past. You can't *know* it's there and *not* call.

Georgie couldn't, anyway.

Whatever was happening, this was the role she'd been given. Neal wasn't the one with a magic phone that could call into the future.

(God, maybe she should test that theory, she could ask him to call her back . . . *No*. No way. What if her mom answered and started talking about Alice and Noomi and divorce? What if Georgie herself answered the phone back in 1998 and said something horrible and immature, and ruined everything? Nineteen-ninety-eight Georgie clearly couldn't be trusted.)

Heather opened the door to the house before Georgie could knock.

"Is there a pizza coming?" Georgie asked.

"No."

Georgie stayed out on the stoop.

"Baked ziti," Heather said, rolling her eyes. "Just come in."

Georgie did. Her mom and Kendrick were eating dinner in the kitchen.

"You're home early," her mom said. "I made a Caesar salad, if you're hungry, and there's puppy chow for dessert."

The pugs started barking under the table.

"Not for you, little mama," Georgie's mom said, leaning over to make eye contact with the pregnant one. *"This puppy chow is for big mamas and daddies. Little mamas can't have chocolate*—I swear, Kenny, they understand everything we say."

Heather was standing to the side of the front door, pulling out the curtain, so she could peek out at an angle.

They were all completely over the fact that Georgie was here. Even the dogs had stopped tracking her every movement with their little whiteless eyes.

Georgie could probably move back home without ever having to talk to her mom about it. Her mom would just start thawing out one more pork chop for dinner and complaining when Georgie left her bag on the table—maybe her mom thought she'd already moved back home.

"Thanks," Georgie said, heading for her room. "I'm not very hungry."

"Are you coming out later?" her mom called after her.

"No," Georgie shouted back, "I'm calling Neal!"

"Tell him we said hello! And that we all still love him! Tell him he'll always be part of this family!"

"I'm not telling him any of that."

"Why not?"

Georgie was halfway down the hall. "Because he'll think I'm crazy!"

She opened her bedroom door, then quickly closed it behind her—then thought about pushing a dresser against it. Instead she rushed over to the closet and started empty-ing things out into her room. She'd buried the phone at the very bottom, under an old sleeping bag, a few rolls of gift wrap, her Rollerblades from grade school . . .

There it was. *There*.

Georgie fell back on her heels and stared at the phone, not sure if she should touch it, not sure if she should rub it three times and make a wish.

She picked up the receiver and held it to her head. No dial tone.

Well, of course, no dial tone—it's not plugged in. It's not plugged in to the space/time portal in the wall behind my bed. (Cue maniacal laughter.)

She crawled over to her bed and shimmied underneath to plug the phone in, half expecting the outlet to zap and spark. Then she pushed out again, untangled her hair from the bedsprings, and leaned against the bed with the phone in her lap.

Right. Here we are. Time to call Neal.

Neal . . .

Georgie held her breath while she dialed his number, then choked when he picked up on the first ring.

"Hello?"

"Neal?"

"Hey," he said. She could hear the quarter-smile in his voice. The one that just barely dented his cheek. "I thought it might be you."

"It is," she said. "It's me."

"How are you?"

"I'm . . ." Georgie closed her eyes and realized she still hadn't properly exhaled. She did it now, bringing up her knees and setting the phone on the floor beside her. This was Neal, he was still there. He was still taking her calls. "Better now," she said, rubbing her eyes into the back of her wrist.

"Me, too," he said, and God, that was good to hear. God, *he* was good to hear.

Georgie and Neal had never spent this much time apart, not since they got married. She was going crazy not talking to him every day, not checking in with him. In the present. In real life.

Was that what was going on here? Was Georgie hallucinating these phone calls because she missed Neal? Because she needed him?

She *needed* him.

Neal was home. He was base.

Neal was where Georgie plugged in, and synced up, and started fresh every day. He was the only one who knew her exactly as she was.

She should tell him about this magic phone insanity. Right now. She *could* tell him, she could always tell Neal anything. Georgie and Neal were bad at a lot of things, but they were good at being on each other's side. Neal was especially good at being on Georgie's side, at being there when she needed him.

She thought of all the times he'd stayed up late to help her with a script. The way he'd lived at her right hand after Alice was born (when Georgie was depressed and in pain and terrible at breastfeeding). The way he never made her feel crazy, even when she was acting crazy, and never made her feel like a failure, even when she was failing.

If there was anyone she could tell about this, it was Neal.

"Georgie? Did I lose you?"

"No," she said. *Jesus.* She could *not* tell Neal. "I'm here."

"Tell me about your day."

Well, first I unplugged my magic phone, then I got into my electric car. . . .

"I worked with Seth on *Passing Time,*" Georgie said— because it was the only true thing that seemed safe to say.

She immediately wished she could take it back. Mentioning Seth was like flipping Neal's off switch; that was as true back then as it was now. (All right, so maybe she couldn't talk to Neal about *everything.*)

"Ah," he said, his voice noticeably cooler.

"What about you?" she asked.

"I . . ." He cleared his throat. She could hear him consciously letting the annoyance go. Neal still did that, too. The irritation would freeze on his face, he'd gather it up, then shake it off. "I helped my mom bake more cookies," he said. "She set some aside for you."

"Thanks."

"Then I ate them."

"Bastard."

He laughed a breath. "And then . . . I met that guy my dad wanted me to meet, the guy with the railroad police."

It took a second for that to click. *Neal's dad's friend, railroad police. Right.* There was a job Neal had thought about—never seriously—back in Omaha. "I still think you're making that up," she said.

"I'm not making it up."

"*Railroad detectives*. It sounds like an hour-long drama on CBS."

"It *sounds* really interesting," Neal said. "Like all the best parts of police work, the thinking and the problem-solving, but not having to walk a beat or answer 9-1-1 calls."

"*This week on* Railroad Detectives," Georgie teased, "*the team discovers a cache of sleepy hoboes. . . .*"

"Something like that."

"Is the railroad looking for oceanographers?"

"No. Thank God. Mike—my dad's friend—said it didn't matter what my degree was in, that any background in the sciences would help."

"Oh," Georgie said. "That's great." She tried really hard to mean it.

"It was good," he said. "Then I came home, ran into Dawn, and ended up getting ice cream with her."

Jesus, Neal's whole day had been a life-without-Georgie dress rehearsal. "Dawn," she said. "That's . . . great. I bet Dawn thinks you should become a railroad detective."

"And you don't?"

"I didn't say that."

"What are you saying?" He sounded cool again.

"*Nothing.* I'm sorry. Just . . . *Dawn.*"

"Are you jealous of Dawn?"

"We've talked about this," Georgie said.

"No, we haven't," Neal disagreed.

He was right; in 1998, they hadn't.

"You're not actually jealous of Dawn," he said.

"Of course I am. She was your fiancée."

"Only sort of. And I broke up with her *for you*."

"You can't have a *sort-of* fiancée, Neal."

"You know I never even meant to propose to her. . . ."

"That makes it worse."

"Georgie. You cannot be jealous of Dawn—that's like the sun being jealous of a lightbulb."

She smiled. But kept arguing. "I can be jealous of anyone who got to you first. If I went down to the malt shop and shared a milk shake with my ex-boyfriend-slash-sort-of fiancé, you'd be jealous."

"Right," Neal snorted. "But I'm not supposed to be jealous when you spend every day with Seth."

"Seth isn't my ex-boyfriend."

"God, no, he's worse."

Rules, Georgie wanted to shout. *Rules, rules, rules!* Weren't all their rules already unspoken by 1998? "You can't compare Seth to Dawn," she said. "I was never *sleeping* with Seth."

There was a loud click, someone picking up another phone. Georgie filled with panic, like she was in junior high and on the phone past curfew—she almost hung up.

"Georgie?" Her mom sounded tentative. Who knows when she'd last picked up the landline.

"Yes, Mom? Did you need to use the phone?"

"No . . . I was just wondering if you wanted some puppy chow."

"Thanks. Still no."

"Is that Neal?"

"It is," Neal said. "Hi, Liz."

Georgie winced. Her mom used to insist that Neal call her "Liz." And then, after he and Georgie got engaged, she'd insisted on "Mom"—which initially made him *really* uncomfortable.

"I feel like I'm cheating on my own mom," he'd said.

"Just try not calling her anything at all," Georgie advised him. *"I got mad at her once, when I was fourteen, and I didn't call her 'Mom' for a year."*

"Oh, honey," Georgie's mom cooed into the phone. "It's still 'Mom.' We're still family. Georgie was supposed to tell you that. None of this affects our feelings for you."

Georgie could tell that Neal was speechless.

"Okay, Mom," Georgie said, "thanks. I'll talk to you later."

"Thanks, Liz," Neal said.

Her mom sighed. "Now, Neal, you tell your mother I said hello—"

Oh God, oh God, oh God. In 1998, Georgie's mom and Margaret hadn't even met yet.

"Mom," Georgie cut her off. "Neal and I were talking about something really important, and I just really need you to hang up now."

"Oh, of course. Neal, honey—"

"Now, Mom. I'm *begging* you." If this went on much longer, Georgie would regress all the way back to toddlerhood.

Her mom sighed. "All right, I can take a hint. Good-bye, Neal. It was so good to hear your voice."

If she even mentioned the girls, Georgie would start screaming. She would. She'd figure out how to explain it later. *"Good-bye,* Mom."

Her mom sighed into the receiver right until the second she hung it up.

Georgie wasn't sure how to recover.

"So," Neal said, "I guess your mom thinks we broke up."

She took a second to feel utterly relieved by his train of thought, then said, "I thought we did, too, up until a few days ago."

"But not now?"

"No," Georgie said, "not now."

"No matter what happens," he said, "I'm never calling your mom 'Mom.' It's too weird."

"I know," she said. "I'll cover for you."

Neal started a sentence, then stopped. Then started again. "Georgie, I—well, I wasn't ever sleeping with Dawn."

"But—" Georgie stopped. "Yes, you were. You were engaged."

"I never slept with her." Neal's voice dropped. "She wanted to wait until marriage. Her first boyfriend was a monster, so she reclaimed her virginity."

"She *reclaimed her virginity*?"

"Leave it, Georgie. She can do whatever she wants with her virginity."

"Right," Georgie said, nodding her head. "Right . . . It doesn't sound like such a bad idea, actually. Maybe I'll reclaim mine before you come back. In the name of Queen Elizabeth."

Neal sounded like he might have laughed.

"Because she was the virgin queen," Georgie said.

"I got it."

Georgie was quiet. *Neal had never slept with Dawn.* She'd always assumed he'd had lots of fabulous young sex with Dawn. Freshly scrubbed Heartland-teenager sex. *"Suckin' on a chili dog outside the Tastee Freeze,"* et cetera.

Did that mean he'd never had sex with anyone but Georgie?

She thought of their first time. At Neal's apartment, in the middle of the night. Laughing and fumbling with the condom—and Georgie wanting to get past this first time together, so they could get to just *be*ing together, whatever that might mean.

Was that Neal's first time ever?

That's exactly the sort of thing he wouldn't tell her. Neal didn't like to talk about sex. And he didn't like to talk about *before*. Before they were together, before Georgie. (He didn't like to talk about *yesterday*.)

She thought of Neal. Practically a teenager, pale as paper. All concentration and broken concentration, laughing through clenched teeth and touching her like she was made of glass.

Neal.

"You can't be jealous of Seth," Georgie offered quietly.

"Really," he huffed.

"Really. That's like the sun being jealous of . . ."

"A comparably sized sun?"

"I was going to say the moon."

"The sun probably *is* jealous of the moon," Neal said. "It's a hell of a lot closer."

"Seth and I are just friends," she said. It was true, it had always been true. *Best* friends—but just friends.

"You and Seth aren't *just* anything."

"Neal . . ."

"He's your soul mate," Neal said. And the way he said it, it was like he'd already thought it through—like he'd thought it through and through, like he'd chosen that word intentionally.

Georgie's jaw dropped against the receiver. "Seth. Is *not*. My soul mate."

"Isn't he? Aren't you planning your life around him?"

"No." Georgie leaned forward. Even in 1998, that hadn't been true. "No. God. I was planning my life around *me*."

"Is there a difference?"

"Neal . . ."

"No, Georgie, let's just get it out there. I'm optional for you—I know that. I know that you love me, I know you want to be with me. But you can imagine your life without me. If I walk away from you now—if I don't come back—you won't have to adjust your grand plan. But Seth *is* your grand plan. It's obvious. I don't think you could imagine going twenty-four hours without him."

"Are you asking me to?"

"No." Neal sounded dejected. "No. I know . . . what you guys have together. I'd never ask you to choose between us."

He never had.

Neal had never liked Seth—that hadn't changed over the years. But he never complained about him. He never complained about all the time Seth and Georgie spent together. About the long hours or the middle-of-the-night texts—or the days when Neal and Georgie took the girls to Disneyland, and Georgie ended up sitting on the curb in Critter Country, talking Seth through some script emergency over the phone.

And Georgie was *so grateful* for that. For Neal's acceptance. (Even if it was just resignation.)

Sometimes she felt like she was walking a fine, precarious line between the two of them. Like there wasn't enough of her to be who she needed to be for them both.

If Neal pushed her, or pulled her—if either one of them did—it would all come crashing down.

Georgie would come crashing down.

But Neal never did. He never seemed jealous. Pissed, resentful, tired, bitter, lost—yeah. But not jealous. He'd always trusted her with Seth.

What would Georgie do if Neal *did* ask her to choose between them?

What would she have done if he'd asked her back in 1998?

She would have been angry. She might have chosen Seth just because Seth wasn't the one asking her to make the choice. And because Seth came first—chronologically. Seth was grandfathered in.

Georgie hadn't known back then how much she was going to come to need Neal, how he was going to become like air to her.

Was that codependence? Or was it just marriage?

"You could," she said.

"What?"

"You could ask me to choose."

"What?" He sounded surprised. "I don't want to."

"I don't want you to either," she said. "But you *could*."

"Georgie, I've seen you two together. You can't even finish a joke without him."

"Those are just jokes."

"Really throwing around the word 'just' tonight, aren't you?"

"You could *ask* me to choose," she insisted.

"I don't *want* to," he said, practically growling.

"I wouldn't even have to think about it, Neal. I'd choose

you. I'd choose you again and again and again. Seth is my best friend—I think he'll always be my best friend—but you're my future." Never mind that this wasn't true yet in 1998. It was *going* to be true. It was inevitably true. "You're my whole life."

Neal exhaled. She could imagine him shaking out his head, blinking. Resetting his jaw.

"Please don't be jealous of Seth," she whispered.

He was quiet.

Georgie waited.

"If you promise me that I don't have to be jealous," Neal said finally, "that I *never* have to be jealous, then I won't be."

"You never have to be, I promise."

"Okay," he said. Then more firmly, "Okay. I'm taking you at your word."

"Thank you."

"Now take me at mine, Georgie, for Christ's sake—I'm not in love with *Dawn*. I never really was. Even if you break up with me and crush my heart, I'm never getting back together with Dawn. I know that the world isn't flat now, I'm not going back."

"So you're saying that, if we break up, you'll definitely hold out for somebody better than Dawn. That's supposed to make me feel better?"

"You've ruined me for Dawn. *That's* supposed to make you feel better."

"Neal, I want to ruin you for *everyone*."

"Christ." His voice got closer, like he was pushing the receiver against his chin. "You *have*. You don't have to be jealous of anyone. But especially not of Dawn, okay?"

"Okay," she said.

He sighed. "Let's never do this again."

"Do what?"

"Be jealous and crappy to each other."

"It's easier for me than for you," she said.

"Why?"

"Because you're right. Seth is worse than an ex-boyfriend. Seth isn't going anywhere."

"Do I have any reason to be jealous of Seth?"

"No."

"Then I'm not. End of story."

Georgie asked Neal more questions about the railroad detectives. She could tell he wanted to talk about it.

Apparently he'd been considering the job more seriously than she'd ever realized.

She tried not to draw attention to the obvious problem with this career plan—that it would mean moving to Omaha. And Georgie was *never* going to move to Omaha.

She was going to work in TV, Neal knew that. And TV meant Los Angeles.

Part of her just wanted to tell him:

This isn't going to happen. We stay in California. You hate it. But you grow your own avocados. So that's something.

You like our house. You picked it out. You said it reminded you of home—something about hills and high ceilings and only one bathroom.

And we're close to the ocean—close enough—and you don't hate it, not like you used to. Sometimes I think you like it. You love me by the ocean. And the girls. You say it sweetens us. Pinks our cheeks and curls our hair.

And Neal, if you don't come back to me, you'll never see what a good dad you are.

And it won't be the same if you have kids with some other, better girl, because they won't be Alice and Noomi, and even if I'm not your perfect match, they are.

God, the three of you. The three of you.

When I wake up on Sunday mornings—late, you always let me sleep in—I come looking for you, and you're in the backyard with dirt on your knees and two little girls spinning around you in perfect orbit. And you put their hair in pigtails, and you let them wear whatever madness they want, and Alice planted a fruit cocktail tree, and Noomi ate a butterfly, and they look like me because they're round and golden, but they glow for you.

And you built us a picnic table.

And you learned to bake bread.

And you've painted a mural on every west-facing wall.

And it isn't all bad, I promise. I swear to you.

You might not be actively, thoughtfully happy 70 to 80 percent of the time, but maybe you wouldn't be anyway. And even when you're sad, Neal—even when you're falling asleep at the other side of the bed—I think you're happy, too. About some things. About a few things.

I promise it's not all bad.

"Georgie? Are you still there?"

"Yeah."

"I thought you fell asleep."

"I'm awake. It's only ten here."

"I was saying that I'd have to wear a gun—would that bother you?"

"I don't know," she said. "I've never thought about it. It's hard to imagine you with a gun." Neal didn't even kill spiders. He teased them onto a piece of paper, then set them down gently on the porch. "Would it bother you?"

"I don't know," he said. "Maybe. I've always hated guns."

"I love you," she said.

"Because I hate guns?"

"Because everything."

"Because everything." She could hear Neal almost smiling. She could almost see him, too.

No . . .

Georgie was picturing *her* Neal. Her almost-forty Neal. Leaner. Sharper. With longer hair and crow's-feet and a bit of gray in the beard he grew every winter. *"What passes for winter,"* he'd say. *"My children are never going to know what it's like to come in from the cold and feel the warmth work its way back into their fingers."*

"It sounds like you're saying they're never going to get frostbite."

"I can't have this conversation with someone who's never built a snowman."

"Our kids have seen snow."

"At Disneyland, Georgie. That's just soap bubbles."

"They don't know the difference."

"What if it was Persephone who kidnapped Hades . . ."

"You're talking fancy again."

Her Neal had lost his baby fat, his soft belly and hobbity hint of a double chin.

Once Alice was born, Neal took up cycling. He went everywhere by bicycle now, hauling a bright yellow trailer. Hauling two little girls, bags of groceries, stuffed animals, stacks of library books . . .

Working motherhood had made Georgie shapeless and limp, and perpetually tired-looking. She never got enough sleep anymore. And she'd never gotten her waist back—or gotten around to buying new clothes for this new (not so new anymore, really) reality. Georgie hadn't even resized her wedding ring after it got too tight to wear during her last pregnancy. It sat in a china saucer on their dresser.

While Neal had come into focus over the years—clean-jawed, clear-eyed—Georgie had lost her own reflection in the mirror.

Sometimes, when she had a day off, they'd walk to the park, the four of them, and Georgie would see how the nannies and stay-at-home moms looked at Neal. That handsome dad with the blue eyes and stubbly dimples and the two laughing, doll-faced satellites.

"Georgie? Am I losing you?"

"No." She pressed the phone to her ear. "I'm here."

"Do we have a bad connection?"

This person on the other end of the line was Neal as he *was*. Before he was quite hers. When he was still circling the possibility of Georgie. This Neal was harsher. Paler. Had a shorter temper. But this Neal hadn't given up on her yet. This Neal still looked at Georgie like she was something brand-new and supernatural. He was still surprised by her, delighted with her.

Even now, as frustrated as he was.

Even now, ten states away and half done with her, this Neal still thought she was better than he deserved. More than he'd ever expected life would give him.

"I love you," she said.

"Georgie, are you okay?"

"Yeah. I'm fine." Her voice broke. "I love you."

"Sunshine." Neal sounded soft, concerned. "I love you, too."

"But not enough," she said, "is that what you're thinking?"

"What? No. That's *not* what I'm thinking."

"It's what you've *been* thinking," she said. "It's what you thought from California to Colorado."

"That's not fair. . . ."

"What if you were right, Neal?"

"Georgie, please don't cry."

"It's what you said, and you said that you meant it. And nothing's changed, has it? Why aren't we *talking* about this? Why are we pretending that everything's fine? It's not fine. You're in Nebraska, and I'm here, and it's Christmas, and we're supposed to be together. You love me. But maybe it isn't enough. That's what you're thinking."

"No." Neal cleared his throat and said it again: "*No*. Maybe I was thinking that. From California to Colorado. But then . . . I got tired. Literally tired—*dangerously* tired, and there was the thing with the aliens. And then sunrise. And the rainbows. I told you about the rainbows, right?"

"Yeah," she said. "But I don't understand the significance."

"There is no significance. I just got *tired*. Tired of being angry. Tired of thinking about dead ends, and everything that isn't or might not be enough."

"So not breaking up with me seemed like a better idea after you'd been awake for twenty-four hours?"

"Don't."

"What if you were right? What if it isn't enough?"

He sighed. "Lately I've been thinking that it's impossible to know."

"To know what?" she pushed.

"Whether it's enough. How does anyone ever know whether love is enough? It's an idiotic question. Like, if you fall in love, if you're that lucky, who are you to even ask whether it's enough to make you happy?"

"But it happens all the time," she said. "Love *isn't* always enough."

"When?" Neal demanded. "When is that true?"

All Georgie could think of was the end of *Casablanca,* and Madonna and Sean Penn. "Just because you love someone," she said, "that doesn't mean your lives will fit together."

"Nobody's lives just fit together," Neal said. "Fitting together is something you work at. It's something you make happen—because you love each other."

"But . . ." Georgie stopped herself. She didn't want to talk Neal out of this, even if he was wrong. Even if she was the only one who knew how wrong he was.

He sounded exasperated. "I'm not saying that everything will magically work out if people love each other enough. . . ."

If *we* love each other enough, Georgie heard.

"I'm just saying," he went on, "maybe there's no such thing as enough."

Georgie was quiet. She wiped her eyes with Neal's T-shirt.

"Georgie? Do you think I'm wrong?"

"No," she said. "I think—oh God, *I know*—that I love you. I love you so much. Too much. I feel like it's going to spin me off my axis."

Neal was quiet for a second. "That's good," he said.

"Yeah?"

"God. Yeah."

"Do you want to get off the phone now?"

He huffed a laugh into the receiver. *"No."*

But maybe he did. Neal was always good about talking

to her on the phone, but he wasn't a fifteen-year-old girl.

"Not even a little bit," he said. "Do you?"

"No."

"I wouldn't mind getting ready for bed. Can I call you back?"

"No," she said, too quickly. Then lied, "I don't want to wake up my mom."

"Okay. Then you call me. Give me twenty minutes. I want to take a quick shower."

"Okay," she said.

"I'll try to pick up on the first ring."

"Okay."

"Okay." He blew a quick kiss into the phone, and Georgie laughed, because Neal seemed like the last guy on earth who would kiss into a phone. But he wasn't.

"Bye," she said, waiting for the click.

CHAPTER 18

Georgie decided to take a shower, too. Her mom said she could borrow some pajamas. All her mom's pajamas came in sets—matching tops and bottoms, or peignoirs with flirty, useless robes.

"Just give me a T-shirt!" Georgie was standing in her mom's bathroom in a towel, shouting through the door.

"I don't have any sleeping T-shirts. Do you want one of Kendrick's?"

"Gross. No."

"Then you'll just have to deal." Her mom opened the door and threw something in. Georgie unfolded a pair of aqua-colored pajama shorts—polyester satin, with cream-colored bows and a matching, low-cut lace-trimmed top. She groaned.

"Have you been talking to Neal all this time?" her mom asked.

"Yeah," Georgie said, wishing she had clean underwear. Not willing to borrow any.

"How is he?"

"Good." She realized she was smiling. "Really good."

"How're the girls?"

"Fine."

"Are you working things through?"

"There's nothing to work through," Georgie said. *Yes,*

she thought. *I think so.* She peeked out of the bathroom. "Where's Kendrick?"

"In the living room, watching TV."

Georgie walked out.

"Look at you," her mom said. "You look so nice. You should let me go shopping with you sometime."

"I have to call Neal back," Georgie said. "Thanks, um, for the pajamas. And everything." She stooped to kiss her mom on the cheek. Georgie tried to do stuff like that more now that she had kids of her own. Alice and Noomi couldn't get enough of Georgie; they practically crawled on her when she was home. It made Georgie feel physically ill to think of them shying away from her—or bristling when she tried to kiss them. What if they went a whole year without calling her "Mom"?

So Georgie tried to be more affectionate with her own mother. When she could.

As soon as she kissed her mom on the cheek, her mom turned her face to catch Georgie on the lips. Georgie frowned and pulled away. "Why do you always *do* that?"

"Because I love you."

"I love you, too. I'm going to call Neal." Georgie tugged at the satin shorts; there was no tugging them to a reasonable length. "Thank you."

She looked both ways before walking out into the hall. She stopped at Heather's room—Heather was lying on her bed. She had her laptop out and was wearing headphones.

She took them off when she saw Georgie. "Hello, Victoria, did you come to tell me a secret?"

"Do me a favor."

"What?"

"I'm starving, but I don't want to walk through the living room like this."

"I think if Dad sees you in Mom's lingerie, it might scar him for life."

Heather called Kendrick "Dad." Which made sense because he'd raised her. And because he wasn't three years older than Heather. "It might scar *me* for life," Georgie said. "Why are all her pajamas lingerie?"

"She's a very sensual woman. I know this because she likes to tell me." Heather got off the bed. "What do you want to eat? I ate all the ziti. And the puppy chow—there wasn't that much left. Hey, do you want me to order you a pizza?"

"No," Georgie said. "I'll take whatever's in the kitchen."

"You could have borrowed some of my pajamas, you know."

"That's very sweet of you," Georgie said. "Why don't you give me as many as you can spare, and I'll fashion something comfy and tentlike out of them."

"I'm sure I have *something* that would fit you."

"Oh my God, stop. Just get me some food. I'm gonna go hide in my room."

"Have you been talking to Neal?"

Georgie grinned. "Yeah."

"That's good, right?"

Georgie nodded. "Go. I'm hungry."

Heather brought back an apple, three prewrapped slices of cheese, and a giant bottle of Mexican Coke. Georgie would have been better off sending Alice.

"Call Neal," Heather said. "I want to say hi to the girls."

"It's after one in the morning there," Georgie said. "They're asleep."

"Oh, right. Time zones."

Georgie unwrapped a slice of cheese and started eating it. "Thank you. Now go."

"You're supposed to wrap the cheese around the apple; it's like a caramel apple."

"That doesn't sound anything like a caramel apple."

"Call him now," Heather said. "I want to say hi."

"No."

Georgie's mom, miraculously, hadn't spoiled anything with Neal, but there was no way Georgie was letting Heather near the phone.

"Why not?" Heather asked.

"You know why not," Georgie said.

"No, I don't."

"Because. We have private . . . stuff to talk about."

"Like divorce stuff?"

"No."

"Like phone sex?"

Georgie grimaced. *"No."*

"Because you can't have phone sex wearing Mom's lingerie."

"I just want to talk to my husband, okay? Privately?"

"Sure. Right after I say hi."

Georgie tried to open the Coke bottle. "Do you have a bottle opener?"

"Yeah, Georgie, I carry one in my jammies. Here." Heather took the bottle and started to twist the cap in the side of her mouth.

"Stop," Georgie said, reaching for the bottle. "You'll ruin your teeth."

Heather sighed dramatically, and handed Georgie the

bottle. Georgie set it delicately in her own mouth and bit down as gingerly as possible.

The phone rang.

Before Georgie could even think about getting to it, Heather grabbed the receiver and shouted, "Hi, Neal!"

Georgie dropped the bottle and launched herself on her sister, digging under Heather's head for the phone.

"It's Heather. . . . Yes, Heather."

"Heather," Georgie whispered. "I'm going to kill you. Let go."

Heather was curled into a defensive ball on the bed, still pushing Georgie (in the face) with one hand, and holding the phone to her head with the other. Her expression went from bratty and victorious to confused. She let go of the phone, abruptly, and Georgie pushed her off the bed.

Georgie grabbed the phone. "Neal?"

"Yeah?" He sounded confused.

"Just a minute."

Heather was standing in the middle of the room, bug-eyed, arms folded. "That's not Neal," she whispered. At least she was whispering.

"It is," Georgie argued.

"Then why didn't he know who I was?"

"He was probably wondering why you were yelling at him."

"That didn't *sound* like Neal."

"Heather, I swear . . ."

"You're having an affair. Oh my God, you're having an affair. Is that why Neal left you?"

Georgie rushed forward and covered Heather's mouth with her hand. Heather's eyes were huge. And tearful. *Oh God.*

"Heather, I swear that I am not having an affair. I promise you."

Heather pulled her head away. "On your life."

"On my *life*."

"On Alice and Noomi's lives," Heather said.

"Don't say that, that's terrible."

"It's only terrible if you're lying."

"Fine. Yes. I swear."

Heather pursed her lips. "I know that's not Neal, Georgie. I know something's wrong here. It's women's intuition."

"You're not a woman yet."

"That's bullshit, I'm old enough to get drafted."

"Please, please, go away," Georgie begged. "I have to talk to Neal. We can talk about this tomorrow morning."

"Fine . . ."

Georgie pushed Heather out the door and closed it. Her heart was thudding. (She really needed to get back to yoga. Or whatever it was people did now. Spin. Georgie hadn't been to the gym since Alice was born.) She wished her bedroom door had a lock. It didn't even latch—her mom said the dogs liked to come in here and sleep on the bed.

Georgie walked back to the phone and picked up the receiver. She held it up to her ear, cautiously. "Neal?"

"Georgie?"

"Yeah."

"Who was that?"

"That was . . . Heather. My cousin Heather."

"Your mom named Heather 'Heather' even though you have a cousin named Heather?"

"Yeah. Sort of. After Heather, my cousin."

"Is she staying with you for Christmas?"

"Yeah."

"Do you have other family there?"

"No. Just Heather."

"I didn't know you had cousins," he said.

"Everybody has cousins."

"But you don't have aunts and uncles."

Georgie sat back down on the floor. "Are you practicing for *Railroad Detectives*?"

"It doesn't seem like you like your cousin."

"I just don't want to waste precious *you* time, talking about Heather."

"Precious me time," Neal said softly.

"Yeah."

"I miss you, Georgie."

"I miss you, too."

"Sorry. I got tired of waiting for you to call."

"It's okay," she said.

"Are you in bed?"

"No, I'm sitting on the floor, eating prewrapped cheese."

"Really," he said. It came out a laugh. "What are you wearing?"

Georgie took a bite of cheese. This was ridiculous. This was all ridiculous. "You don't want to know."

"It's snowing here."

Georgie felt a pull in her stomach. She'd still never seen snow.

It never snowed when she was in Omaha, even in December—Margaret said Georgie brought the sun with her.

But it was snowing now for Alice and Noomi.

And it was snowing in 1998 for Neal.

"Really?" she said.

"Yeah." Neal sounded soft and warm. He sounded tucked in. "Just started."

Georgie climbed up into her bed and clapped softly to turn off the light. "Tell me about it."

"I can't," he said. "You don't have any frame of reference."

"I've seen snow on TV."

"That's usually fake."

"How is real snow different?"

"It's less like powder. It's sticky. It doesn't scatter when you walk through it, not usually. What's it like in your head?"

"I don't know. I've never thought about it. It's like snow."

"Think about it."

"Well . . . it looks like crystal—snowflakes do—but I know it's soft. I guess I imagined that it would feel almost ceramic? But instead of shattering, it would crumble in your hands."

"Hmmm . . ."

"Is that right?" she asked.

"Almost not at all."

"Tell me."

"Well, it's ice," he said.

"I know it's ice."

"You're partly right—it's soft. Have you ever had shaved ice? Did you have one of those Snoopy Sno-Cone Machines?"

"Of course not, my mom never bought me anything good."

"But you've had shaved ice."

"Yeah."

"So you know how that's soft. How it's solid, but soft. How it compresses when you push your tongue into the roof of your mouth."

"Yeah . . . ," she said.

"Well, it's like that. Like ice. But soft. And light. And almost whipped with air. And sometimes, like tonight, it's thick—and it sticks together in clumps, like cotton candy and wet feathers."

Georgie laughed.

"I wish you were here," he said. "To see it. If you were here, you'd be sleeping in the basement—there's a foldout couch."

She knew about the couch. "I don't like basements."

"You'd like this one. It's got lots of windows. And a foosball table."

Georgie climbed under the covers. "Oh, well, *foosball*."

"And a whole wall of board games."

"I like board games."

"I know. . . . You're in bed now, aren't you?"

"Hmm-mmm."

"I can tell. Your voice has given up."

"Given up what?" she asked.

"I don't know. Being upright. And on-the-ball. Clever. All the things you have to be all day long."

"Are you saying I'm done being clever?"

"I'm saying," he said, "I like you when you've given everything up for the day."

"I like you on the phone," Georgie said. "I've always liked you on the phone."

"Always?"

"Mmm."

"If you were here," Neal said, "you'd be sleeping in the

basement. And I'd notice it was snowing, and I wouldn't want you to miss it. I'd come downstairs. . . ."

"Don't, you'll traumatize Margaret if you get caught sneaking into my room."

"Pfft. I'm stealthy. I'd come down and wake you up. And I'd let you borrow a pair of my boots and an old coat."

"Make it your letterman's jacket."

"It's not warm enough," he argued.

"This is hypothetical snow, Neal. Make it your letterman's jacket."

"I don't get it—you think wrestling is gross, but you like my letterman's jacket."

"You didn't wrestle *in* the jacket," she said.

"It could be real, you know. This scenario. Next Christmas."

"Mmm."

"So I'd take you outside in borrowed boots and my letterman's jacket, out to the backyard—I've told you how there are no streetlights, right? You can see the stars. . . ."

Georgie had stood in that backyard with Neal, his backyard that felt like the edge of a forest, a dozen times over the years. There hadn't ever been snow, but there were stars.

"And I'd watch you meet the snow," he said.

"Meet it?"

"Feel it. Taste it. I'd watch it catch in your hair and eyelashes."

She rubbed her cheek into her pillow. "Like in *The Sound of Music*."

"And when you got too cold, I'd hold you close. And everywhere I touched you, the snow would melt between us."

"We should talk on the phone more at home."

He laughed. "Really."

"Yeah. Just call each other from the next room."

"We could get cell phones," he said.

"Brilliant idea," she agreed. "But you have to promise to answer yours."

"Why wouldn't I answer?"

"I don't know."

"And then," he said, "when you got too cold for me to keep you warm—which would be too soon, because you're spoiled by the sun—I'd take you back inside. And we'd shake off the snow and leave our wet boots in the mudroom."

"Why's it called a mudroom?"

"Because it's the room where you take off your muddy things."

"I love that your house plans for you to get muddy. Like it's in the architecture."

"And then I'd follow you back downstairs. . . . And you'd still be so cold. And your pajama pants would be wet. Your face would be flushed, your cheeks would be numb."

"That sounds dangerous," she said.

"It's not dangerous. It's normal. It's nice."

"Hmm."

"And I wouldn't be able to stop touching you," Neal said, "because I've never touched you cold."

"You're hung up on the cold."

His voice dipped into a rumble. "I'm hung up on you."

"Don't talk like that," Georgie whispered.

"Like what?"

"That voice."

"What voice?" he rumbled.

"You know what voice. Your *Would you like me to seduce you?* voice."

"I have a Mrs. Robinson voice?"

"Yes," she said. "You're a minx."

"Why can't I seduce you, Georgie? You're my girl-friend."

She swallowed. "Yeah, but I'm sleeping in my childhood bedroom."

"Georgie. I've had my way with you in that childhood bedroom. Just last week, in fact."

"Yeah, but you're in *your* childhood bedroom." *And you're actually, practically your childhood self.* Georgie couldn't talk dirty with this Neal. It would be like cheating on *her* Neal—wouldn't it?

"Have you blacked out all of last summer?" he asked.

She smiled and looked away, even though he couldn't see her. "The Summer of Spectacular Phone Sex," she said. Of course she remembered the Summer of Spectacular Phone Sex.

"Exactly," he said. "The Summer of Conjugal Long Distance."

Georgie had forgotten that nickname. It made her laugh. "No. I haven't forgotten."

"Is something wrong?"

"I can't have spectacular phone sex with you." *I haven't had phone sex for fifteen years.* "I'm wearing my mother's lingerie."

Neal laughed. Genuinely. Out loud, which almost never happened. "If you're trying to turn me on, I have to tell you, sweets, it's not working."

"I'm *actually* wearing my mother's lingerie," Georgie said. "It's a long story. I didn't have anything else to wear."

She could hear him smiling, even before he started talking. "Well, Christ, Georgie—take it off."

Neal.

Neal, Neal, Neal.

"I'll call you tomorrow."

"No," she said, "just stay."

"I'm falling asleep." He breathed a laugh. It sounded muffled. She could picture his face in the pillow, the phone resting on his ear—she was imagining a cell phone. *Wrong.*

"That's okay," she said.

"I might be asleep already," he murmured.

"I don't mind. It's nice. I'll fall asleep, too. Just set the phone close, so I can hear you wake up."

"And then I'll explain to my dad that I was on a long distance call for ten hours because sleeping on the phone seemed romantic at the time."

God. Long distance. Georgie had forgotten about long distance—did that still exist? "It would be romantic, though," she said. "Like waking up in each other's heads."

"I'll call you when I wake up."

"Don't call me," she said. "I'll call you."

He snorted a little.

"I didn't mean it like that," she said. "But seriously: Don't call me, I'll call you."

"Okay, you call me, sunshine. Call me as soon as you wake up."

"I love you," Georgie said. "I love you like this."

"Asleep?"

"Unlocked," she said. And then, "Neal?"

"Call me before you get dressed," he said.

She laughed. "I love you."

"Love you, too." His voice was a slur.

"I miss you," she said.

He didn't answer.

Georgie felt her own eyes closing. The receiver slid along her cheek—she clutched it, lifting it back up. "Neal?"

"Mmm."

"I miss you."

"Just a few more days," he mumbled.

"Good night, Neal."

"Good night, sweetheart."

Georgie waited for him to hang up, then set the receiver on its hooks and slid partway off the mattress to put the phone back on the nightstand.

MONDAY
DECEMBER 23, 2013

CHAPTER 19

The first time Georgie woke up, it was just after dawn, and it was because she wasn't wearing pants. Which was alarming at first. And then funny. And then she pulled the covers up over her head and tried to go back to sleep. Because it felt like she'd been dreaming, dreaming something good, and like maybe she'd be able to get back to it if she didn't completely open her eyes.

She fell asleep thinking that she couldn't remember the last time she felt so warm—and that maybe "warm" was the same as "in love"—and obviously she was in love with Neal, she'd always been in love with Neal, but when was the last time she'd talked to him for six hours, just talked to him? Just him, just her. Maybe this *was* the last time, she thought. And then she fell back to sleep.

The second time Georgie woke up, it was because somebody was shouting. Two somebodies were shouting. And banging on her bedroom door.

"Georgie! I'm coming in!" *Was that Seth?*

"Georgie, he's *not* coming in!" *And Heather . . .*

Georgie opened her eyes. The door opened and immediately slammed shut.

"Fuck, Heather," Seth whined. "That was my finger."

Georgie sat up. She was wearing her mom's skimpy tank top. Clothes, she needed clothes. She spotted Neal's T-shirt on the floor and made a desperate grab for it, yanking it over her head.

"I can't just let you waltz into my sister's bedroom!" Heather shouted.

"Are you protecting her honor? Because that ship has sailed."

"It hasn't sailed. He's just visiting his mom."

"What?" Seth sounded winded. The door opened, and he spotted Georgie before it slammed shut again. "Georgie!"

The door flew back open, and Seth and Heather fell in, practically on top of each other.

"Oh my God," Georgie said. "Get off my sister."

Heather was pulling at the neck of Seth's sweater.

"Tell *her* to get off *me*," he said.

"Get off!" Georgie shouted. "This is like a nightmare I haven't even had yet."

Heather let go and stood up, folding her arms. She looked as suspicious of Georgie as she did of Seth. "I answered the front door, and he ran past me."

Seth straightened his cuffs furiously, glaring at Georgie. "I *knew* you were here."

"Brilliant deduction," Georgie said. "My car's parked outside. What are you doing here?"

"What am *I* doing here?" He gave up on his cuffs. "Are you kidding me? I mean, are you *kidding* me? What are *you* doing here! What are you *doing,* Georgie?"

Georgie rubbed her face in Neal's T-shirt and glanced over at the phone—which was sitting next to her old alarm clock, which said noon. "Jesus," she groaned. "Is it really almost noon?"

"Yes," Seth said. "Noon. And you're not at work, and

you're not answering your phone, and you're still wearing those ridiculous clothes."

"My battery's dead."

"What?"

She pulled the comforter tight around her waist. "I'm not answering my phone, because my battery's dead."

"Oh, good," he said, "that explains why you're at your mom's house, having an epic lie-in."

The doorbell rang. Heather looked at Georgie. "Are you okay?"

Seth threw his hands in the air. "Seriously! Heather! I think you can trust me to be alone with your sister, who has been my best friend *longer than you have been alive.*"

Heather pointed at him, threatening. "She's fragile right now!"

The doorbell rang again.

"I'm fine," Georgie said. "Get the door."

Heather stomped out into the hall.

Seth ran a hand through his hair and shook his head. "Okay. Let's not panic, we've still got time—and I've got coffee. There are still twelve workable hours left today, right? And then at least that many tomorrow. And maybe five or six on Christmas?"

"Seth . . ."

"What did she mean by 'fragile'?"

"Look, Seth, I'm sorry. Just let me get dressed."

"You've got your special Metallica T-shirt on," he said. "Looks like you're already dressed."

"Just let me change, then. And brush my teeth and wake up. *I'm sorry.* I know we need to work on the scripts."

"Jesus, Georgie"—he sat down hard on the bed, facing her—"do you think I care about the scripts?"

She folded her legs up under the comforter. "Yes."

Seth's head fell into his hands. "You're right. I do. I care a lot about the scripts." He looked up, despondently. "But finally getting our dream show won't be that rewarding if you move back in with your mom and start sleeping eighteen hours a day."

"I'm sorry," she said.

He rucked both hands through his hair. "Stop. *Saying* that. Just . . . tell me what's going on with you."

She glanced over at the yellow phone. "I can't."

"I already know."

"You do?" *No, he couldn't.*

"I know it's Neal. I'm not blind."

"I never thought you were blind," Georgie said. "Just self-absorbed."

"You can talk to me about this."

"I really can't," she said.

"The universe won't unravel, Georgie."

"Something else might."

Seth sighed. "Just . . . did he leave you?"

"No."

"But you guys aren't talking."

No, she thought, *not since Wednesday.* Then—*yes, all night long.*

"What makes you say that?" she asked.

Seth looked up, almost like he was embarrassed for her. "The way you've been taking your laptop with you to the bathroom, just in case your phone rings."

"I have to leave it plugged in," she said.

"Get a new phone."

"I'm going to. I've been busy."

Seth drew his lovely auburn eyebrows together. He

looked like a concerned junior senator. Like the actor who'd get cast to play a concerned junior senator. Like the star of a lighthearted procedural on the USA Network. "Can't you just tell him this is all my fault? Throw me under the bus."

"That doesn't actually work," Georgie said, fisting her hands in the comforter in her lap. "Making you seem like an asshole just makes me seem like a person with asshole loyalties."

Seth rolled his eyes. "He thinks I'm an asshole no matter how you make me out."

She sighed and looked at the ceiling. "God. Seth. This is why we can't talk about this."

"What? I'm not saying that he's an asshole. I'm saying that I know he thinks I am."

"Neal is not an asshole."

"I know," Seth said.

"And I hate that word."

"I know."

She wanted to rub her eyes, but she didn't want to let go of the comforter.

"I mean, he is *sort of* an asshole . . . ," Seth said.

"Seth."

"What? That's his shtick, isn't it? You know that's his shtick. He's like a Samuel L. Jackson character."

"I can't stand Samuel L. Jackson."

"I know, but you like that whole 'You wanna mess with me, punk, huh? Do ya?' thing. You love that."

"Shut up, you don't even know Neal."

"I know him, Georgie. I've been sitting one seat away from him my whole fucking life. I secondhand-smoke know him. It's like we've got shared custody of you."

"No"—Georgie pressed her fingertips into her

forehead—"this is why we don't talk about this. You don't have any custody."

"I have some. Weekdays."

"*No.* Neal is my husband. He has full custody."

"Then why isn't he here trying to figure out what's wrong with you?"

"Because!" Georgie shouted.

"Because why?"

"Because I fucked up!"

Seth was angry. "Because you didn't go to Omaha?"

"Most recently because I didn't go to Omaha. Because I *never* go to Omaha."

"You go once a year! You bring me back that Thousand Island dressing I like."

"I mean, metaphorically. I always choose the show. I always choose work. I'm forever not going to Omaha."

"Maybe you should ask yourself why not, Georgie."

"Maybe I should!" she practically shouted.

Seth stared at his lap.

Georgie stared at hers. This wasn't them—Seth and Georgie never fought. Or rather, they *always* fought; they bickered and they insulted and they mocked. But they never fought about anything that mattered.

She knew that Seth knew things weren't great between her and Neal.

Of course Seth knew. He'd been sitting right next to her for twenty years. He'd watched it all go bad—at least that's how it would look from his perspective—but he never mentioned it.

Because there were *rules*.

And because some things were sacred. Not Georgie's life, but *work*—work was sacred. Seth and Georgie checked their lives at the door, and they worked. And there was something really beautiful about that. Something freeing.

No matter how badly they messed up their lives, the two of them would always have the show, whatever show they were on, and they'd always have each other—they protected that.

They protected work so they'd always have it there, an oasis that ate up their days.

God. *God.* This was how Georgie had ruined everything.

By being really good at something. By being really good *with* someone. By retreating into the part of her life that was easiest.

She started crying.

"Hey," Seth said, reaching out to her.

"Don't," Georgie said.

He waited until she was just sniffling. "Did you get to work on the script last night?"

"No."

"Are you coming in today?"

"I—" She shook her head. "—I don't know."

"We can work here, if you want. Change of scenery might do us good."

"What about Scotty?"

Seth shrugged. "He's already working from home. He even finished an episode. It's . . . not bad. It doesn't sound like us, but it's not bad. It's something."

Work. Georgie should go to work. She was missing Christmas so she could work on the show. If she didn't work on the show, this whole week would be a waste; Georgie would have destroyed her marriage for nothing.

She was about to tell Seth, *"Fine, fine, I'll come in, I'll work,"* when the phone rang.

The landline.

She and Seth both looked at it. It didn't ring again.

"Come on," Seth said. "I brought coffee. I don't know where it ended up—I handed it to your sister to get her out of my way. God, she's protective, have you been getting death threats?"

Someone thumped down the hall, and the door opened. Heather shoved her head and shoulders through. "It's for you." She scowled at Georgie. "It's *Neal*."

Georgie's heart skipped a beat. (Great. Now she was having heart palpitations.) (Wait. Neal could call the kitchen phone, too? This was out of control.) "Thanks. Hang up when I pick up?"

"You want me to hang up on him?"

"No," Georgie said, "I'll get it in here."

"Can you do that?"

"Are you serious?"

Heather scowled some more. "Sorry I'm not up on your twentieth-century technology."

"Go to the kitchen, wait until you hear me pick up, then hang up."

"Just pick up now," Heather said.

Georgie looked at the phone, just out of reach, and at Seth—and not at her mom's pajama shorts lying on the floor. "In. A minute," she said.

"Fine." Heather watched Georgie closely, like she was trying to crack her game. "I'll just go talk to Neal while I wait."

"Don't talk to him, Heather."

Heather's eyes had narrowed to slits. "I'll just say hi to Neal, ask him about the girls. . . ."

Georgie kicked Seth. "Pick up the phone."

"What? You want *me* to talk to Neal?"

"Nobody's talking to Neal. Pick up the phone—" She kicked him again. "—then hand it to me. And you—" She pointed at Heather. "—are a terrible sister. And a worse person."

Georgie kicked Seth one more time. He stood and picked up the receiver—holding it in the air for a few seconds, pinching the handle like it was a bomb—then tossed it to Georgie.

Heather waited in the doorway. *Hang it up,* Georgie mouthed. *Now.*

She held the phone up to her ear and waited for the click. She could hear voices at Neal's house—his parents. She could hear Neal breathing.

Heather rattled the phone onto the hook in the kitchen.

"Hello?" Georgie said.

"Hey," Neal answered.

Georgie felt her face get all soft; she looked down so Seth wouldn't notice. "Hey. Can I call you back?" She hoped this was the right Neal. (She didn't mean the *right* Neal, she meant the *young* one.)

"I know I wasn't supposed to call," he said, "but it was getting late, and I thought—I don't know what I thought, that I wanted to talk to you, I guess."

This was the right Neal. "It's okay," she said, "but can I call you back?"

"Yeah," he said. "Sorry."

"Don't be sorry. I'll call you right back."

"Good morning, Georgie."

Georgie looked at the clock. "It's almost two there, isn't it?"

"Yeah," Neal said. "But . . . not there, right? I called now because I didn't want to miss telling you good morning."

"Oh." She felt her face go globby. "Good morning."

"A-ha!" Seth said.

Georgie looked up at him, stricken.

He leaned against the closet, pleased with himself. "You're not wearing pants."

"Is that Seth?" Neal asked.

Georgie closed her eyes. "Yeah."

She could hear Neal's defenses coming up—and falling down, like Iron Man's armor snicking into place. She could hear it from across the country and fifteen years away.

Neal's voice was central air: "Did he just say that you weren't wearing pants?"

"He's being an idiot."

"Yeah. Well. You're calling me back, right? When you're done with Seth? Is that what's happening?"

"Yeah," Georgie said. "That's what's happening."

"Right." He exhaled roughly into the phone. "Talk to you soon."

He hung up.

Georgie threw the receiver at Seth, *hard*. But not hard enough—the cord caught and coiled back in on itself, falling to the floor. For a second, she was worried that she'd broken it. (Could she just plug in a new phone? Apparently the brown Trimline was magic, too, so she could always call Neal from the kitchen.)

"It's not enough for you to ruin my marriage *now*," she seethed, "is it? You have to ruin it everywhere at once."

Seth eyebrows jumped up—he looked like she *had* hit

him with the phone. He looked like he wanted to shout, *"Rules, rules, rules!"*

"Ruin your marriage . . . ," he said.

Georgie let out a breath and shook her head. "I shouldn't have said that." She kept shaking her head. "I'm sorry. I'm just . . . Why did you open your mouth?"

"You think I'm ruining your marriage?"

"No. Seth. I don't. I think *I'm* ruining my marriage. You're just an accessory."

"I'm not an accessory—I'm your best friend."

"I know."

"I'm *always* going to be your best friend."

"I *know*."

"Even if this—"

"Don't," she said.

He fell back against the closet, kicking it gently, then resting his foot against it like he was modeling orange chinos. (He was wearing orange chinos.) Then he folded his arms. "What does that even mean," Seth asked, " 'everywhere at once'?"

"It doesn't mean anything. I'm just tired."

"And scared," he said quietly.

She looked down at the comforter. "And scared."

"And talking to me about it is clearly a *catastrophic* idea. . . ."

She pulled her lips into her mouth and bit them, nodding.

"So let's not talk about it, Georgie. Let's just write."

Georgie looked up at him. Seth was being as sincere as he knew how—his face was so open, she practically didn't recognize it.

"It's the only thing I can fix for you," he said.

Her eyes dropped to the phone. "I have to call Neal back."

"Fine. You call Neal back. Then get dressed. I'll track down our coffee and find a place to set up. . . . And then you'll come out when you're ready—and I won't mention that you sleep pantless, but I'll always know from now on, Georgie, *always*—and we will write ourselves a script. We'll go Amy Sherman-Palladino on its ass."

"I love Amy Sherman-Palladino."

"I know," he said, crunching his eyebrows at her meaningfully. "I'm your *best friend*."

"I know."

"I'm going out to the kitchen now."

"Seth . . ."

"And you'll be out in a minute."

"Seth, I can't right now. I have to call Neal back."

His head fell back against the closet. "I can wait."

"I don't want you to wait."

"Georgie."

"Seth. I have to fix what I can."

"What am I supposed to do in the meantime?"

"Go to work," she said. "Write."

"And you'll come in to the office later?"

"Probably."

"But you'll definitely come in tomorrow."

"Yes."

He bounced his head gently against the fiberboard. "Fine. Just . . . fine." He kicked off the door. *"Four days,"* he groaned. "We have four days to make this happen."

"I know."

"All right . . . but if it turns out you can't actively pick up the pieces of your marriage today, you may as well come write with me."

"Stop talking about my marriage. For all time."

Seth stopped at the door and grinned back at her. "Well, come on—you're gonna see me to the door, right?"

Georgie folded her arms in the comforter. "Let Heather kick you out. It'll cheer her up."

"I always thought Heather liked me," he muttered, letting the door swing closed behind him.

Georgie didn't wait for Seth to leave the house, she didn't wait for her head or eyes to clear—she didn't stop to process the fact that *Neal* had called *her,* twice now, which meant her magic phone worked both ways, which might mean . . . *Who knows what that might mean? It's a magic phone. It's not like it has rules.*

She dialed Neal's number so fast, she hit a wrong number and had to start all over.

His dad answered. Just to flip Georgie the fuck out again.

"Hi, Paul—Mr. Grafton, it's Georgie. Is, um, is Neal there?"

"You can call me Paul," he said.

"Paul," Georgie said, and she felt like crying again.

"You caught us just in time," he said. "Here's Neal."

A shuffling noise then—"Hello?"

"Hi," Georgie said.

"Hi," Neal said. Coolly. But maybe not angrily. It was always so hard to tell with him. "Seth give you a break?"

"He left."

"Oh."

"Are you leaving?" she asked. "Your dad said—"

"Yeah. We're going to see my grandma's sister. She's in a nursing home."

"That's nice of you."

"It really isn't. She's in a nursing home, and she'll be alone on Christmas. It's pretty much the very least we can do."

"Oh," Georgie said.

"Sorry. I just . . . hate nursing homes. My great aunt doesn't have kids of her own, so we—"

"I'm sorry."

"You're sorry." Neal huffed. "I thought you were *sleeping*."

"When?"

"When I called."

"I *was* sleeping," she said.

"You were with Seth."

"He'd just woken me up."

"You were supposed to call *me* when you woke up."

"I was *going* to call you."

"Eventually," he said.

"Neal. You promised you'd never be jealous of Seth."

"I'm not jealous of Seth. I'm angry with you."

"Oh."

"I have to go," he said. "I'll call you when I get back."

Don't call me, Georgie almost answered. "Okay. I'll be here."

"Okay."

She wasn't going to say "I love you" now just to see if he'd say it back. "I'll be here," she said again.

"Okay." He hung up.

CHAPTER 20

Neal hung up.

Because it was that easy for him.

For a second, Georgie wished he knew—who she really was, *when* she really was, everything. Neal wouldn't just hang up on her like that if he knew he was hanging up on the future. You don't hang up a magic phone.

Georgie wandered out to the kitchen, hungry.

Heather was standing at the front door, talking to someone. Georgie spotted the pizza delivery car through the picture window and wondered if it would be rude to interrupt and take the pizza from them, or if, without the pizza, their little flirtation would collapse in on itself.

She started the coffeemaker and rooted through the fridge, not finding anything.

After a few more minutes, Heather walked into the kitchen, smiling.

"Where's the pizza?" Georgie asked. "I'm starving."

"Oh. I didn't order a pizza."

"But the pizza boy was here."

Heather stepped past Georgie and leaned into the fridge. "It was a wrong pizza."

"There's no such thing as a wrong pizza," Georgie said. "All pizzas are right from conception."

"It was the wrong address," Heather said. "Probably

just a mix-up because we order from them so often."

"Heather, I'm serious, there's no such thing as a wrong pizza. That boy wanted to talk to you."

Heather just shook her head and opened the vegetable drawer.

"How long has this been going on?" Georgie asked.

"Nothing's going on."

"How long have you been ordering pizzas for sport, not sustenance?"

"How long has Seth been your wake-up service?"

Georgie pushed the fridge door closed—Heather had to jerk back to get out of the way. "Out of line," Georgie said.

Heather looked like she wanted to say something else, something worse, but pressed her lips closed and folded her arms.

Georgie decided to walk away. She stopped at the edge of the kitchen. "I'm going to take a shower. Come get me if Neal calls."

Heather ignored her.

"Please?" Georgie said.

"Fine," Heather agreed, not even bothering to turn her head.

Georgie checked the yellow phone before she got into the shower, just to make sure there was a dial tone and that the ringer was turned up. (As if somebody might have snuck in and messed with it.)

Once, in junior high, she'd been so worried about missing a call from a boy, she'd dragged the phone into the bathroom with her every time she had to go. (He never did call.) (Which didn't discourage Georgie even a little bit.)

She stood under the shower until the water ran cold,

then stole some more of her mom's yoga pants and a sweat-shirt with a pug on it, and walked out to the laundry room.

When Georgie was growing up, the washing machine and dryer sat out against the garage with a little plastic canopy over them. But Kendrick had built her mom a laundry room onto the back of the house, with a tile floor and a sorting table. Georgie'd still be able to hear the kitchen phone out here, if it rang.

She opened the washing machine and dropped in her jeans and T-shirt and bra. . . .

It was a very depressing bra.

It'd been pink once, sometime between Alice and Noomi, but now it was a grayish beige, and one of the underwires kept sneaking out through a rip between Georgie's breasts. Sometimes the wire crept almost all the way out and sprung like a hook from the neck of her shirt; sometimes it bent the other way and poked her. You'd think that would prompt Georgie to buy some new bras, but instead she just pushed the wire back as soon as no one was looking, then forgot about it until the next time that bra came up in her rotation.

Georgie was bad at all shopping, but bra shopping was the worst. You couldn't do it online, and you couldn't have somebody else do it for you.

Bra shopping had always been the worst—even when her breasts were still young and lovely. (If only Georgie could figure out how to call *herself* in the past, she'd tell her-self how young and lovely she was. *"This is the ghost of bra-shopping future: Everybody's a little lopsided, roll with it."*)

She closed the washing machine lid, set the dial to GEN-TLE, then sank down on the floor in front of the dryer and leaned against it. It was warm and humming, and Georgie felt like one of those rhesus monkeys who preferred the cloth mother.

It wasn't supposed to go like this.

Everything had seemed so good when Georgie fell asleep last night. Better than good. Maybe better *than ever* . . .

Which was weird. When she was talking to Neal in the past, they got along better than they did in their shared past *or* their shared present. Maybe these were the versions of themselves that were meant to be together—mature Georgie and mostly unjaded Neal. Too bad they couldn't go on this way.

How long *could* this go on?

It was December 23rd.

Georgie knew what happened back in 1998: Neal ended up on her doorstep on Christmas Day. That meant that Neal—landline Neal—would have to leave Omaha tomorrow morning, in the past, to propose to her.

Would that still happen . . . Would Neal still propose? Or had Georgie screwed that up an hour ago, in one fell swoop of Seth?

Maybe she'd screwed it up the very first time she called Neal in the past.

Yesterday, Georgie had wondered if she was supposed to talk Neal out of loving her—if that was the point of this magic, to save him from her. But what if she'd talked him out of it just by opening her mouth?

She was thinking in hot, helpless circles when Heather walked down the back steps into the laundry room. She was carrying one of those Campbell's soups that you can heat up in the microwave, then drink out of the can. Chicken & Stars.

"Do you ever feed yourself?" Heather asked. "Or does Neal just set out a dish for you every morning?"

"Sometimes I order things," Georgie said.

"What do you feed the girls?"

"Neal feeds the girls."

"What if Neal isn't home?"

"Yogurt."

Heather handed Georgie the soup, a peace offering, then sat down next to her, against the washer.

"Thanks," Georgie said.

Heather still looked wary of Georgie. She took a deep breath and let it out through her teeth. "I know something's going on, so you may as well tell me—are you sleeping with Seth?"

Georgie took a sip of soup and burned her mouth. *"No."*

"Do you have a boyfriend who sort of sounds like your husband, but isn't your husband, but is also named Neal?"

"No."

"Is something really weird going on?"

Georgie turned her head toward Heather and tipped it against the dryer. "Yeah . . ."

Heather mirrored her, laying her head against the washer. "I can't even remember you without Neal," she said.

Georgie nodded slowly, then took another, more careful, drink of soup. "You were in our wedding, you know. Do you remember?"

"I think so," Heather said, "but I might just be remembering the photos."

Heather was supposed to be the flower girl, but none of Georgie's friends had been able to afford the trip to

Nebraska, so Heather became her only bridesmaid—besides Seth, who just assumed he'd be standing up for Georgie.

Georgie wasn't even sure she should invite Seth (because the wedding was in Omaha, and because *Neal*), but Seth started calling himself Georgie's best man, and she wasn't sure how to argue. . . .

He wore a brown three-piece suit and a pale green tie to the wedding. Heather wore lavender shantung and a green cardigan. Seth carried her down the aisle.

And he insisted that Heather come along for Georgie's bachelorette party—a "bridal-party only" dinner at some thousand-year-old Italian restaurant near Neal's house. They ate spaghetti with sugar-sweet tomato sauce, and Seth talked nonstop about the sitcom he was working on, the one he'd just convinced to hire Georgie. Georgie drank too much Paisano, and Heather fell asleep at the table. "Good thing I'm the designated driver," Seth said.

There was a photo from the next day, at the ceremony, of Seth signing the marriage certificate as Georgie's witness. Heather was standing on tiptoe to watch. Seth in his brown waistcoat. Georgie in her white dress. Neal beaming.

Georgie took another gulp of soup. "You were adorable," she told Heather. "I think you thought it was *your* wedding—Neal danced with you, and you blushed the whole time."

"I remember that," Heather said. "I mean, I've seen the pictures. I looked just like Noomi."

Georgie and Neal hadn't had a traditional church wedding—or much of a reception. They got married in Neal's backyard. The lilacs were in bloom, and Georgie carried a handful of branches that his mom had gathered into a bouquet.

Everything was on the cheap. She and Neal had both just graduated, and Georgie didn't start on the sitcom until they got back from their honeymoon. (Five days in rural Nebraska, in a cabin somebody owned on a muddy river.) (The five best days.)

They'd tried to pay for the whole wedding themselves; her mom and Kendrick were already digging deep to buy plane tickets, and Georgie didn't want to ask Neal's parents for help.

Georgie was the one who suggested they get married in Omaha. She knew Neal would like it. Their breakup, their almost breakup, was still fresh in her memory, and Georgie wanted Neal to look back on their wedding day and feel happy—about all of it. She wanted him to *be* happy that day, to be completely in his element.

Neal's family ended up helping out anyway. His parents bought the cake, and his aunts made cream cheese mints and sandwiches. The pastor who'd baptized and confirmed Neal was there to marry them. And after the ceremony, Neal's dad moved his stereo out onto the patio and played deejay.

The only song Georgie insisted on was "Leather and Lace."

That had started out as a joke.

"Leather and Lace" was playing in a restaurant on one of their first dates, and Georgie cracked herself up telling Neal that it was "our song." Then they both tried—and failed—to think of a more ridiculous "our song." (Neal suggested "Gypsies, Tramps & Thieves"; Georgie pushed for the theme from *Taxi*.)

After that, "Leather and Lace" kept coming on the radio at significant moments in their relationship. . . .

Once when Neal was kissing her in the car outside her mom's house.

Once on a road trip to San Francisco.

Once when Georgie thought she was pregnant, and they were waiting in line at Walgreens to buy a Clearblue Easy. (Neal with his hand on her back. Georgie holding the pregnancy test like it was a pack of gum. Stevie Nicks crooning about having her own life and being stronger than you know. At some point, "Leather and Lace" just became their song. For real.

When it started to play on their wedding day, on Neal's parents' patio, Georgie got all choked up.

Was that the moment she realized she was actually getting married?

Or was it just the moment she realized she'd landed a guy who would dance with her, totally sincerely, forehead to forehead, to "Leather and Lace"? *("Stay with me, stay-ay.")*

After "Leather and Lace," Neal danced with his mom to "Moon River." (The Andy Williams version.) Then Georgie danced with Seth, and Neal danced with Heather to "Both Sides Now." (The Judy Collins version.)

A few hours later, when everyone else had gone or gone inside—Seth left for the airport right after the cake—Neal and Georgie stayed out on the patio, slow-dancing to whatever came on the oldies station.

They'd never really danced together before that day. Or since. And, truthfully, they weren't doing much dancing even then. . . . Neal held Georgie with one hand on the small of her back and one on the back of her neck, and

Georgie leaned against him with both hands on his chest, and they swayed from side to side.

It wasn't dancing. It was just a way to make the wedding last. A way to stay in the moment, rolling it over and over in their heads. *We're married now. We're married.*

You don't know when you're twenty-three.

You don't know what it really means to crawl into someone else's life and stay there. You can't see all the ways you're going to get tangled, how you're going to bond skin to skin. How the idea of separating will feel in five years, in ten—in fifteen. When Georgie thought about divorce now, she imagined lying side by side with Neal on two operating tables while a team of doctors tried to unthread their vascular systems.

She didn't know at twenty-three.

That day, out on the patio, it just felt like the biggest day of her life so far, not the biggest day of her life from now on. Not the day that would change everything. That would change *her*, at a cellular level. Like a virus that rewrites your DNA.

That day, that evening, out on the patio . . .

Georgie pretended to dance. She clung to Neal's shirt. They rubbed their noses together. "You're my wife," Neal said, and then he laughed, and she tried to catch his dimples with her teeth. (Like if she caught them, she might get to keep them.)

"Yours," she said.

Maybe Georgie had gotten a *glimpse* of it then, the way infinity unspooled from where they were swaying. The way everything she was ever going to be from then on was irrevocably tethered to that day, that decision.

Neal was wearing a navy blue suit, and he'd waited to

get his hair cut until the day before the wedding, so it was a little too short.

"Yours," she said.

Neal squeezed the back of her neck. "Mine."

The dryer stopped.

"I've never been in love," Heather said. "I don't think I'm susceptible."

Georgie set down her soup can and pushed her glasses up to rub her eyes. "How could you possibly know that?"

Heather shrugged. "Well, it hasn't happened yet, has it?"

"Maybe you haven't ordered enough pizza."

"I'm being serious, Georgie."

"Okay—*seriously*, Heather, you're only eighteen. You have plenty of time to fall in love."

"Mom said she'd been in love three times by my age."

"Well"—Georgie frowned—"she's *unusually* susceptible. She's got a compromised immune system when it comes to love."

Heather played with the drawstring on her sweatshirt. "I haven't even really dated anybody yet."

"Have you tried?" Georgie asked.

Her sister wrinkled her nose. "I don't want to try."

"It'll happen in college."

"*You* dated in high school," Heather insisted. "Did you fall in love before Neal?"

"Why are you asking me this?"

"Because I need to talk to somebody," Heather said, "and Mom is aberrant."

"Can't you talk to your friends?"

"My friends are at least as clueless as I am. Did you fall in love before Neal?"

Georgie thought about it. There was a guy in the eleventh grade who'd been something more than just another moving target—for a few weeks, then it passed. And then there were the years she'd sat on the couch with Seth.

"Maybe," Georgie said. "Maybe I came really close to falling in love, cumulatively, over two or three relationships."

"But not like with Neal."

"Not like with Neal."

"How'd you know he was the one?"

"I didn't know. I don't think either of us knew."

Heather rolled her eyes. "*Neal* knew—he proposed to you."

"It's not like that," Georgie said. "You'll see. It's more like you meet someone, and you fall in love, and you *hope* that that person is the one—and then at some point, you have to put down your chips. You just have to make a commitment and hope that you're right."

"No one else describes love that way." Heather frowned. "Maybe you're doing it wrong."

"*Obviously* I'm doing it wrong," Georgie said. "But I still think love feels that way for most people."

"So you think most people bet everything, their whole lives, on hope. Just *hoping* that what they're feeling is real."

"Real isn't relevant," Georgie said, turning completely to face Heather. "It's like . . . you're tossing a ball between you, and you're just hoping you can keep it in the air. And it has nothing to do with whether you love each other or not. If you didn't love each other, you wouldn't be playing this stupid game with the ball. You love each other—and you just *hope* you can keep the ball in play."

"What's the ball a metaphor for?"

"I'm not sure," Georgie said. "The relationship. Marriage."

"You're really depressing," Heather said.

"Maybe you shouldn't be talking about marriage to someone whose husband just left her."

"He didn't leave you," Heather said. "He's just visiting his mom."

Georgie looked down at the empty soup can in her lap.

"I keep waiting for you to say that it's all worth it . . . ," Heather said.

Georgie swallowed. "That's a meaningless thing to say."

They sat quietly for a minute until one of the pugs— the bulging pregnant one—scuttled down the stairs into the laundry room. Watching a pug run down stairs is a lot like watching a pug fall down stairs. Georgie winced and looked away. It ran over to her and froze, barking aggressively.

"I don't like you either," she said, turning back to the dog.

"It's the shirt," Heather said. "She hates that shirt."

Georgie looked down at the pug that was BeDazzled on her borrowed shirt.

"They're very territorial," Heather said. "Here, move—let her climb into the dryer."

"I may not like her," Georgie said, "but I don't want to *cook* her."

"She likes it," Heather said, pushing Georgie over and opening the dryer door. "It's warm." She lifted the dog into the dryer, on top of the clothes.

"What if it's too hot in there?"

"Then she'll jump out."

"This is so dangerous," Georgie said. "What if you don't know she's in there, and you start the dryer?"

"We check first."

"I wouldn't have checked."

"Well, now you will. Look—she likes it."

Georgie watched the little dog settle down on a pile of darks, glad that her own clothes were still in the washer. She frowned at the dog, then at Heather. "Remind me never to ask you to babysit again."

Georgie's bra fell apart completely in the washing machine. Her mom had a Speed Queen with an old-fashioned agitator, and the loose underwire had wrapped around the center and caught on something inside the drum. Georgie yanked the wire free.

It hadn't even been ninety minutes since Neal hung up on her. He might not have made it to his aunt's nursing home in Iowa yet. Georgie couldn't just sit here, waiting all day. She should go to work. . . . God, no, she couldn't deal with Seth right now.

She held up the bra, trying to decide whether she could get by on one underwire, then shoved it into the dryer with the rest of her clothes (dislocating the pug first) and ran back into the house.

Heather was sitting on the couch, messing with her phone.

"Do you want to go to the mall?" Georgie asked.

"On the day before Christmas Eve? Sure, that sounds like a great idea."

"Okay. Let's go."

Heather was already narrowing her eyes; she narrowed

them to a squint. "Aren't you going to put on a bra?"

"I'm going to the mall to buy a bra."

"Why don't you just go home and pick up some clothes?"

Georgie thought of her house. Sitting dark and too far away, almost everything just as Neal had left it. "I need to get back here before Neal calls."

"So take your phone with you."

"He's calling *here*—are you coming?"

"Nah," Heather said. "I'll stay. That way there's some-body to answer the phone when *Neal* calls." She put his name in air quotes.

They frowned at each other.

"Come with me," Georgie said. "I'll buy you some-thing."

"What?"

"I might have to go to the Apple Store."

Heather leapt up from the couch, then froze. "I can't be bribed; I won't keep your dirty secrets."

"I don't have any dirty secrets."

Georgie's cell phone was still plugged in to the car lighter and woke up as soon as she turned on the car. She had seven missed calls and four voice mails from Seth, plus two missed calls and one voice mail from Neal's cell. Georgie stopped—halfway in her mom's driveway and halfway in the street—to play that voice mail. She held her breath, waiting to hear Neal's voice. To hear *now*-Neal's voice.

"Mom?" It was Alice. "Grandma wants to know if we're allowed to watch *Star Wars, Episode Five*. I told her yes, but she said there's a lot of violence. And Daddy went to see Grandpa at the cemetery, and he didn't take his phone, so we can't get his permission. I told Grandma it's okay—that we just close our eyes when Luke cuts Darth Vader's head off—but she doesn't believe me. So call us back, okay? I love you—". Alice kissed into the phone. "—bye."

Georgie set the phone down on the dashboard and backed into the street.

"Are you okay?" Heather asked.

"I'm fine," Georgie said, shoving her glasses up and wiping one eye with the back of her hand.

" 'Cause we just left the house, and you're already driving like an asshole."

"I'm fine," Georgie said.

CHAPTER 21

There was no parking at the mall—they circled and circled before they found a spot. Then Georgie opened her glove compartment and dug out her driver's license and credit card.

"Don't you have a purse?" Heather asked.

"I'm not usually in purse-necessary situations."

"I thought moms were supposed to carry big purses with first-aid kits and packets of Cheerios."

Georgie scowled at her.

"You're practically homeless," Heather said, "aren't you? If Neal doesn't come back, you're gonna have to forage for food and water."

Georgie shoved the phone and cards into her pocket. "We're not wasting time here," she said. "There won't be any hanging out at the Orange Julius, scamming for hot guys."

"I'm not twelve, Georgie."

"In and out. We get the bra, we get a new battery for my phone, then we're out of there."

"Are you buying me a new phone? Because I think I'd rather have an iPad."

"Who said I was buying you a phone?"

"It was implied. Besides, Mom says you're good for it."

"Just hurry. I don't want to miss Neal."

*

"Jingle Bell Rock" was playing inside the mall, and inside the store, and inside the dressing room in the Intimates Department.

There was already a jumble of bras on the floor, and Georgie was trying on more, facing away from the mirror. She was so distracted, she kept forgetting to pay attention to which ones fit.

Just pick one, Georgie. Or buy them all. It doesn't matter. You're just killing time.

Jesus, what a weird time to kill time. The fate of her future hung in the balance, and there was nothing she could do at the moment but run out the clock. At least, not until Neal called back.

He would call back, right?

What if he didn't, what if he was too angry? What if he was *still* angry tomorrow morning?

Georgie had to talk to Neal, to make things right again. She had to make sure that he still got into his car tomorrow, his tomorrow, and showed up at her door on Christmas Day.

But what if he didn't?

Did Georgie really believe that the last fifteen years would just unravel? Had she committed so completely to this bizarre scenario that she thought her marriage was going to start fading out, like Marty McFly in the middle of "Earth Angel"?

What else *could* she think? She had to keep playing along—the stakes were too high.

If Neal didn't show up to propose to her in 1998 . . .

Twenty-two-year-old Georgie would never know what she was missing. That girl thought it was already over, that she'd already lost him.

Georgie collapsed that week after Neal left for Omaha.

She spent the whole time in a fog. Lying in her bed, deliberately not calling him. Why should she call him? What was she supposed to say—sorry? Georgie *wasn't* sorry. She wasn't sorry that she knew what she wanted to do with her life. She wasn't sorry that she was making it happen.

It's not like Neal was offering her some compelling alternate plan: *"Georgie, I want to be a sheep farmer—it's in my blood, and I can't do it anywhere but Montana."* (Was that where sheep were farmed?) *"I need you. Come with me."*

No, Neal was just saying, *"I hate it here, I hate this. I hate that you want this."*

All he was offering Georgie were negatives.

And then he'd taken even those off the table. He'd left without her—broken up with her on his way out of town.

Georgie had genuinely believed they were broken up.

For the first few days that Neal was gone, she felt it like an actual breach between her ribs, a tear at the bottom of her lungs. Georgie would wake up in a panic sure that she'd run out of air—or that she'd lost the ability to hold it inside of her.

Then the breath would hit her like a baseball to the heart.

The air was right there; she just had to think about it. *In, out. In, out.* She wondered if she was going to have to spend the rest of her life reminding herself to breathe. Maybe that would be her internal monologue from now on. *In, out. In, out.*

Neal didn't call to apologize to Georgie that week, either.

Why should he? she thought at the time. What did he have to apologize for? For not wanting exactly what Georgie wanted? For realizing what his limitations were?

Good for him for knowing himself so well.

Good for him for figuring it out.

Neal loved her, Georgie knew that. He couldn't keep his hands off her—he couldn't keep his *ink* off her; he was always doodling on her stomach or her thigh or her shoulder. He kept a set of Prismacolor markers by his bed, and when Georgie took a shower, the water ran rainbows.

She knew Neal *loved* her.

Good for him for realizing it wasn't enough to make him happy. That was very mature of him. He was probably saving them both a lot of heartache.

Oh God, oh God, oh God.

In-out, in-out, in-out.

Stay with me, stay-ay.

By that Christmas morning, Georgie hadn't made any emotional progress from the breakup. She wasn't feeling any better or stronger.

She was pretty sure that every Christmas from then on would be tainted by Neal leaving. Like Georgie would never be able to hear "Jingle Bells" again without feeling Neal drive away from her with a tow chain in her stomach.

Seth kept calling to check on her, but she didn't want to talk to him. She didn't want to hear him tell her how much better off she was without Neal.

Georgie wasn't better off. Even if Neal was right— even if they'd never make it work together, even if they were fundamentally *wrong* for each other—she still wasn't better off without him. (Even if your heart is broken and attacking you, you're still not *better off* without it.)

Her mom made Georgie come out to the living room Christmas morning to watch Heather open her presents. Heather was three, just old enough to understand that everything under the tree was for her. Georgie sat on the couch in flannel pajama pants and a ratty T-shirt, and ate pancakes with her fingers.

Kendrick was there. He was still new then. He brought Georgie a movie-theater gift certificate with a bow on it. Heather got a talking Teletubby, which she was currently spazzing out over.

He—Kendrick, not the Teletubby—kept trying to talk to Georgie, and he was trying so hard, Georgie didn't have the heart to ignore him. (But she didn't have any heart at all, so that made conversation difficult.) When the doorbell rang, Kendrick jumped up to answer it, probably just to get away from Georgie.

"It's your friend Neal," he said when he came back to the living room.

"You mean Seth," she said.

Kendrick scratched his goatee—he used to have a ridiculous goatee—"Neal's the little one, right?"

Georgie set down her plate and got off the couch.

"Why didn't you invite him in?" her mom asked Kendrick.

"He said he'd rather wait outside."

Georgie didn't believe it was Neal. She *couldn't* believe it was Neal. First of all, because Neal was in Omaha—he wouldn't have skipped Christmas in Omaha. And second, because they were broken up. And third, because if Georgie *did* believe it was Neal, and then it turned out that it wasn't? That might be it. That might finish her.

The front door was still open when she got there.

Neal was standing on the other side of the screen, biting his lip and squinting up her block, like he was waiting for her to come from the other direction.

Neal.

Neal, Neal, Neal.

Georgie's hand trembled as she pushed the screen door open.

Neal turned to her, and his eyes got wide. Almost like he hadn't let himself believe it was really going to be her.

He took a step back, so Georgie stepped out onto the front porch. She wanted to grab him. (It was probably safe to grab him—Neal probably hadn't come to her house on Christmas morning just to break up with her *extra* hard, right? He wouldn't have come back just to tell her he was leaving?)

Neal's eyes were thin, and his face was tight. He looked like she was still hurting him. "Georgie," he said.

Georgie started crying instantly. From zero to eleven. "Neal."

Neal shook his head, and she jerked forward to hug him. Even if he *had* come just to make sure she knew they were really over, Georgie was going to get one more desperate embrace out of this.

His arms came around her shoulders, and he held her so tight, they rocked back and forth. "Georgie," Neal said, then started pulling away.

She didn't let him.

"Georgie," he said, "wait."

"No."

"Yes. Wait. I need to do something."

She still didn't let go; Neal had to unwind her arms and take a step back.

As soon as he was away, he dropped to one knee. Georgie thought maybe he was going to apologize, that he was falling at her feet. "No," she said, "you don't have to."

"Shhh. Just let me do this."

"Neal . . ."

"Georgie, please."

She folded her arms and looked miserable. She didn't want him to say he was sorry. That would take them right back into the heart of their sorry situation.

"Georgie," he said. "I love you. I love you more than I hate everything else. We'll make our own enough—will you marry me?"

Georgie stopped, in the middle of fastening a bra behind her back, and turned to face herself in the dressing room mirror.

Oh . . .

CHAPTER 22

Christmas.

On one knee.

Looking straight through her.

"We'll make our own enough," he'd said.

Last night on the telephone, Georgie had asked Neal if love was enough.

And fifteen years ago, he'd answered her.

Was that . . . could it just be a coincidence?

Or did it mean . . .

That it had already happened.

That *this*—all of this, the phone calls, the fighting, the four-hour conversations—had *already happened*. For Neal. Fifteen years ago.

What if Georgie wasn't disrupting the timeline with these phone calls—what if this *was* the timeline? What if it had been the timeline all along?

"We'll make our own enough," Neal had said that day at her door.

Georgie remembered him saying it, remembered that it sounded nice—but all she was focused on at the time was the ring in his hand.

Could it be that Neal was referring to a conversation he'd thought she was a part of?

"What if it isn't enough?" Georgie asked him last night.

"We'll make our own enough," he promised her in 1998. *"Will you marry me?"*

CHAPTER 23

"O*h.*"

Georgie gaped at herself in the mirror. "Oh my God," she gasped.

"It can't be that bad," Heather said from outside the fitting room. "You're not even forty."

"No, I . . ." Georgie walked out of the mauve cubicle, pulling her mother's pug sweatshirt down over her head. "I need to go home now."

"I thought Neal was calling you at our house."

"Right, I need to go there. Now."

The attendant met them just outside the room. "Did any of those work out?"

"This one's fine," Georgie said. She reached under her shirt and snapped the tags off the bra, handing them to the salesperson. "I'll take this one." She started walking toward the cash register.

Neal had never told Georgie why he changed his mind—why he forgave her, why he came back to California and proposed. And Georgie had never asked. She hadn't wanted to give him an opportunity to reconsider. . . .

But maybe *this* was why. Maybe *she* was why. Now.

"I'm sorry," the salesperson said. "I can't let you wear that out. Store policy."

Georgie stared at her. She was a thin, white woman, a

little younger than Georgie, with taupe-colored lipstick. She'd kept trying to come into the dressing room with Georgie to make sure the bras were fitting correctly. "But I'm buying it," Georgie said.

"I'm sorry, ma'am. Store policy."

"Fine," Georgie said, "I need to go—I'll just take it off and do all this some other day."

"But you already removed the tags. You have to purchase it."

"Right." Georgie nodded. "Fine."

She reached up behind her to unclasp the bra, then after a few seconds of maneuvering, pulled it out one of her sleeves and dropped it on the counter.

"Ring it up twice," Heather said. "She'll take two."

The salesperson went to get another bra.

"You are such a badass," Heather said, grinning at her. "Have I mentioned that I want to be you when I grow up?"

"I don't have time for this. We need to leave. Now."

"But we were going to the Apple Store. Georgie, *please*. I want an iPad, I've already named it."

"You can order it online. We need to leave."

"Seriously? You're really buying me an iPad? Can I also order a pony?"

When Neal left California that Christmas, he and Georgie were as good as broken up, and when he came back, he wanted to marry her. And in between, in between . . .

Maybe *this*. Maybe *her*.

Maybe this week, these phone calls—*everything*—had already happened. Somehow, sometime . . .

And Georgie just had to make sure that it happened again.

"Georgie? Hey."

Heather shoved the bag of bras into Georgie's chest. Georgie caught them.

"Sorry to interrupt your aneurysm," Heather said, "but you said that time was of the essence here."

"Right," Georgie said, "right." She followed Heather to the car, then handed her the key fob. "You drive."

"Why?" Heather asked.

"I need to think."

Georgie climbed into the passenger seat and tapped her dead phone against her chin. She didn't even bother plugging it in.

CHAPTER 24

Georgie set the yellow rotary phone in front of her on the bed and stared at it. She resisted the urge to check the dial tone, just in case Neal called at that exact second.

This changed everything.

Didn't it?

If Neal had already proposed to her in the past, then Georgie must have already convinced him in the future. It didn't matter what happened now. What she said. Whether he called her back.

Whatever Georgie did next had *already* happened. She was walking in her own footsteps—there was nothing she could mess up.

She leaned close to the phone and lifted the receiver to her ear, slamming it down again as soon as she heard a dial tone.

Is that what this whole week was about, preserving the status quo? Maybe she should be grateful for that. . . .

But Georgie had thought—she'd hoped—that this wrinkle in time was offering her a shot at something better.

God, what good is a magic phone, anyway? It isn't a time machine.

Georgie couldn't change the past—she could only talk at it. If Georgie had a proper time machine, maybe she could actually *fix* her marriage. She could go back to the moment that everything started to go bad, and change course.

Except . . .

There hadn't really been a moment like that.

Things didn't *go* bad between Georgie and Neal. Things were *always* bad—and always good. Their marriage was like a set of scales constantly balancing itself. And then, at some point, when neither of them was paying attention, they'd tipped so far over into bad, they'd settled there. Now only an enormous amount of good would shift them back. An impossible amount of good.

The good that was left between them didn't carry enough weight. . . .

The kisses that still felt like kisses. The notes Neal stuck to the refrigerator when Georgie got home late. (A sleepy cartoon tortoise with a word bubble telling her there were leftover enchiladas on the bottom shelf.) Shared glances when one of the girls said something silly. The way Neal still put his arm around her when they all went to the movies. (He was probably just more comfortable that way.)

So much of what was still good between them was through Alice and Noomi—but Alice and Noomi were so solidly *between* them.

Georgie was pretty sure that having kids was the worst thing you could do to a marriage. Sure, you could *survive* it. You could survive a giant boulder falling on your head—that didn't mean it was good for you.

Kids took a fathomless amount of time and energy. . . . And they took it first. They had right of first refusal on everything you had to offer.

At the end of the day—after work, after trying to spend

some sort of meaningful time with Alice and Noomi—Georgie was usually too tired to make things right with Neal before they fell asleep. So things stayed wrong. And the girls just kept giving them something else to talk about, something else to focus on. . . .

Something else to love.

When Georgie and Neal were smiling at each other, it was almost always over Alice and Noomi's heads.

And Georgie wasn't sure she'd risk changing that . . . even if she could.

Having kids sent a tornado through your marriage, then made you happy for the devastation. Even if you *could* rebuild everything just the way it was before, you'd never want to.

If Georgie could talk to herself in the past, before the scales tipped, what would she say? What could she say?

Love him.

Love him more.

Would that make a difference?

When Georgie was eight months pregnant with Alice, she and Neal still hadn't settled on a day care.

Georgie thought maybe they should get a nanny. They could almost afford one. She and Seth had just started working on their third show, a CBS sitcom about four mismatched roommates who hung out in a coffee shop. Neal called it *Store-Brand Friends*.

Neal was working in pharmaceutical research then. He'd thought about graduate school for a while but didn't know what he wanted to study, so he got a job in a lab. Then he got another job in another lab. He hated it, but at least he worked better hours than Georgie. Neal was done every day by five—and home making dinner by six.

There was a nice day care they were considering on the studio lot. They went and visited, and Georgie put their name on the waiting list.

It was going to be fine, Neal said. It was all going to be fine.

It was just happening so fast.

They'd always assumed they'd have kids someday, but they hadn't really talked through the details. The closest they'd come was on that first date, when Georgie said that she wanted kids and Neal hadn't argued.

After they'd been married for seven years, it seemed like they should probably get on with it—the trying, not the talking. Georgie was already thirty, and lots of her friends had had fertility problems. . . .

She got pregnant the first month they stopped using condoms.

And then it was *happening*. And they still didn't talk about it. There was no time. Georgie was so tired by the time she got home from the show, she fell asleep most nights on the couch during prime time. Neal would wake her up and walk behind her up their narrow staircase, his hands supporting her hips and his head resting between her shoulder blades.

It was all going to be fine, he said.

Georgie was thirty-seven weeks along when they went out to celebrate their eighth wedding anniversary. They walked to an Indian restaurant near their house—their old house in Silver Lake—and Neal talked her into having a glass of wine. *("One glass of red wine isn't going to hurt at this point.")* They talked about the studio day care some more; it was Montessori, Georgie said—for probably the third time that night—and the kids had their own vegetable garden.

There was an Indian family sitting one table over. Georgie was terrible at guessing kids' ages before she had her own, but the family had a little girl who must have been about a year and a half. She was toddling from chair to chair, and she reached out and grabbed Georgie's armrest, smiling up at her triumphantly. The girl wore a pink silk dress and pink silk leggings. She had a cap of black hair and gold studs in her ears. "Oh—sorry," the girl's mother said, leaning over and sweeping the child up onto her lap.

Georgie set her glass down too hard, and wine splashed out onto the yellow tablecloth.

"Are you okay?" Neal asked, his eyes dropping to her stomach. He'd been looking at Georgie differently since she started to show, like she might split open at anytime without warning.

"I'm fine," she said, but her chin was wobbling.

"Georgie—" Neal took her hand. "—what's wrong?"

"I don't know what we're doing," she whispered. "I don't know why we're doing this."

"Why we're doing what?"

"Having a baby," she said, glancing tearfully over at the pink-swathed toddler. "We're just—all we ever talk about is what we're going to do with it when we're not there. Who's going to *raise* it?"

"We are."

"From six to eight P.M.?"

Neal sat back in his chair. "I thought you wanted this."

"Maybe I was wrong. Maybe I shouldn't get what I want." *Maybe I don't deserve it.*

Neal didn't tell her it would all be fine. He seemed too shocked to speak. Or maybe too angry. He just watched Georgie cry—his brow low, his jaw forward—and refused to finish his chana masala.

The next morning he told her he was quitting his job.

"You can't quit your job," Georgie said. She was still lying in bed. Neal had brought her a mug of hot black tea and a plate of scrambled eggs.

"Why not?" he said. "I hate it."

He did hate it. He'd been there three years, the pay was terrible, and his boss was an unrepentant egomaniac who liked to brag about "curing cancer."

"Yeah," she said, "but . . . do you even *want* to stay home?"

Neal shrugged. "You're going to be miserable if we put this baby in day care."

"I'll get over it," Georgie said, knowing that she would and feeling guilty about that, too.

"You don't want me to stay home?"

"I haven't thought about it, have you?"

"There isn't anything to think about," he said. "I can do this. You can't. We don't need my paycheck."

"But . . ." Georgie felt like she should argue, but she didn't know where to start. And, actually, she really, really *liked* this idea. She already felt better about the baby, knowing that it would be with Neal, that they wouldn't be turning it (they didn't know the gender yet, but they'd set-tled on "Alice" or "Eli") over to a stranger nine hours a day.

"You're sure?" she asked, moving to get out of bed. She was huge—Georgie got huge with both pregnancies—and she was having spasms in her lower back every time she sat up. Neal bent in front of her so she could put her arms around his neck, then pulled her upright with his hands on her hips. "It's a big sacrifice," she said.

"Taking care of my own child isn't a sacrifice. It's what parents do."

"Yeah, but are you *sure*? Don't you want to think about this?"

Neal was looking at Georgie's face, not smiling—just meeting her eyes without flinching, so she'd know he was serious. "I'm positive."

"Okay," she said, and kissed him, already feeling so relieved. And feeling some sort of evolutionary satisfaction. Like she'd made the right decision picking this man; he was going to find all the best sticks for their nest and chase off all the predators.

They stood together, curled over the mass of baby between them, and Georgie felt like everything was going to be fine.

That's how Neal had become a stay-at-home dad.

That's how Neal had thrown away his own career before he'd even figured out what he wanted from it.

What would happen now? If they stayed together? (God, was she really asking that question?)

Noomi would start school next year. Would Neal go back to work then? What would he want to do—what would he want to be?

A railroad detective?

CHAPTER 25

Neal didn't call her back.

Georgie lay on her bed and watched the phone. She was trying to figure out whether she could see the magic if she looked hard enough. Whether the phone shimmered or glittered or made some sort of spooky *Freaky Friday* noise when it was doing its thing.

One of the pugs, the boy, wandered into the room. He stood next to the bed barking until Georgie hauled him up with her.

"I don't like you," she said. "I don't even know your name. In my head, I call you 'the Sweaty One' and the other one 'the One Who Looks Like It Bit a Brick.'"

She did know their names. They were Porky and Petunia.

Porky nuzzled his flat face into Georgie's stomach and whimpered. She rubbed her knuckles into the skin at the back of his neck.

The door was open, and Heather leaned in.

"I'm still fine," Georgie said. Heather had been checking on her ever since they got back from the mall and Georgie had run to her room to brood over the phone.

"I brought you some Pringles," Heather said.

"I don't want any Pringles."

Heather walked over and sat on the bed. "Well, now you're just lying." She shook a stack of chips out onto the bedspread, and Georgie and Porky started eating them. When the can was empty, Heather wiped her fingers on Georgie's borrowed velour pants and lay down on the bed next to the dog. "Are you okay?"

Georgie didn't answer. She started crying instead.

Porky climbed into her lap.

"He hates it when people cry," Heather said.

"Well, I hate him, so he's making it worse."

"You don't hate him."

"I do," Georgie said. "His face is always wet, and the best thing he smells like is bacon bits."

"Why don't you just call Neal?"

"He probably isn't home. Besides, I don't want to talk to him if he doesn't want to talk to me."

"Maybe you'll change his mind."

Georgie tried to smooth out the wrinkles over Porky's eyes.

"If you and Neal split up," Heather asked, "will you move back in here?"

"Why? Am I in your way?"

"No. I kind of like having you here. It's like having a sister." Heather elbowed Georgie. "Hey. You're supposed to say, 'We're *not* splitting up—Neal's just visiting his mom.'"

Georgie shrugged.

After another minute or so, Heather elbowed her again. "I'm hungry," she said.

"Where's Mom?"

"At her work Christmas party."

"We could make some more cheesy apples," Georgie said.

"I ate all the cheese slices." Heather turned on her side

and rested her head in her hand. "I guess we could order a pizza. . . ."

Georgie forced a smile she knew wouldn't happen on its own. "That sounds perfect."

"I guess I could call Angelo's," Heather said.

"Perfect," Georgie said, "but tell them we don't want any of those wrong pizzas. If we get a wrong pizza, we're sending it back."

Heather smiled back at her. "Do you like artichoke hearts?"

"I love artichoke hearts. I love all hearts."

Heather bounced up and pressed redial on her phone. She ordered the pizza, already jiggling her leg and biting at her lip. "I'll wait in the living room for it," she said as soon as she ended the call.

"Good idea," Georgie agreed.

Georgie and Porky went back to their melancholy staring. Georgie at the phone. Porky at Georgie.

"I'm sorry," Georgie said, scratching under his collar. "But I really don't like you." She thought of Noomi. Noomi liked the pugs; she said they looked like really ugly kitties. "Meow," Noomi would say, getting as close to Porky's face as he'd let her. (Which, to Porky's credit, was pretty close.)

"Meow," Georgie said now.

Porky sneezed.

Both the pugs loved Neal. Georgie knew he fed them table food. (Because he was a soft touch. And because he hated her mom's cooking.) As soon as Neal sat down on the couch, the pugs would start nipping at his jeans until he had both of them in his lap. That's how Neal ended up every Thanksgiving afternoon and every other Christmas —with two little girls and two little dogs sacked out in his lap. Neal, tired and bored, but smiling at Georgie from across the room, his dimples playing hide-and-seek with her.

She felt the tears welling up on her again.

Porky whined.

"Oh God," Georgie said, sitting up. "I have to do something."

She took one more look at the phone. It didn't ring.

"Come on." She set the dog on the floor and left the room.

"What're you doing?" Heather asked. She'd taken down her hair and spritzed the curls with something, and she was waiting by the door—literally, leaning against the frame.

"Losing my mind," Georgie said.

"Can't you do that in your room?"

"I thought you were worried about me."

"I was. I will be. But now—" Heather pointed emphatically at the door. "—there's a pizza coming."

"That's what happens when you order one."

"*Right,*" Heather said, goggling her eyes at Georgie. "The *pizza* will be here any minute."

"Oh, right." Georgie said. "I'll just . . . ."

The doorbell rang. Heather jumped.

"I'll just get my clothes out of the dryer."

Heather nodded.

"It might take a while . . . ," Georgie continued. "You just . . . shout or something when the pizza gets here."

Heather nodded again. The doorbell rang again. Georgie felt like telling Heather that none of this mattered, that her pizza-boy dramatics were nothing compared to

Georgie's magic, life-destroying phone of destiny—but instead she turned deliberately toward the laundry room.

As soon as Georgie was through the door, she heard the whimpering.

Porky was standing outside the open dryer, barking at it. "Damn it, Heather." Heather must have let Petunia into the dryer again—to take a nap on Georgie's warm, clean clothes.

Georgie stomped down the back steps, irritated with every living thing in the house. Porky looked up at her and barked. "What's the problem?" Georgie asked. "Do you want to drool all over my clothes, too?"

She leaned over the dryer door to look for the other one, lumpy old Bit-a-Brick. That's when Georgie saw the blood. "Oh God . . ."

Porky started barking again. Georgie crouched in front of the dryer, trying not to block the light. All she could see was a pile of clothes streaked with blood. Neal's Metallica T-shirt was on top, moving; she pulled it out of the way. Petunia was curled underneath, gnawing at something, something dark and wriggling.

"Oh God, oh God—Heather!" Georgie shouted. She jumped up and ran back in the house. *"Heather!"*

When she got to the kitchen, Heather was standing at the front door, staring at Georgie like she was planning how to kill her later. The pizza boy was standing . . .

Oh. The pizza boy was a girl.

Smaller than Heather; wearing dark jeans, a short-sleeved white T-shirt under thin leather suspenders, and a ball cap that said ANGELO's. The girl looked kind of like Wesley Crusher, but prettier and with nicer arms. It was a good look.

Huh, Georgie thought, then said out loud: "*Heather*. It's Petunia."

"What?"

"Petunia's having a baby."

"*What?*"

"Petunia!" Georgie said, more urgently. "She's having puppies in the dryer!"

"No, she's not. She's having a C-section in two weeks."

"Great!" Georgie shouted. "I'll go tell her!"

"Oh God!" Heather shouted back. She ran past Georgie toward the laundry room. Georgie ran behind her as far as the door.

Heather knelt in front of the dryer and immediately screamed. Porky was running back and forth across the tile floor—it sounded like someone rattling their fingernails against a metal desk. He was already hoarse from barking. "Oh God, oh God, oh God," Heather chanted.

"Whoa," someone said.

The pizza girl stepped around Georgie on the stairs. "Whoa," she said again, crouching behind Heather.

"She's gonna die," Heather said.

The girl touched her shoulder. "She's not."

"She *is*. Their heads are too big, she has to have a C-section. Oh God." Heather took a few crazy breaths. "Oh my God."

"She's going to be fine," Georgie said. "She was built for this."

"She *wasn't*," Heather said, crying now. "Pugs are bred to be useless. We have to take her to the vet."

"I think it's too late for that," pizza girl said, looking into the dryer. "There are puppies in there." Porky ran by the dryer again, and the girl scooped him up, running her hand over his skull and whispering, *"Hush."*

"Right," Georgie said.

Heather was still crying and breathing like she was making every effort to pass out.

"Right," Georgie said again. "Heather, move."

"Why?"

"I'm going to help Petunia."

"You don't even like her."

"Move."

Pizza girl tugged on Heather's elbow, and Heather moved back.

"My OB didn't like me either," Georgie murmured. "Get out your phone, Heather. Google 'pugs in labor.'"

"I would if I had a smartphone!" Heather snarled.

"I've got it," ever-more-impressive pizza girl said. "Here—" She handed Porky to Heather. "—maybe you guys could get some clean towels."

"Have you done this before?" Heather asked hopefully, taking the dog and wiping her face in its fur.

"No," the girl said, "but I watch Animal Planet."

"Google," Georgie said, reaching into the dryer. Petunia had burrowed under the T-shirt again and was shivering, worrying something with her mouth. Georgie tried to nudge more clothes away, so she could see.

"Okay, okay," pizza girl said. "It's loading. Okay, here we go—'giving birth can be especially challenging for both pugs and pug owners .'"

"So far, so good . . . ," Georgie said. "It's too dark, I can't see anything."

"Oh." The girl held her key chain over Georgie's shoulder. "There's a flashlight."

"That's handy." Georgie took the heavy key chain and

found the stainless steel light.

"It helps when I'm delivering pizzas at night, to get the credit card numbers—okay, it says here that pugs have complicated pregnancies, and we should be financially prepared for a C-section. . . ."

"Skip ahead," Georgie said. Petunia was wet and splotched with blood. The thing in her mouth was moving. *Oh, God, she's eating it.*

"She's eating the puppies!" Heather shrieked. She was leaning behind Georgie holding a stack of towels and three bottled waters.

"She's not eating it," pizza girl said, putting her hand on Heather's arm. She held up her phone so they both could see. "It's in its sac. They're born in sacs, and the mom chews them out. It's a good sign that she's chewing them free. It says that pugs are notoriously bad mothers. If she didn't do it, we'd have to."

"We'd have to chew them out?" Georgie asked.

The girl looked at Georgie like she was insane—but still managed to look patient. "We'd use a washcloth," she explained.

"I brought washcloths!" Heather said.

The girl smiled at Heather. "Great job."

"What else does it say?" Georgie asked.

Still-competent-but-clearly-distracted pizza girl looked back at her phone. "Um . . . okay, *puppies*—there can be one to seven."

"Seven," Georgie repeated.

"Sacs . . . ," the girl said, *"chewing* . . . Oh, she's supposed to chew the umbilical cord, too."

"Great."

"And placentas—there's a placenta for each puppy.

That's important. You need to look for the placentas."

"What do the placentas look like?"

"Do you want me to Google that?"

"No," Georgie said, "keep reading."

Petunia was still working on the wriggly thing with her teeth. "Good girl," Georgie said. "Probably."

She patted blindly around Petunia and recoiled when she felt something else soft and warm.

"What?" Heather asked, still half in a panic.

"I don't know," Georgie said, reaching back in. She found it again, warm and *wet*. Was it a puppy? Georgie held up what looked like a bag of blood, then dropped it. "Placenta."

"That's one," the girl said enthusiastically.

"Aren't you supposed to be reading?" Georgie reached back in.

"There's nothing else. *Make the dog comfortable. Make sure she helps the puppies get free. Count the placentas. Make sure they nurse . . . .*"

Georgie felt something else wet under Petunia and grabbed it instinctively. "Jesus," she said. "Another baby." Still in its sac. It looked like a raw sausage. Georgie reached for one of Heather's towels and started rubbing at the membrane. "Like this?"

Pizza girl looked up from her phone. "Harder, I think."

Georgie scrubbed at the lump till the skin around it tore and she could see the grayish pink puppy inside.

"Is it alive?" Heather asked.

"I don't know," Georgie answered. The puppy was warm, but not warm as life. Georgie kept rubbing it clean, tears falling on her hand. Petunia whined, and Heather's girl reached past Georgie into the dryer to pet her.

Heather knelt next to Georgie. "Is it *alive*?" She was crying, too.

"I don't know." The puppy twitched, and Georgie rubbed harder, massaging it with her hands.

"I think it's breathing," Heather said.

"It's cold." Georgie brought the puppy up to her chest and tucked it inside her sweatshirt, rubbing. The puppy shuddered and squeaked. "I think . . ."

Heather hugged Georgie. "Oh God."

"Careful," Georgie said.

Pizza girl sat back from the dryer cradling another puppy against her white shirt.

"Oh my God," Heather said, and hugged her, too.

There were three puppies.

And three placentas.

Eventually Georgie thought to call her mom.

And then she called the vet, who talked them through cutting the last umbilical cord and making Petunia comfortable.

The puppies got a sponge bath. Georgie took charge of the one she was still holding inside her shirt. Then they all got tucked back into the dryer with clean towels. "It's her little nest," Heather said, patting the dryer like it had helped.

Georgie tried to put the Metallica shirt in the washer, but Heather grabbed onto it, making a disgusted face. "Georgie, no. This is an intervention."

"Heather. That's Neal's shirt. From high school."

"It gave its life for a good cause."

Georgie let go. Heather handed the T-shirt to pizza girl, who was starting to clean up.

Pizza girl's name was Alison, and Heather's face followed her around the room like a sunflower chasing daylight.

"I still don't like you," Georgie said to Petunia, reaching in and stroking the dog's slack stomach. "Look at you, nursing like a champ. Now who's a notoriously bad mother?"

The puppies were clean, but Georgie and Heather and Alison were still sticky with blood and fetal juices—and pug vomit, Georgie was pretty sure.

Their mom looked horrified when she finally ran into the laundry room, kitten heels clicking on the stairs.

"It's fine," Georgie tried to assure her. "Everything is fine."

"Where are my babies?" her mom asked, taking in the pile of bloody towels and the pile of bloody girls. Heather and Alison were sitting together in front of the dryer. Alison was cuddling Porky, who'd been stashed in the hall bathroom for most of the action. Her stained white T-shirt made her look like a butcher.

"They're right here," Heather said. "In the dryer."

Georgie's mom hurried over, and Alison quickly got up to make room. *"My little mama,"* Georgie's mom said, *"my little hero."*

Alison took a step back. "I guess . . . ," she said, looking over at Heather.

Heather's head was in the dryer.

"I guess I should go," Alison said. After a few more seconds, she handed Porky to Georgie (who immediately handed him over to Kendrick), then wiped her hands on her jeans and started walking toward the door.

"Alison," Georgie said, "thanks. You were a lifesaver. If I ever have another baby, I want you to deliver it."

Alison waved her hand, like it was nothing, and kept walking.

"Who was that?" Kendrick asked as soon as she was out of sight.

"Pizza—," Georgie said, but stopped when Heather's head whipped up, her face full of dread. "Heather, can you help me with something in the kitchen?" Georgie leaned over and grabbed her sister's sleeve, then pulled her up the steps and into the house, just as the front door was closing.

"What are you doing?" Georgie demanded.

"Nothing," Heather said, jerking away. "What are *you* doing?"

"Making sure you don't let that incredibly attractive, steady-handed girl walk away."

"Georgie, I don't want to talk about this."

"Heather, that girl just helped us deliver babies."

"Because she's a nice person."

"*No.* Because she's willing to wade through blood and amniotic fluid just to impress you."

Heather rolled her eyes.

"What is wrong with you?" Georgie asked. "You obviously want to kiss that girl. *I* kind of want to kiss that girl. So go do it. Or go, I don't know, make progress in that general direction."

"It's not that easy, Georgie."

"I think it might be."

"I'm not you. I can't just . . . *take* what I want. And Mom's here, and she'll figure out that I'm gay—"

"She's gonna figure it out anyway. She won't care."

"*Eventually* she won't care. I'll tell her eventually. Just, not while I'm living here. I don't want to, it's not worth it—none of this is worth it. I mean, what? I humiliate myself? And freak out Mom, and probably get hurt . . . And just ruin everything for the chance that *maybe* I'm supposed to be with this girl I don't even know?"

"*Yes,*" Georgie said. "That's how it works. Exactly."

Heather folded her arms. "Oh, you don't know how it works—you told me so yourself. And that's after spending your whole life trying to figure it out. It's not worth it."

Georgie couldn't stop shaking her head. "Oh my God, Heather—forget what I said. Don't listen to *me*. Why would you listen to me? Of course it's worth it."

"But it's not even anything," Heather said, glancing miserably at the door. "It's just a chance."

"The chance to be happy."

"Or the chance to be heartbroken, like you?"

"The chance to be *alive*. To be . . . *Heather,* forget everything I said before. *It's worth it*. Do you think I wouldn't risk everything to bring Neal to that door right now? That's how it works. You keep risking everything. And you keep hoping you can keep him from walking away."

"Her."

"Whoever. Jesus."

The doorbell rang, and they both turned. After a second, the door opened, and Alison stepped carefully through, pushing her long bangs out of her eyes. "Sorry," she said. "I thought everybody might still be out back—I think I left my keys on the dryer. . . ."

"I'll get them," Georgie said before either of the girls could say anything more. "I'll be right back." She squeezed Heather's arm on the way to the laundry room, then sat down next to her mom, pointing out which puppy was hers.

She left Alison's keys sitting on top of the dryer.

CHAPTER 26

Georgie's mom lent her another pair of velour pants. And a T-shirt that said PINK.

Heather lent Alison a DECA T-shirt that hung too wide around the other girl's neck.

They made a new nest for the dogs next to the Christmas tree, and Georgie's mom decided that she and Kendrick couldn't go to San Diego for Christmas and leave the puppies alone. "I guess we'll keep you company, Georgie."

Everyone agreed that Alison couldn't just go back to work, not after *everything*. She spent ten tense minutes on the phone, trying to explain the situation to Angelo.

"Did you get fired?" Heather asked when Alison walked back into the living room.

Alison shrugged. "I'm going back to Berkeley next week, anyway."

On the bright side, she had three large pizzas in the back of her car, plus an order of lasagna, some very cold fried mushrooms, and a dozen parmesan bread twists.

"God bless us, every one," Georgie said, cracking open one of the boxes.

Fortunately for Heather, their mom only had eyes for the puppies and didn't even notice Heather and Alison on the couch, giggling at each other with cheeks full of pizza.

Georgie herself was three giant slices in when the

phone rang in the kitchen. The landline.

Heather looked at Georgie, and Georgie dropped her pizza, practically stepping on Porky on her way to the phone.

She got there on the third ring. "Hello?"

"Hey," Neal said. "It's me."

"Hey," Georgie said.

Heather was standing behind her. She held out her hand. "Take it in your room," she said. "I'll hang it up."

"Neal?" Georgie said into the phone.

"Yeah?"

"Just a minute, okay? Don't go anywhere. Are you going anywhere?"

"No."

Heather was still reaching for the phone; Georgie held the receiver against her chest. "Promise me you won't talk to him," she whispered.

Heather put her hand on the receiver and nodded.

"On Alice and Noomi's lives," Georgie said.

Heather nodded again.

Georgie let go of the phone and ran down the hall. Her hands were trembling when she picked up the yellow phone. (That never used to happen to her when she was upset; she was probably pre-diabetic.)

"Got it," she said. She heard the kitchen phone click. "Neal?"

"Still here."

Georgie sank onto the floor. "Me, too."

"Are you okay?"

"Yeah," Georgie said, "yeah. I've just had the weirdest day. Plus, I guess I . . . I didn't think you were going to call back."

"I said I would."

"I know, but . . . you were angry."

"I—" Neal stopped and started his sentence again. "We ended up staying with my aunt for a while. It was hard to leave. She was really happy to see us, so we stayed for dinner at the nursing home. And that was depressing and kind of gross, so we went to Bonanza on the way home."

"What's a Bonanza?"

"It's like a cafeteria-buffet-steakhouse thing."

"Is everything in Nebraska named after Westerns?"

"I guess so," he said.

"I'll bet your Italian restaurants are named after Sergio Leone movies."

"What made your day so weird?"

Georgie started laughing. It sounded like a laugh played backwards.

"Georgie?"

"Sorry. It's just . . ." *What made her day so weird?* "I delivered three puppies and found out that Heather is gay."

"What? Oh—for a second, there, I thought you were talking about your sister. Your cousin is gay?"

"It doesn't matter," Georgie said.

"How did you deliver puppies? Whose puppies?"

"That doesn't matter either. But I think we're keeping one."

" 'We'—you and your mom? Or 'we,' *we*?"

"We, we, we," Georgie said. "All the way home."

"Georgie?"

"Sorry."

"You delivered puppies?"

"I don't want to talk about it."

"What *do* you want to talk about?"

"I don't know. I need another second." Georgie pulled the phone away from her ear and dropped it on the carpet. At some point, she'd started breathing like Heather during the pug emergency. Georgie smoothed her hair back and redid her ponytail, taking off her glasses and rubbing her eyes.

This is it, Georgie, get back in the game.

No, this wasn't a game. It was her life. Her ridiculous life.

It doesn't matter what you say now, she told herself. *Neal's going to propose on Christmas. He already did. He said, "We'll make our own enough." It's fate.*

Unless . . .

Unless it wasn't. Maybe Neal had just said that "enough" thing because it was on his mind that day, not because of their phone calls. Had he given Georgie any other clues over the years that these conversations happened? (This would be easier to figure out if Neal were the sort of guy who *ever* gave away clues.)

This was Georgie's last chance to talk to Neal before he left for California. Her last chance to *make sure* he left— what was she supposed to say?

She took a deep breath, *in,* then pushed it, *out.* Then picked up the phone.

"Neal?"

"Yeah. I'm here."

"Do you believe in fate?"

"What? What kind?"

"Like, do you believe that everything is already decided? That we're destined for it?"

"Are you asking if I'm a Calvinist?"

"Maybe." Georgie tried again: "Do you think that everything is already *decided*? Already written. Is the future just sitting there waiting for us to get to it?"

"I don't believe in destiny," he said, "if that's what you mean. Or predestination."

"Why not?"

"There's no accountability in it. I mean, if everything is already set in stone, why try? I prefer to think that we're choosing in every moment what happens next. That we choose our own paths—Georgie, why is this important?"

"I don't know." She sounded far away from herself in the receiver.

"Hey . . . *Georgie*."

"Yeah?"

"I'm sorry I kept you waiting."

"Just now?"

"No," he said. "Today. All day."

"Oh. It's okay."

Neal huffed. Frustrated. "I hate that you thought I wouldn't call—I hate that everything is so tentative between us right now. When did everything get so tentative?"

"I think when you left for Omaha without me."

"I just came home for Christmas."

Georgie's voice was barely there when she reached for it. "That's not true."

She could hear Neal clenching his jaw. "All right," he said. "You're right."

Georgie was quiet.

Neal was quiet, too.

"I didn't break up with you," he said finally. "You know that, right?"

"I know," she said. "But we're still broken."

Neal growled. "Then we'll fix it."

"How?"

"When did you get so hopeless, Georgie? The last time we talked, everything was fine."

"No, the last time we talked you were pissed with me about Seth." She rested her tongue between her teeth and thought about biting all the way through.

"Because you were putting him first again."

"I wasn't," she said. "He just showed up. He woke me up."

"He just showed up *in your bedroom*."

"*Yes.*"

Neal growled again. "I hate that. I hate that so much, Georgie."

"I know, Neal."

"That's all you can offer me? You *know*?"

"I can tell you I'll never invite him into my bedroom," she said. "But sometimes he just shows up. You said you didn't want me to choose between you."

"And you said you would choose *me*."

"I would," she said. "I do."

Neal huffed.

Georgie waited.

"Why are we fighting?" he asked. "Are you punishing me because I didn't call you today?"

"*No.*"

"Then why are we fighting?"

Why were they fighting? They shouldn't be fighting. Georgie was supposed to be wooing him, making him forgive her, making him love her—letting it all happen.

"Because," she sputtered. "Because I want to!"

"What?"

"I just want to get everything out. I want every horrible thing on the table. I want to fight about it all now, so we never have to again!" She was shouting.

Neal was seething. "I don't think that's possible."

"I can't do it!" she said. "I can't keep fighting with you about the same things over and over again. I can't keep *not* fighting about the same things over and over again. I can't go another day, pretending you're not pissed with me, pretending everything's fine, talking in that stupid cheerful voice I use when I know you're just quietly hating me."

"Georgie." Neal sounded surprised. And hurt. "I never hate you."

"You do. You will. You hate what I do to your life, and that's the same as hating me—that's just as bad. If you hate your own life because of me, that's worse."

"Jesus. I don't hate my life."

"You will."

"Is that a threat?"

She forced down a sob. "No. It's a promise."

"What the—" Neal stopped. He never swore in front of her, she wasn't sure if he ever swore, period. "—what's wrong with you tonight?"

"I just want to get it over with."

"What? Us?"

"No," she cried. *"Maybe.* I want to say every terrible true thing. I don't want to trick you into coming back to me, Neal. I don't want to tell you it's all going to be okay when I know it isn't."

"You're not making sense."

"It's *not* going to be okay. If you come back. If you

forgive me or whatever it is you need to do. If you tell yourself that you'll just get used to it. To Seth and L.A. and my job . . . You're wrong. You'll *never* get used to it. And you'll blame me. You'll hate me for keeping you here."

Neal's voice was cold. "Stop telling me that I hate you. Stop using that word."

"It's your word," she said, "not mine."

"Why are you being like this?"

"Because I don't want to trick you."

"Why do you keep saying that?"

"Because part of me *does* want to trick you. Part of me wants to say whatever I have to say to make sure you'll still want me. I want to tell you that it'll be different—*better*. That I'll be more sensitive, that I'll compromise more. But I won't be, Neal, I know I won't be. And I don't want to *trick* you. Nothing is ever going to change."

Neal was quiet.

Georgie imagined him standing on the other side of the kitchen, their kitchen, staring into the sink. Lying next to her in bed, facing the wall. Driving away from her without looking back.

"*Every*thing is going to change," Neal said before she was ready for it. "Whether we want it to or not. Are you—Georgie, are you saying you don't want to be better to me?" He didn't give her a chance to answer. "Because I want to be better to you. I *promise* to be better to you."

"I can't promise you that I'll change," she said. Georgie couldn't make promises that her twenty-two-year-old self wouldn't keep.

"You mean you don't want to."

"No," she said, "I—"

"You can't even promise me that you'll try? From this

moment onward? Just *try* to think about my feelings more?"

Georgie coiled the yellow cord around her fingers until her fingertips went white. "From this moment onward?"

"Yeah."

She couldn't make promises for her twenty-two-year-old self. But what about for this version of herself? The one that was on the phone with him. The one that was still refusing to let him go.

"I . . . I think I can promise that."

"I'm not asking you to promise me that everything will be perfect," Neal said. "Just promise me that you'll try. That you'll think about how it feels for me when Seth is in your bedroom. That you'll think about how long you're leaving me waiting when you're at work. Or how I might be feeling when I'm stuck at a stranger's party all night. I know I've been a jerk, Georgie—I'm going to try not to be. Will you try with me?"

"From this moment onward?"

"Yeah."

From this moment onward, from this moment onward. She grabbed on to the idea and held tight. "Okay," she said. "I promise."

"Okay. Me, too."

"I'll be better to you, Neal." She steadied herself against the bed. "I won't take you for granted."

"You *don't* take me for granted."

"Yes," she said, "I do."

"You just get caught up—"

"I take for granted that you'll be there when I'm done doing whatever it is I'm doing. I take for granted that you'll love me no matter what."

"You do?"

"Yes. Neal, I'm so sorry."

"Don't be sorry," he said. "I *want* you to take that for granted. I *will* love you no matter what."

Georgie felt herself sliding out of control again. "Don't say that. Take it back."

"No."

"Take it back."

"You're crazy," he said. "No."

"If you say that, it's like you're telling me that all the insensitive things I do are okay. It's like you're just handing me 'no matter what.' You're pre-pardoning me."

"That's what love is, Georgie. Accidental damage protection."

"No, Neal. I don't deserve that. And it isn't even true. Because if I had that, already, you wouldn't have left."

"I'm sorry," he said. The *s* in "sorry" slurred, like his mouth was pressed against the phone. "I won't leave again."

"You will," she said. "And it'll be my fault."

"Jesus, Georgie. You're all over the place. I can't talk to you if you're going to be like this."

"Well, I'm *going* to be like this. I'm going to be worse than this."

"I'm getting off the phone," he said.

She shook her head. *"No."*

"Then we're starting over."

"No!"

"Yes. We're starting this whole conversation over." He still wasn't shouting, but his voice was building like something that was about to blow.

"I don't want to," she panted. "It doesn't work. Everything bad and everything good has already happened."

"I'm going to hang up now, Georgie. And we're both going to take some deep breaths. And when I call back, we're *starting over.*"

"*No.*"

He did it then.

Neal hung up.

Georgie tried to take a deep breath—it caught in her throat like a millstone.

She dropped the receiver on the hook and wandered out into the hall, to Heather's bathroom. Georgie hardly recognized her own face in the mirror. She looked pale and witless, a ghost who'd just seen a ghost. She rinsed her face with cold water and sobbed tearlessly into her hands.

So this was how Georgie talked her husband into proposing to her. By practically begging him not to. By finally freaking the fuck out.

Neal would be freaking out, too, if he was the one with a magic phone. . . .

Neal *did* have a magic phone, and he didn't even realize it.

God, why had she said all those horrible things? Georgie looked in the mirror again. At the woman Neal had ended up with.

She'd said them because they were true.

Georgie went back to the bedroom and looked down at the yellow phone.

She picked up the receiver and listened for the dial tone, then dropped it on the floor and climbed into bed.

That noise the phone makes when you leave it off the hook? It stops after a while.

TUESDAY
CHRISTMAS EVE , 2013

CHAPTER 27

When Georgie woke up, she couldn't believe she'd fallen asleep. (How could she have fallen asleep? She'd probably fall asleep during an air raid.) She sat up and looked at the clock, 9 A.M., then at the phone splayed out on the carpet.

What had she done?

She crawled out of bed, hands first, hanging the phone up before she even landed on the floor. It took a few tries and a few minutes before she got a dial tone again. Then she dialed Neal's house impatiently, catching her finger in the next number before the dial had completely unwound. . . .

Busy signal.

What had she done?

Neal's mom must be on the phone. Or his dad. *(Jesus. His dad.)*

Georgie thought about how you used to be able to break into someone's call, if you had an emergency. You could call the operator and she'd interrupt. That had happened to Georgie once in high school, before they got call waiting; one of her mom's friends needed to get in touch with her mom, and Georgie had been on the phone for two hours with Ludy. When the operator cut in, Georgie felt like it was the voice of God. It took a while before she could talk on the phone again without imagining that the operator was there listening.

She hung up the phone and tried again. Still busy.

She hung up—and it rang.

Georgie jerked the receiver back to her ear. "Hello?"

"It's just me," Heather said. *"I'm calling from inside the house."*

"I'm fine," Georgie said.

"I can tell. Fine people are always telling everybody how fine they are."

"What do you want?"

"I'm leaving in a little bit, and Mom wants you to come out for breakfast and say good-bye. She's making French toast."

"I'm not hungry."

"She says depressed people need to be reminded to eat and bathe. So you should also probably take a shower."

"Okay," Georgie said.

"Okay, bye," Heather said. "Love you."

"Love you, bye."

"But you're actually coming out to say good-bye, too, right?"

"Yes," Georgie said, "bye."

"Love you, bye."

Georgie hung up and tried Neal's number again. Busy.

She looked over at the clock—five after nine. What time would Neal have to leave Omaha if he was going to drive to California by tomorrow morning? What time had he gotten here that Christmas Day?

She couldn't remember. The week they were broken up was a weepy blur. A weepy blur fifteen years in her rearview mirror.

Georgie picked up the phone again. *One, four, oh, two . . .*

Four, five, three . . .

Four, three, three, one . . .

Busy.

"Take a shower!" her mom shouted down the hall. "I'm making French toast!"

"Coming!" Georgie yelled at the door.

She crawled over to her closet and started pulling things out.

Rollerblades. Wrapping paper. Stacks of old *Spoons*.

At the back of the closet was a red and green box meant for Christmas ornaments. Georgie had written SAVE in big letters on every side with a black Sharpie. She pulled it out and opened the lid, kneeling on the floor next to it.

The box was completely full of papers. Georgie had started a second Save Box after she and Neal got married (it was at their house somewhere, in the attic), but by then, she had a computer and the Internet, and all her saves became bookmarks and screenshots—jpegs that she dragged onto her desktop, then forgot about, or lost the next time her hard drive failed. Georgie never printed out photos anymore. If she wanted to look at old Christmas pictures, she had to go searching through memory cards. They had a box of videotapes from when Alice was a baby that they couldn't even watch because the cassettes didn't fit into any of their machines.

Everything at the top of this Save Box was from just before Georgie moved out of her mom's house. Just before her and Neal's wedding. (*Which has already happened,* she reminded herself.)

She found the receipt for her wedding dress—three hundred dollars, used, from a consignment store.

"I hope whoever wore it first is happy," Georgie'd said to

Neal. *"I don't want leftover bad-marriage mojo."*

"It doesn't matter," Neal said. *"We're going to be so happy, we'll neutralize it."*

He *was* happy then. During their engagement. She'd never seen him so happy.

As soon as Georgie said yes, as soon as the ring was on her finger—it stopped at the second knuckle of her ring finger, so he slipped it onto her pinkie—Neal jumped up and hugged her. He was smiling so big, his dimples reached theretofore unknown depths.

He held her by the base of her spine and the back of her neck, and kissed her face all over. "Marry me," he kept saying. "Marry me, Georgie."

She kept saying yes.

The memory was fuzzy in her head now, which seemed impossible—how could she have let any of those details go? At some point, her brain must have taken the whole scene for granted. She and Neal were so fundamentally married now, it didn't seem important how they got there.

She remembered that he was happy. She remembered the way he cupped the back of her head and said, *"From this moment onward. From every moment onward."*

God—had Neal really said that? Had she really only half-understood her own proposal?

Georgie dug back into the Save Box in earnest. . . .

Her college diploma.

Some stupid chart she'd torn out of *Spy* magazine.

The last *Stop the Sun* strip. The one where Neal's dapper little hedgehog went to heaven.

Ah—there. Polaroids.

Georgie's mom was the last person on earth to give up her Polaroid camera; she'd always lacked the follow-through to get 35-millimeter film developed.

There were three snapshots in the box from the day Neal proposed—all three taken inside the house, in front of the Christmas tree. Georgie was wearing a baggy T-shirt from her high school improv group that said NOW, GO!—and she looked like she'd spent the whole week crying. (Because she had.) Neal was wearing rumpled flannel and had been driving through the night. But still, they both looked so young and fresh. Skinny Georgie. Chubby Neal.

Only one of the pictures was in focus: Georgie rolling her eyes and holding her hand up to show the too-small ring, and Neal grinning. This might be the only photo ever taken of Neal grinning. This might be the only time he'd ever grinned. When he smiled big like that, his ears stuck out at the top and the bottom, like wrong-facing parentheses.

After these photos were taken, Georgie's mom had forced pancakes on Neal, and he'd admitted that he'd gone the last two nights without sleep. *"I pulled over for a few hours in Nevada, I think."* Georgie dragged him to her room and pushed him onto the bed, taking off his shoes and his belt, and unbuttoning his jeans, so she could rub his hips and his stomach and the small of his back. She burrowed with him under her comforter.

"Marry me," he kept saying.

"I will," she kept answering.

"I think I can live without you," he said, like it was something he'd spent twenty-seven hours thinking about, *"but it won't be any kind of life."*

Georgie laid the Polaroids out on the floor. Three moments in motion. There he was—there he was happy and hopeful. Her Neal. The right one.

"Georgie!" her mom shouted. "Come on!"

She laid the photos out on the floor and waited for them to go black.

CHAPTER 28

Her mom opened the bedroom door without knocking and walked in. "I was coming," Georgie said.

"Too late," her mom replied. "We're driving Heather out to Dr. Wisner's now."

Georgie always forgot that Heather had a different last name. They all had different last names. Her mom was Lyons, Heather was Wisner, Georgie was McCool. Georgie'd wanted to be Grafton, but Neal wouldn't let her. *"You don't come into this world with a name like Georgie McCool and throw it away on the first pretty face."*

"You're not that pretty."

"Georgie McCool. Are you kidding me—you're a Bond girl. You can't change your name."

"But I'm going to be your wife."

"I know. And I don't need you to change anything."

"Have you talked to the girls today?" her mom asked.

"Not yet," Georgie said. "I talked to them yesterday."

Had she talked to the girls yesterday? Yes. Alice. Something about *Star Wars*. No . . . that was a voice mail.

Had she talked to them the day before?

"You should just come along with us," her mom said, "for the ride. The fresh air will do you good."

"I better stay," Georgie said. "Neal might call."

What would it mean if he called now? That he was still in Nebraska? That all bets were off?

"Bring your phone," her mom said.

Georgie just shook her head.

Her mom settled down onto the floor next to her. She and Georgie were wearing matching lounge pants. Her mom's were teal, Georgie's were pink. Her mom reached over Georgie's lap and picked up one of the Polaroids—a blurry one of Neal looking at Georgie and Georgie looking off camera.

"God, do you remember that?" her mom sighed. "That boy drove halfway across the country in one day; I don't think he even stopped for coffee. He's always been king of the grand gesture, hasn't he?"

Down on one knee. Waiting outside Seth's frat house. Inking cherry blossoms across her shoulders.

He always had.

Her mom set down the photo and squeezed Georgie's velveteen knee, shaking it a little. "It's going to get better," her mom said. "It's just like those commercials say. 'It gets better.'"

"Are you talking about that campaign for gay kids?"

"It doesn't matter what it's for. It's true about everything. I know you feel awful now; you're right in the thick of it. And it's probably going to get worse—I don't know how you're going to work this out with the girls. But time heals all wounds, Georgie, every single one of them. You just have to get through this. Someday you and Neal will both be happier. You just have to survive, and give it time."

She started kissing Georgie's face. Georgie tried not to flinch away. (And failed.) Her mom sighed again and stood up. "There's French toast for you in the kitchen. And plenty of leftover pizza . . ."

Georgie nodded.

Her mom stopped at the door. "Do you think if I give my 'it gets better' speech to your sister, she'll admit she has a girlfriend?"

Georgie almost laughed. "She doesn't think you know."

"I didn't," her mom said. "Kendrick kept telling me, ever since she wore that suit to Homecoming, but I told him it was perfectly normal for a busty girl to want to de-emphasize her curves. Look at you—you're not gay."

"Right . . . ," Georgie said.

"But if she's going to hold a girl's hand on my couch— even a really handsome girl—well, I'm not blind."

"Alison seems nice."

"It's fine with me," her mom said. "The women in our family have terrible luck with men, anyway."

"How can you say that? You have Kendrick."

"Well, *now* I do."

Georgie came out to the living room to say good-bye to Heather, then took a shower and put her mom's clothes back on. She couldn't believe she'd specifically gone to a lingerie store without buying new underwear.

She thought about going out to the laundry room and digging Neal's T-shirt out of the trash. . . .

The first time she'd stolen that shirt had been the first weekend she'd stayed at his apartment. Georgie had been wearing the same clothes for two days, and she smelled like sweat and salsa—but she hadn't wanted to go home to change. Neither of them wanted the weekend to end. So she took a shower at Neal's apartment, and he gave her a pair of track pants that were too small for her hips, and the Metallica T-shirt, and a pair of striped boxers.

She'd laughed at him. "You want me to wear your underwear?"

"I don't know." Neal blushed. "I didn't know what you'd want."

It was a Sunday afternoon; Neal's roommates were at work. Georgie came back from the shower, wearing his T-shirt and the boxers—those were too small, too—and Neal pretended not to notice.

Then he'd laughed and pinned her to his mattress.

It was so rare to make Neal laugh. . . .

Georgie used to tease him about being a waste of dimples. "Your face is like an O. Henry story. *The world's sweetest dimples and the boy who never laughs*."

"I laugh."

"When? When you're alone?"

"Yeah," he said. "Every night when I'm sure everyone is asleep, I sit on my bed and laugh maniacally."

"You never laugh at me."

"You want me to laugh at you?"

"*Yes,*" she said. "I'm a comedy writer. I want *everyone* to laugh at me."

"I guess I'm not much of a laugher."

"Or maybe you just don't think I'm funny."

"You're very funny, Georgie. Ask anybody."

She pinched his ribs. "Not funny enough to make you laugh."

"I never feel like laughing when things are funny," he said. "I just think to myself, 'Now, that's funny.'"

"My life is like an O. Henry story," Georgie said, "*the funniest girl in the world and the boy who never laughs*."

"'The funniest girl in the world,' huh? I'm laughing on the inside right now."

Neal's dimples dimpled even when he was just thinking about smiling. And his blue eyes shone.

They'd kept having this conversation over the years, but it had gotten a lot less playful.

"I know you don't watch our show," Georgie would say.

"You wouldn't watch your show if it wasn't your show," Neal would answer. While he was folding laundry. Or slicing avocados.

"Yeah, but it *is* my show. And you're my husband."

"The last time I watched it, you said I was being smug."

"You *were* being smug. You were acting like it was beneath you."

"Because it *is* beneath me. Christ, Georgie, it's beneath *you*."

It didn't matter that he was right. . . .

Anyway.

The first time she'd borrowed that T-shirt, Neal had laughed and pinned her to his bed.

Because he didn't laugh when he thought something was funny—he laughed when he was happy.

CHAPTER 29

Everyone was gone now. Her mom had left the TV on in the living room, so the pugs could listen to Christmas carols.

Georgie sat at the kitchen table and stared at the Touch Tone Trimline phone mounted on the wall.

Neal wouldn't call now, from the past. She didn't really want him to.

She just didn't want this to be over.

Georgie wasn't ready to *lose* Neal yet. Even to her past self. She wasn't ready to let him go.

(Somebody had given Georgie a magic phone, and all she'd wanted to do with it was stay up late talking to her old boyfriend. If they'd given her a proper time machine, she probably would have used it to cuddle with him. *Let somebody else kill Hitler.*)

Maybe the Neal she'd talked to all week was on his way to California, maybe he wasn't, maybe he was a figment of her imagination—but *that* Neal still felt like he was within reach. Georgie still believed she could make things right with him.

Her Neal . . .

Her Neal didn't answer anymore when she called.

Her Neal had stopped trying to get through to her.

And maybe that meant that he wasn't hers. Not really.

Neal.

Georgie stood up and walked over to the phone, running her hand down the cool bow of it before lifting it off the cradle. The buttons lit up, and she carefully pressed in Neal's cell number. . . .

The call immediately went to voice mail.

Georgie got ready to leave a message—though she wasn't sure what to say—but she didn't get a beep. "We're sorry," said one voice. "This mailbox is . . . full," said another. The call disconnected and Georgie heard a dial tone.

She crumpled against the wall, still holding on to the receiver.

Did it even matter whether Neal was on his way to her in 1998—if he didn't come back to her *now*? What good was it to win him in the past, just to lose him in the future?

In a few days, Neal would bring the girls home to California. She'd meet them at the airport. What would he and Georgie have to say to each other after ten days of silence?

They were frozen in place when Neal left last week. Now they were frozen through.

The dial tone switched to the off-the-hook signal. Georgie let go of the receiver, and it bounced lazily on the spiral cord.

Is this how Neal had felt? Last night? (In 1998.) When Georgie left the phone off the hook? He'd already been so upset, he already sounded so scared—it must have driven him crazy when he couldn't get through to her. How many times had he tried?

Georgie had always thought it must have been a powerful romantic urge that made Neal drive all night to get to her on Christmas morning. But maybe he got in the car because he couldn't get through to her. Maybe he just needed to see her and know that they were okay. . . .

Georgie stood up in slow motion.

Neal. King of the grand gesture. Neal who crossed the desert and found his way through the mountains to reach her.

Neal.

Georgie's key fob was on the counter, where Heather had left it. She grabbed it.

What else did she need? Driver's license, credit card, phone—all in the car. She could sneak out the garage door and leave the house locked up. She checked on the puppies on her way out.

Georgie could do this.

There was nothing else left for her to do.

CHAPTER 30

Georgie ducked under the garage door as it was closing.

"You shouldn't do that," someone said. "It's dangerous."

She turned—Seth was sitting on the front steps.

"What are you doing?" she asked.

He shook his head. "Just trying to figure out what to say to you when I knock on the door. I'm expecting you to be out of your mind. Possibly high. *Definitely* dressed like a lunatic. I might not say anything at all; I might just knock you unconscious—I'll need something heavy, I was thinking about that old yellow phone of yours—and drag you back to the office."

Georgie took a few steps toward him. He was wearing dark, sharply cuffed jeans and pointy oxfords, with a green cardigan that Bing Crosby could have worn to sing "White Christmas."

She looked up into his eyes. He looked awful.

"I don't suppose you were just heading in to work," he said.

She shook her head.

"Or that you've been writing."

She watched him.

"*I* haven't been writing," Seth said—then laughed. It was a real laugh, even though it sounded painful. He shoved his hands in his hip pockets and looked out at the lawn. "That's not true, actually. . . . I've been writing you a lot of e-mails. 'Hey, Georgie, what's up?' 'Hey, Georgie, is this funny?' 'Hey, Georgie, I can't do this by myself. I've never even tried before, and now I know that I can't, and it's terrible.'" He looked over at her. *"Hey. Georgie."*

"Hey," she said.

They held each other's eyes, like they were holding on to something hot. Seth was the first to look away.

"I'm sorry," she said.

He didn't answer.

She took another step forward. "We can reschedule the meeting. Maher Jafari likes us."

"I'm not sure we can," he said. "I'm not sure it matters."

"It matters."

He jerked his head back to her. "Then when should we reschedule it, Georgie? Have you penciled in next week to stop losing your mind? How's January look for Neal? Think he might find some time to cut you some slack?"

"Seth, don't . . ."

He stood up from the stairs and walked toward her. "Don't what? Talk about Neal? Should I just pretend everything's okay? Like you do?"

"You don't understand."

He raised his hands, frustrated. "Who understands better than me? I've been there since the beginning. Right there."

"I can't talk about this now. I have to go." She turned away, but Seth grabbed her arm and held it.

His voice was soft. "Wait."

Georgie stopped and looked back at him.

"I've been thinking," he said. "You asked me if I would try to change anything if I could go back to the past. And I told you that I would—*and I would*—but I didn't tell you . . ." He let out a loud breath. "Georgie, maybe it's not supposed to be like this, you know?"

She shook her head. "No."

"I always think about that Halloween. When Neal was such a dick to you? And you asked me to take you home, and I did. And I—I left you there alone. Maybe I wasn't supposed to. Maybe I was supposed to stay."

"No. Seth . . ."

"Maybe we're not supposed to be this way, Georgie."

"No."

"How do you *know*?" He squeezed her arm. "You're not happy. I'm not happy."

"You usually seem happy."

"Maybe compared to you."

"No," she said. "You seem genuinely happy."

"You only see me when I'm with you."

Georgie inhaled faintly, then gently pulled her arm away.

"I . . ." Seth drew his hands back into his pockets. "This is the only relationship I've ever been able to make work. *This one.* I love you, Georgie."

The words pushed her eyes closed.

She opened them. "But you're not in love with me."

Seth laughed again, just as painfully. "It's been so long since that was an option, I don't even know anymore. . . . I know it kills me to see you like this."

His collar was caught in his sweater. She reached up and smoothed it out.

"It kills me," she said, "to see you like this."

They were standing close, face-to-face, looking in each other's eyes. In all the times they'd stood next to each other, Georgie was pretty sure they'd never stood exactly here.

"That's what I'd change," Seth said. "If I could go back."

"We can't go back," she whispered.

"I love you," he said.

She nodded.

He leaned closer. "I need to hear you say it."

Georgie didn't look away; she thought it through, and finally said, "I love you, too, Seth, but—"

"Stop," he said. "Just . . . stop. I know." His shoulders relaxed, and he shifted his weight at an angle away from her. It was enough to make their posture ordinary again.

They were both quiet.

"So—" Seth looked down the driveway. "—where are you headed?"

"Omaha," she said.

"Omaha," he repeated. "You're forever going to Omaha. . . ." He reached out, quickly, and pulled the top of her head against his lips. Then he was moving away, striding gracefully toward his car. "Don't forget my salad dressing."

CHAPTER 31

Georgie had never driven herself to the airport.

She'd only flown by herself once, when she was eleven, to visit her dad in Michigan. It hadn't gone well, and she hadn't gone back. And then her dad died when she was in high school, and when her mom asked if Georgie wanted to go to the funeral, she said no.

"You didn't go?" Neal was shocked when she'd told him. You could tell he was shocked because he raised his left eyebrow two millimeters. (Neal's face was like a flower blooming—you'd need time-lapse photography to really see it in action. But Georgie'd become such a student of his face, she could read most of the twitches.)

"I didn't know him," Georgie said. They were sitting on the foldout couch in Neal's parents' basement. It was the second or third Christmas after they were married, and they'd come to stay for almost a week.

His mom put them in the basement, with the foldout, even though there was a double bed up in Neal's old bedroom. *"She doesn't want us to disturb the sanctity of your bedroom,"* Georgie teased. His parents hadn't touched Neal's room since he left for college. All his high school wrestling clippings and team photos were still taped to the wall. There were still clothes in the closet.

"It's like when you go to Disneyland," Georgie would say, *"and they show you a replica of Walt's office, exactly as he left it."*

"Would you prefer dog photos?"

"To weird sweaty photos of you in a nineteenth-century bathing costume?"

"It's called a singlet."

"It's incredibly disturbing."

Neal's mom kept all their family photo albums in the basement. The week Georgie and Neal stayed there, she hauled out the whole stack. "If you're ever President of the United States," Georgie said, a large floral-patterned album spread over her lap, "historians will thank your mom for taking such good notes."

"Only child," he said. "She wanted to get all the memories she could out of me."

Neal had been a solid, stolid child. Round and wide-eyed as a toddler. Looking frankly at the camera on his fifth birthday. More hobbity than ever during grade school—with his T-shirt tucked over his tummy into his maroon Toughskins, and his shaggy '70s hair. By middle school, he'd started standing with his feet planted and his shoulders slightly forward. Not daring you to knock him down—he wasn't that kind of short guy. Just looking like someone who *couldn't* be knocked down. By high school, he was broad and steely. An immovable object.

Georgie sat on the couch looking through the albums, and Neal sat next to her, idly playing with her hair; he'd seen all these pictures before.

She stopped at a photo of Neal and Dawn dressed up for some high school dance. *Jesus, they really were right out of a John Cougar Mellencamp video.*

"Yeah," he said, "but still . . ."

"Still, what?" Georgie smoothed the plastic over the photo.

"He was your dad."

She looked away from high school Neal, up at the Neal sitting next to her. Neal at twenty-five. Softer than in high school. With less tension around his eyes. Looking like he'd probably kiss her in a minute, when he was done making whatever point he was making.

"What?" Georgie asked.

"I just don't understand how you could skip your father's funeral."

"He didn't feel like my father," she said.

Neal waited for her to elaborate.

"He was only married to my mom for ten minutes—I don't even remember living with him, and he moved to Michigan when I was four."

"Didn't you miss him?"

"I didn't know what I was missing."

"But didn't you miss *something*? Like even the idea of him?"

Georgie shrugged. "I guess not. I never felt incomplete or anything, if that's what you're asking. I think fathers must be kind of optional."

"That is a fundamentally wrong statement."

"Oh, you know what I mean." Georgie went back to the photo album. There were dozens of photos from Neal's graduation day. He looked pained in these—like, after eighteen years, he'd finally lost patience with his mom's photo-vigilance. His dad was in nearly every photo, too, looking much more tolerant.

"I really *don't* know what you mean," Neal said.

Georgie turned the page. "Well, they're nice, if you have one—if you have a good one—but dads aren't *necessary*."

Neal sat up straighter, away from her. "They're absolutely necessary."

"They must not be," she said, turning toward him on the couch. "I didn't have one."

Neal's eyebrows were grim and his mouth was flat. "That doesn't mean you didn't need one."

"But I *didn't* need one. I didn't have one, and I'm fine."

"You're not fine."

"I am so," she said. "How am I not fine?"

He shook his head. "I don't know."

"You're being uncharacteristically irrational," Georgie said.

"I'm not being irrational. No one else in the world would argue with me about this. Dads aren't optional. My dad wasn't optional."

"Because he was there," she said. "But if he wasn't there, your mom would have filled in the gaps. That's what moms do."

"Georgie—" He pulled his arm away from her shoulders and hair. "—you're being warped."

She hugged the photo album against herself. "How am I being warped? I'm just sitting here being the product of a perfectly well-adjusted single-parent family."

"Your mom isn't well adjusted."

"Well, that's true. Maybe kids don't need moms, either." She was teasing now.

Neal wasn't. He stood up from the couch, shaking his head some more.

"Neal . . ."

He walked toward the stairs, away from her.

"Why are you getting so mad about this?" she said. "We don't even have kids."

He stopped halfway up the stairs. He had to lean down below the ceiling to make eye contact with her. "Because we don't even have kids, and you already think I'm optional."

"Not *you*," she said, not wanting to admit she was wrong—not really wanting to sort out what she did mean. "Men, in general."

Neal stood up again, out of sight. "I can't talk to you right now. I'm going upstairs to help with dinner."

Georgie pushed the photo album back down into her lap and flipped to the end.

"Where are you flying today?" the woman behind the counter asked without looking up at Georgie.

"Omaha."

"Last name?"

Georgie spelled out McCool, and the woman started clacking at her console. She frowned. "Do you have your reservation number with you?"

"I don't have one," Georgie said. "I need one. That's why I'm here."

The ticket agent looked up at Georgie. She was a black woman in her late fifties, early sixties. Her hair was pulled up into a bun, and she was eyeing Georgie over a pair of gold-framed reading glasses. "You don't have a ticket?"

"Not yet," Georgie said. She'd walked up to the first counter she came to. She didn't know if this airline even flew to Omaha. "Can I get one here?"

"Yes . . . You want to fly out today?"

"As soon as possible."

"It's Christmas Eve," the woman said.

"I know." Georgie nodded.

The woman—her nametag said ESTELLE—raised her eyebrows, then looked back down at her console, clacking away again.

"You want to get to Omaha," she said.

"Yes."

"Tonight."

"Yes."

She clacked some more. Every once in a while, she'd make a discontented *hmmm*-ing noise.

Georgie shifted on her feet and rattled her keys against her leg. She'd already forgotten where she'd parked.

The ticket agent—Estelle—walked away and picked up a phone that was attached to the wall. It seemed like a special phone. There was an orange light built into the wall above it. *Now, that's what a magic phone should look like,* Georgie thought.

Then Estelle came back to her clackity-clack console. "All right," she sighed, after a minute.

Georgie licked her lips. They were chapped, but she didn't have any lip balm.

"I can get you to Denver tonight on United. From there, you're just going to have to cross your fingers. We've got delays across the system."

"I'll take it," Georgie said. "Thank you."

"Don't thank me," Estelle told her. "I'm the lady who's about to get you stranded in the Denver airport on Christmas Eve. ID?"

Georgie handed over her driver's license and credit card.

The ticket was exorbitantly expensive, but Georgie didn't blink.

"You could fly to Singapore for this much," Estelle said.

"Nonstop . . . Do you have anything to check?"

"No," Georgie said.

Estelle held her hand over a printer, waiting for the tickets. "What's in Omaha anyway? Besides two feet of snow."

"My kids," Georgie said, then felt her heart squeeze. "My husband."

The other woman's face softened for the first time since Georgie had stepped up to the counter. She handed Georgie her boarding passes. "Well, I hope you get there sooner than later. Hurry up. You've got twenty minutes to get to your gate."

For the next twenty minutes, Georgie felt like the heroine of a romantic comedy.

She even decided what song would be playing on her soundtrack—Kenny Loggins doing a big, triumphant, live version of "Celebrate Me Home." (Slow and gentle at the beginning, building up to an irresistible crescendo. Excessive amounts of blue-eyed soul.)

She ran through the airport. No luggage to drag, no kids to hang on to.

She ran by other people's families. By loving elderly couples. By volunteer carolers wearing red and green sweaters.

With every step, Georgie felt more sure of herself.

This was what she should have done ten minutes after Neal left last week. Flying across the country to reunite with your true love was always the right move. (Always.) (In every case.)

Everything would be all right if Georgie could just get to Neal. If she could hear his voice. If she could feel his arms around her.

Just like everything had been all right when he'd showed up on her doorstep fifteen years ago. (Tomorrow morning.) As soon as she'd seen his face that day, she'd forgiven him.

Her plane was already boarding when Georgie—flushed and breathless—arrived at the gate. A pretty blond flight attendant took her ticket and smiled. "Have a great flight—and Merry Christmas."

CHAPTER 32

The plane didn't take off.

Everyone got buckled up. They turned off their electronic devices. The pretty flight attendant told them which exit to head for in case of catastrophe or near-certain death. Then the plane taxied for a few minutes.

Then a few minutes more.

There was twenty minutes, probably, of taxiing.

Georgie was sitting between an extremely polished and sanded woman who tensed every time Georgie bumped her thigh and a boy about Alice's age wearing a THIS SUUUUUUUCKS T-shirt. (He was way too young to watch *Jeff'd Up,* in Georgie's opinion.)

"So, you like Trev?" she asked him.

"Who?"

"Your T-shirt."

The kid shrugged and turned on his phone. A minute later, the flight attendant came by and asked him to turn it off.

After forty minutes of taxiing, Georgie realized the boy was the uptight woman's son. She kept leaning over Georgie to talk to him.

"Would you like to trade seats?" Georgie asked her.

"I always leave an empty seat between us," the woman said. "Usually that means we end up with extra space because nobody wants to sit by themselves in the middle."

"Did you want to sit together?" Georgie asked. "I don't mind moving."

"No," the woman answered. "Better stay where we are. They use the seat assignments to identify bodies."

The captain came on the intercom to apologize because he couldn't turn the air-conditioning on—and to tell them to just "hang in there, we're fifth in line to take off."

Then he came back to say they weren't in line anymore. They were waiting for news from Denver.

"What's happening in Denver?" Georgie asked the flight attendant the next time she stopped to tell the boy to turn off his phone.

"Snowpocalypse," the flight attendant said cheerfully.

"It's snowing?" Georgie asked. "Doesn't it always snow in Denver?"

"It's a blizzard. From Denver to Indianapolis."

"But we're still leaving?"

"The storm is shifting," the flight attendant said. "We're just waiting for confirmation, then we'll take off."

"Oh," Georgie said. "Thanks."

The plane returned to the gate. Then taxied out again. Georgie watched the boy play a video game until his phone died.

All the tension and adrenaline she'd felt in the airport drained out through her feet. She was hungry. And sad. She slumped forward in her seat, so she wouldn't brush against the woman next to her.

Georgie kept thinking about her last phone conversation with Neal, their last fight. Then she started wondering if it might actually *be* their last fight. If she'd scared him away from proposing, wouldn't it erase all the fights they'd had since?

By the time the captain came back with good news— "We've got a window"—Georgie'd run out of urgency. *This is purgatory,* she thought. *Between places. Between times. Completely out of touch.*

Everyone around her cheered.

Georgie wasn't a good flier. Neal always held her hand during takeoff and turbulence.

Now that there were too many people in their family to sit in one row, they'd sit across from each other two and two—Georgie and Neal in both aisle seats, so he could take her hand if he needed to.

Sometimes he didn't even look up from his crossword, just reached out for her when the plane started to shake. Georgie always tried not to look scared, for the girls' sake. But she always was scared. If she made a noise or took too sharp of a breath, Neal would squeeze her hand and look up at her. *"Hey. Sunshine. This is nothing. Look at the stewardess over there—she's dozing. We'll be fine."*

Georgie's plane ran into turbulence an hour into the flight to Denver. The woman sitting next to her wasn't bothered by it, except for when the lurching shifted Georgie's hips into hers.

Her son had already fallen asleep against Georgie's right side. Georgie leaned against him, clenched her fists and closed her eyes.

She tried to imagine Neal, driving through this blizzard to get to her.

But there was no blizzard in 1998.

And maybe Neal wasn't trying to get to her.

She tried again to remember what she'd said to him last night on the phone. She tried to remember what he'd said back.

Neal probably thought she was a maniac. She should have just told him about the magic phone. Full disclosure. Then they could have solved it together. They could have Sherlocked and Watsoned it from both ends of the timeline.

Or Neal could have figured it all out—he was the Sherlock and the Watson in their relationship.

The plane heaved, and Georgie pressed her head back into her seat, forcing herself to hear Neal's voice. *It's nothing. We'll be fine.*

The sun was setting in Denver. The plane circled (and shook) for forty-five minutes before there was a break in the storm they could land through.

When she finally stepped out onto the jetway, Georgie was sure she was going to throw up, but the feeling quickly passed. It was cold in the tunnel. She hurried by the untouchable lady and her son, and got out her boarding pass for Omaha.

Georgie'd missed her next flight, but there had to be another one—Omaha was the biggest city between Denver and Chicago. (Neal said so.)

She took a few confused steps into the airport. The gate was so full, people were sitting on the floor, leaning against the windows. Every gate, up and down the concourse, was full.

Georgie needed to get to the other side of the terminal. She found a people mover and walked quickly. It felt like time was moving faster for her than for the people she was passing. No one else seemed to be in a hurry. And most of the shops were shuttered and dark, even though it was only six. *Christmas Eve,* she thought. And then, *Snowpocalypse.*

When she got to her gate, every seat was taken. People were standing around a muted TV, watching the Weather Channel. There was a sign over the desk with three flight numbers, all delayed. Technically she hadn't missed her flight—because it had never taken off.

Georgie got in line, just to make sure that staying put was her best bet to get to Omaha.

When she finally got to the desk, the airline employee was surprisingly upbeat. "Your *best* bet is to Apparate."

"Sorry?"

"Just a little Harry Potter humor," he said.

"Right."

Georgie hadn't read the Harry Potter books. But she'd gone to see most of the movies with Seth on days when he felt like getting out of the office. She didn't care about wizards, but she thought Alan Rickman was dreamy.

"When did you start lusting after middle-aged guys?" Seth asked.

"When I became middle-aged."

"Rein it in, Georgie. We're still thirty-somethings."

"God, I loved that show."

"I know," he said.

"That's proof that I'm middle-aged," she said. *"I miss* Thirtysomething."

The Starbucks next to her gate was closed. And the McDonald's. And the Jamba Juice. Georgie bought a turkey sandwich from one vending machine and an iPhone charger from another. She got terrible coffee at the only place that was open, a Western-themed sports bar, then walked back to the gate and found a spot against the wall to lean against.

The glass behind her was cold. Georgie squinted out the window. She couldn't see anything—no snow, nothing more than shadows—but she could hear the wind. It sounded like she was still in the airplane.

Across from her, a woman was breaking a cookie in half and splitting it between her kids, two girls small enough to share a seat. They had napkins folded in their laps and boxes of milk. The woman was sitting next to her husband, and his arm hung lazily over the back of her chair, stroking her shoulder absently.

Georgie wanted to move closer to them. She wanted to brush crumbs from the littlest girl's coat. She wanted to talk to them. *"I have this, too,"* she'd say to the woman. *"This exactly."*

But did she?

Still?

Georgie kept testing herself, cataloging her memories, tracing them backwards. Alice's seventh birthday. Noomi's first Disneyland Halloween. Neal mowing the lawn. Neal getting frustrated in traffic. Neal shifting toward her in his sleep when Georgie had insomnia.

"You okay?"

"Can't sleep."

"Come here, crazy."

Neal teaching Alice how to make Jiffy Pop. Neal doodling a sleepy gerbil on Georgie's arm . . .

Georgie could never remember the difference between a gerbil, a hamster, and a guinea pig—so Neal had taken to drawing them on her when he was bored. *"Cheat sheet,"* he'd say, writing *I am a guinea pig* in a word balloon on her elbow.

She ran her hand up over her blank arm. The little girl across from her knocked over her milk—Georgie leaned in and caught it. The mother smiled at her, and Georgie smiled back. *I have this, too,* Georgie's smile said.

She missed her girls. She wanted to see them. There were photos on her phone. . . .

Georgie scanned the gate for an outlet and found one on the wall a few feet down; two people were already plugged in. She walked over and asked if she could charge when they were done. "I just need a minute," she said, "just to check something."

"Go ahead," a twenty-something boy said. He was Neal's age—1998 Neal. The boy unplugged his phone and moved a few inches away to give her room.

Georgie knelt down awkwardly between him and a woman who was typing on her laptop. She broke open the new charger and dug her phone out of her pocket, then plugged it in and waited for the white apple to appear.

Nothing happened.

"Has it been dead awhile?" the boy asked. "Sometimes it takes a few minutes."

Georgie waited a few minutes.

She plugged and unplugged it at both ends. She pushed the two buttons.

A tear fell onto the screen. (Hers, obviously.)

"Do you want to use my phone?" the boy asked.

"No, that's okay," Georgie said. "Thanks." She unplugged her phone and stood up, rocking backwards awkwardly once she was on her feet. She turned away. Then back. "Actually, uh, yeah. Could I use your phone?"

"Sure." He held it up to her.

Georgie took the phone and dialed Neal's cell phone number. *"We're sorry. This mailbox is . . . full."* She gave the kid back his phone. "Thanks."

Her spot on the wall, by the little girls, was gone. A woman was sitting there now with her toddler.

Georgie checked the sign over the desk again. Still delayed. One of the other flights had been canceled. She walked away from the gate and dropped her phone in the trash.

Then she thought better of it and reached into the trash can to get it back. (It was right on top.) (Airport trash is relatively clean.) An older man wearing a big puffy jacket watched her. She tried to wave her phone around, so that he wouldn't think she was digging for food.

Then she shoved it in her pocket and walked over to the people mover. She rode it as far as she could in one direction, then came all the way back, then got on again.

Just because Georgie couldn't see the photos of her kids on her phone didn't mean that the photos weren't still there.

Just because she couldn't see the photos of her kids on her phone didn't mean that her kids weren't still there.

Somewhere.

Noomi's bed with a dozen stuffed kitties. Alice's paper dolls. Noomi chewing on her pigtail, Neal pulling it out of her mouth. Noomi chewing on her other pigtail, Neal tying her pigtails in a knot on top of her head.

Neal in the kitchen. Neal making hot chocolate. Neal making Thanksgiving dinner. Neal standing by the stove when Georgie got home late for work. "I wasn't sure what you wanted to pack, but I washed everything in your hamper.

Don't forget that it's cold there—you always forget that it's cold."

If Georgie could just look at her photos, she'd feel better.

If she just had a little proof—not that she needed proof—but if she could just have a little proof that they were still there. She rubbed her naked ring finger. She emptied her pockets for signs of life: All she had was a credit card and a driver's license, both in her maiden name.

It got darker in the airport.

Airports are always dark at night, and this one was even darker with all the sleeping storefronts and the snow. Georgie could still hear the wind, even though she was nowhere near the windows now. The whole building keened with it.

At some point, she stepped off the people mover. The ground was too still beneath her, and she staggered. When she recovered her bearings, she went to the nearest bathroom and stood in front of the full-length mirror.

As soon as the room was mostly empty, she lifted up her T-shirt and ran her hand along the stretch marks and the ropy scar under her belly.

Still there.

CHAPTER 33

Georgie knew something was wrong because she'd been through this once before, and that time, the baby had come right out.

With Alice, there'd been an incision, then a slippery pull—like someone had just hooked a wide-mouthed bass and yanked it out of Georgie's guts. Then a nurse had rushed away with the baby, Georgie thanking God for the screams.

The slow part, after Alice, had been putting Georgie back together again. Neal told her that the doctors actually took out her uterus and set it in on her stomach, then poked around inside her abdomen to make sure everything checked out.

Neal had been sitting right next to her that day, when Alice was born.

He was sitting right next to her now. Georgie's hands were strapped to her side, and he was holding one.

Georgie knew something was wrong this time because the incision happened, and she felt the pressure of the doctor's hands inside her—but then there was no baby. There was no rush of movement. The nurse who was supposed take the baby away stood tensely behind the doctor (and the intern and the two medical students), empty-handed.

Georgie knew that something was wrong because of

the tension in Neal's jaw. Because of the way he was watching everyone.

She felt more pressure inside—more hands, more than just two.

The anesthesiologist kept talking to her in a low murmur. *"You're doing just fine, Mom. You're doing great."* Like it took special talent to lie still on the table. (Maybe it did.) She was poking Georgie's chest with a toothpick. *"Can you feel this?"* Yes. *"Can you feel this?"* No. *"It might feel like you can't breathe,"* the anesthesiologist said, *"but you can. Just keep breathing, Mom."*

They were all talking now, doctors and nurses; everything that came out of their mouths was numbers. The table suddenly ratcheted upwards, so that Georgie was lying at a mild incline, her head toward the floor.

This isn't good, she thought calmly, looking up at the lights.

It seemed smart to stay calm in this situation, with her body wide open, her blood pumping who knows where. She could see someone's arm reflected in the light fixture above her—the sleeve was red.

Then Neal squeezed Georgie's hand.

He'd turned away from the doctors and the place where the baby was supposed to be, and was hovering over Georgie's shoulder. His jaw was tense, but his eyes were fierce and open.

Maybe this was why Neal always had his guard up. His eyes, unguarded, could burn tunnels through mountains.

Georgie kept breathing. In, out. In, out. *"You're doing great, Mom,"* the anesthesiologist hummed. Georgie knew she was lying.

Neal's eyes were pouring fire on her. If he always

looked at Georgie like this, it'd be uncomfortable. If he always looked at her like this, maybe she'd never look away.

But she'd never doubt that he loved her.

How could she ever doubt that he loved her?

Neal was saying good-bye to her with that look. He was begging her to stay. He was telling her that she was doing just fine—just keep breathing, Georgie.

How could she ever doubt that he loved her? When loving her was what he did better than all the things he did beautifully.

The anesthesiologist pushed a plastic mask onto Georgie's mouth.

Georgie didn't look away from Neal.

When she woke up, later that night, in a recovery room, she realized that she hadn't expected to.

There was a hospital bassinet pulled close to her bed, and Neal was asleep in the chair.

CHAPTER 34

The airport had brought out cots and laid them out in the hallway between gates. It looked like an army field hospital.

Georgie didn't feel like she could sleep in front of strangers like that—or at all, tonight. Though she wished she had a blanket. . . . If any of the airport stores were open, she'd buy one of the giant blue and orange Broncos sweatshirts in the window displays.

People were sleeping around her, too, in chairs, and against the wall. They slept with their heads on their purses and their hands on their carry-ons. Like they were worried about pickpockets. Georgie wasn't worried about pickpockets; she had nothing to steal.

It must be late. Or early. Georgie'd lost track of time completely—she kept checking her dead phone out of habit. The airport hadn't dimmed the lights, but it was still too dark to read without a book light. The wind seemed to be pushing the darkness into the terminal.

There was a lull in the storm. Or maybe it was just dying down—Georgie didn't know how blizzards were supposed to end.

There was a gate change, then another wait. Then she was boarding, only half-conscious of which flight was hers and where it was going.

"Omaha?" the flight attendant asked when Georgie stepped onto the plane.

"Omaha," Georgie replied.

The plane was only about fifteen rows long, with just two seats across. She'd never been on a plane this small; she'd only heard about planes this small when they crashed.

Georgie wondered if the pilots were as tired as she was. Why even bother taking off, at this point? In the middle of the night? Unless the flight crew was heading home, too.

WEDNESDAY
CHRISTMAS DAY, 2013

CHAPTER 35

The sun was rising when they left Denver, and now Omaha was a blinding white below them. Georgie gripped her armrests through the landing and stood up in her seat before the seat belt light went off.

She'd done it. She was here now. She was close.

Alice. Noomi. *Neal*.

The Omaha airport seemed abandoned. The coffee shop was closed. And the little magazine stand. Always before, when Georgie'd walked past the security checkpoint, Neal's parents—or just his mom—had been waiting right there, in the little row of chairs.

There was only one person sitting there today. A young woman in a heavy purple parka. She jumped out of her chair and started running toward Georgie. Then someone else ran past Georgie the other way—the boy from the Denver airport who'd lent her his phone.

The girl jumped into his arms, and he swung her in an ecstatic, lopsided circle. The joy of it hit Georgie like a shock wave. The boy's duffel bag fell to the ground. His face disappeared in the girl's long, wavy dark hair.

Georgie walked past them, holding her breath.

Keep moving. So close. It's almost over.

The main terminal was empty except for the dozen or so people from Georgie's plane and a security guard. If the girls were here, Georgie would have let them run ahead.

Alice could even have done cartwheels, if she wanted. There was no one in the building to bother.

Georgie started running down the escalator. She was close. *So close.* She ran to the exit and pushed through the revolving door—then stopped.

Everything was covered in snow.

Like—well, like on TV. The parking garage across the street looked like a gingerbread house topped with thick white icing.

The snow looked as *soft* as icing. Smooth, but almost furry. She pushed through the doors and stepped outside, feeling chilled through after her first inhale. (Her T-shirt wasn't any protection from the cold. Her *skin* wasn't any protection.)

God. Oh my God. Have the girls seen this?

Georgie leaned over an empty planter, pressing her hand into the snow, watching her fingers make four canyons. The snow was light, but kept its form. She moved her palm up, shaping a soft curve.

She expected the snow to feel cold, but it didn't. Not at first. Not until it started to melt between her fingers. She'd brushed some onto her feet, and they were cold now, too. She tried stamping the snow off her ballet flats, and looked up and down the drive for the taxi stand. There weren't even any cars.

Georgie folded her arms and walked down the sidewalk, looking for a sign.

"Can we help you find something?" someone said.

Georgie turned. It was the ecstatic young couple. Still hanging on each other, as if neither of them could quite believe the other was finally here.

"Taxi stand?" Georgie said.

"You're looking for a taxi?" the boy asked. The man. She should probably call him a man. He must be twenty-two, twenty-three; his hair was already thinning.

"Yeah," Georgie said.

"Did you call for one?"

"Uh." Georgie was shivering, but she was trying not to let on. "No. Should I call for one?"

The boy looked at the girl.

"There aren't really taxis here," the girl said apologetically —but also like Georgie might be an idiot. "I mean, there are a few, if you call ahead. . . . But it's Christmas."

"Oh," Georgie said. "Right." She looked up and down the drive again. "Thanks."

"Do you need to use my phone?" the boy offered.

"That's okay," Georgie said, turning toward the door. "Thanks again."

She heard them talking quietly. She heard the boy say something about Joseph and Mary and no room at the inn. "Hey, do you need a ride somewhere?" he called out to Georgie.

She looked back at them. The boy was grinning. The girl looked concerned. They were probably part of some fresh-faced Nebraska death cult who hung out at airports on holidays, picking up strays.

"Yes," she said. "Thank you."

"You don't have a bag?" the girl asked.

"No," Georgie said, then couldn't think of anything to say next that could possibly make her lack of bag/coat/socks make sense.

"All right," the boy said. (Georgie still couldn't call him a man.) "Where to?"

"Ponca Hills," she said.

The boy turned to the girl. They were all sitting in the front of an old red truck, the girl squished in the middle. The heat didn't work, and the front windshield was already fogged over. He wiped it with the sleeve of his green canvas coat.

"That's out north," the girl said, taking out her phone. "What's the address?"

The address, the address . . . "Rainwood Road," Georgie said, relieved to remember even part of Neal's parents' address, then hoped that Rainwood Road didn't stretch the entire length of the city.

The girl typed it into her phone. "Okay," she said to the boy. "Turn right up here."

Georgie wondered how long they'd been apart.

The boy kept kissing the girl's head and squeezing her leg. Georgie looked out the window to give them privacy— and because the whole city looked like some sort of fairy wonderland. She'd never seen anything like it.

The idea that *this* just fell from the sky.

And then looked like *that*. Like Tinker Bell had painted it on.

How did people ever get used to it?

Georgie didn't realize at first that it must be difficult to drive in. They were moving slowly, but the truck still slid through a red light. "I can't believe you drove in this," the boy said.

"I wasn't going to leave you at the airport," his girl-friend said. "I was careful."

He grinned and kissed her again. Georgie wondered if they were getting close to Neal's neighborhood. Almost no one else was on the road. A few people were out shoveling.

They must be close. Georgie recognized that park. That bridge. That bowling alley. The girl gave the boy directions. Georgie recognized a pizza place that she and Neal had walked to. "We're close," she said, leaning forward and resting a hand on the dash.

"Rainwood should be your next right," the girl said.

"Yeah . . . ," the boy agreed. But the truck stopped moving.

His girlfriend looked up from her phone. "Oh."

Georgie looked up the hill, but didn't see what the problem was.

The boy sighed and scrubbed at his dirty blond hair, then turned to Georgie. "We might get halfway up that hill. But I'm not sure we'd get down. Or out."

"Oh . . . ," Georgie said. "Well. It's close. I can walk from here, I know the way."

They both looked at her like she was crazy.

"You're not wearing a coat," he said.

"You're not even wearing shoes," the girl said.

"I'll be fine," Georgie assured them. "It's five blocks, tops. I won't freeze to death." She said it like she knew something about freezing to death, which she clearly didn't.

"Wait a minute." The boy got out of the truck, then hopped back inside thirty seconds later with his duffel bag. He unzipped it, and clothes spilled out. He started heaping them in the girl's lap. "Here," he said, pulling out a thick, gray wool sweater. "Take this."

"I can't take your sweater," Georgie said.

"Take it. You can mail it back to me—my mom sews my address inside everything. Take it, it's no big deal."

"Just take it," the girl said.

"I'm trying to think if I have extra boots. . . ." He shoved his clothes back into the bag. "I might have some waders in the back."

The girl rolled her eyes, and for a minute she looked just like Heather.

"Or—why don't you tell me where you're going?" he said to Georgie. "I'll run up to the house and come back with your shoes and your coat or whatever."

"No," Georgie said. She pulled the sweater on over her head. "You've done enough, thank you."

"You can't walk through the snow barefoot," he insisted.

"I'll be fine." Georgie opened the passenger door.

He opened his door, too.

"Oh for Christ's sake," the girl said. "You can wear my boots." She reached for the floor. Georgie noticed she was wearing a small engagement ring. "You can have them. I don't even like them."

"Absolutely not," Georgie said. "What if you get stuck in the snow?"

"I'll be fine," she said. "He'd carry me across the city before he let me get my feet wet."

The boy grinned at the girl. The girl rolled her eyes again and finished pulling off her boots. "Just take them," she said. "He's got it in his head that you're our Christmas mission. If we don't help you, he'll never get his wings."

Georgie took the boots. Knockoff Uggs. They looked about her size.

She kicked off her patent leather ballet flats—a birthday gift from Seth, so undoubtedly expensive. (Seth always bought Georgie clothes for Christmas, usually to replace the most pathetic item in her wardrobe. Good thing he didn't know about her bras.) "You can have these," Georgie said, "if you want them."

The girl looked dubious.

"We'll wait here for a while," the boy said. "Come back if you need help."

Right, Georgie thought, putting on the boots. *If my husband doesn't recognize me. If my in-laws don't live there anymore. If everyone I know is either dead or not born yet because I ruined time. . . .* "Thank you."

"Merry Christmas," the boy said.

"Be careful," his fiancée warned. "There might be ice."

"Thank you." Georgie swung her legs out of the truck and jumped onto the ground, catching the door as her feet slid out from beneath her.

No one had shoveled yet on Rainwood Road. Georgie vaguely remembered that there weren't any sidewalks; she and Neal had walked in the street that time they went to get pizza, their hands swinging between them.

The snow came up to the top of Georgie's calves—she had to lift her feet high to make any progress. Her ears and eyelids were freezing, but after a block of climbing, her cheeks were flushed, and she was panting.

God, she'd never even been able to imagine this much cold before.

How could people live someplace that so obviously didn't want them? All that romance about snow and seasons. . . . You shouldn't have to make a special effort not to die every time you left your house.

Everything was so quiet, Georgie's breath sounded thunderous. She looked back, but she couldn't see the red truck anymore. She couldn't see any signs of life. It was easy to imagine that every house she passed was empty.

Georgie felt tears in her eyes and tried to pretend it was because of the cold, or the fatigue, and not because of what was waiting for her—or not waiting for her—at the top of the hill.

CHAPTER 36

Neal grew up in a brick colonial house with a circular driveway. His mom was overly proud of it; the first time Georgie visited, a few months after they got engaged, his mom told her the driveway was one of the reasons they'd bought the house.

"I don't get it," Georgie said later, after she'd snuck up from the basement to Neal's room, and he'd shoved her up against the wall, under his Eagle Scout certificate. *"It's like there's a road in your front yard,"* she said. *"How is that a good thing?"* Neal had huffed a smile into her ear, then pushed the neck of her pajamas open with his nose.

Georgie walked up the drive now, wrecking the post-card perfection of the snowy front yard with her tracks.

She opened the storm door and knocked—the front door pushed open under her hand. Because in Omaha, apparently, nobody even *closed* their front doors. Georgie could hear Christmas music and people talking. She knocked again, peeking into the house.

When no one answered, she stepped cautiously into the foyer. The house smelled like apple-cinnamon Glade and pine needles. "Hello?" Georgie said, too quietly. Her voice was shaking, she'd tracked in snow—she felt like she was breaking in.

She tried it a bit louder: "Hello?"

The door from the kitchen opened partway, and the

music—"Have Yourself a Merry Little Christmas"—
swelled. Neal stepped out. Half a room away from her.

Neal.

Milk chocolate hair, pale skin, a red sweater she'd never
seen before. A look on his face she'd never seen before.
Like he didn't know her at all.

He stopped.

The kitchen door swung to and fro behind him.

"Neal," Georgie whispered.

His mouth was open. Lovely mouth, lovely matching
lips, lovely dents like handholds for Georgie's teeth.

His eyebrows were low and stern, and when he closed
his jaw, there was a tense pulse in the corners of his cheeks.

"Neal?"

Five seconds passed. Ten. Fifteen.

Neal right there. In jeans and blue socks and a strange
sweater.

Was he happy to see her? Did he even know her? *Neal?*

The door flew open behind him. "Daddy? Grandma
says—"

Alice walked into the room, and Georgie felt like
someone had just kicked her in the back of the knees.

Alice jumped. Just like kids do in the movies. For joy.
"Mommy!" She ran for Georgie.

Georgie's phone slid out of her hand as she dropped to
the floor.

"Mommy!" Alice shouted again, landing in Georgie's
arms. "Are you our Christmas present?"

Georgie held Alice so tight, it probably hurt, and covered the side of the girl's face with kisses. Georgie didn't
see the kitchen door open again, but she heard Noomi
squeal and meow, and then there were two of them in her

arms, and Georgie was falling sideways off her knees, trying to hold on.

"Missed you," she said between kisses, blinded by pink skin and yellow-brown hair. "Missed you so much."

Alice pulled back, and Georgie tightened her arm around her. But Neal was lifting Alice up and away. "Daddy," Alice said, "Mommy's here. Were you surprised?"

Neal nodded and lifted Noomi up, too, setting them both aside. Noomi meowed in protest.

Neal held his hands out to Georgie, and she took them. (So warm in her freezing fingers.) He pulled her to her feet, then let go. He still wasn't smiling, so she didn't smile either. She knew she was crying, but tried to ignore it.

"You're here," he said without moving his lips.

Georgie nodded.

Neal moved quickly, taking her face in his hands—one on her cold cheek, one under her jaw—and pulling it into is.

She felt relief blow through her like a ghost.

Neal.

Neal, Neal, Neal.

Georgie touched his shoulders, then the back of his hair—still sharp—then the tops of his ears, rubbing them between her fingers and thumbs.

She couldn't remember the last time they'd kissed like this. Maybe they'd never kissed like this. (Because neither of them had ever almost fallen off a cliff.)

"You're here," he said again.

And Georgie nodded, stepping forward just in case he was thinking of pulling away.

She was here.

And it didn't fix anything. It didn't change anything.

She still had her job. And the meeting maybe. She still

had Seth to sort out—or not. Georgie hadn't made any real decisions. . . .

But for once she'd made the right choice.

She was here.

With Neal. Whatever that meant from now on.

He kissed her like he knew exactly who she was. He kissed her like he'd been waiting for her for fifteen years.

Alice and Noomi jumped on their parents' feet and hugged their legs.

There was a dog in there somewhere, and Neal's mom talking about setting an extra place at the table.

"You're here," Neal said, and Georgie held him by the ears so he couldn't pull away.

She nodded.

BEFORE

Neal parked the Saturn in Georgie's driveway. He leaned forward and rested his head against the steering wheel. Christ, he was going to fall asleep.

That would make a great Christmas surprise—Georgie knocking on his window later, asking him if he'd move his car.

He bounced his head on the wheel.

Come on, Neal. You can do this. She might say no, but at least you can ask the question.

He tried not to think of the last time he'd asked this question, when he already knew Dawn would say yes, and he already knew he didn't want her to.

Dawn would've said yes if he'd asked her again this week; he could tell by the way she'd been looking at him.

Christ, he could see it. The wedding. The marriage. The rest of his life with Dawn. It would all be so pleasant and predictable, he didn't even have to live it to know the ending.

He couldn't predict the next ten minutes with Georgie. Not ever. But especially not today. *The next ten minutes . . .* She might say no—she'd been begging him to break up with her on the phone all week.

But all she'd done was convince him that he couldn't.

Even fifteen hundred miles away, even on the phone, Georgie was more alive than anything else in his life.

He felt his cheeks warm, just thinking about seeing her again. That's what Georgie did to him. She pulled the blood to the surface of his skin. She acted on him. Tidally. She made him feel like things were happening. Like *life* was happening—and even if he was miserable sometimes, he wasn't going to sleep through it.

He ran his hand over his pocket. The ring was still there.

It had been there since he left the nursing home; his great-aunt had pressed it into Neal's hands—*"I don't need this anymore. I never really needed it, but Harold liked to see it on my finger."* It was a family ring, she said. It should stay in the family.

Neal made up his mind as soon as he saw it.

The future was going to happen, even if he wasn't ready for it. Even if he was *never* ready for it.

At least he could make sure he was with the right person.

Wasn't that the point of life? To find someone to share it with?

And if you got that part right, how far wrong could you go? If you were standing next to the person you loved more than everything wasn't everything else just scenery?

Neal unbuckled his seat belt.

AFTER

"It doesn't look real."

"What does it look like?"

"Like a Very Special Christmas Episode."

"Hmmm . . ." Neal's mouth was warm on the back of her neck. "A two-parter," he said. "With some sort of *Christmas Carol* gimmick."

"Exactly," Georgie said. "Or *It's a Wonderful Life*."

Neal's mouth was warm and wet. "Are you cold, George Bailey?"

"No," she said.

"You're shivering."

"M'not cold."

He held her tighter anyway.

"It just falls like this?" she asked.

"Mm-hmm."

"Even when no one's watching?"

"I think so, but I guess I can't prove it."

"I can't believe I almost missed this."

"But you didn't miss it," he said.

"I almost did. . . ."

"Don't. We've already been through it."

"We haven't," she said. "Not really."

"We've been through it enough."

"But, Neal I—I just really missed you."

"Okay, but you can stop now. I'm right here. Stop missing me."

"Okay."

The snow kept falling. In slow motion.

"I missed you, too," Neal said. "I missed you telling me."

"Telling you what?"

"Everything. What you're thinking. What you're worried about. What you want for dinner."

"You missed me saying that I feel like Thimpu chicken again?"

"I didn't miss you saying *that*—I just missed you *saying*, you know?"

"Maybe," she said.

"Tell me something now, Georgie."

"What?"

"Tell me what I missed," he said, then squeezed her: "Are you sure you're not cold?"

"No."

"You're still shivering."

"I . . ." She turned her head, so she could see his face. "Petunia had her puppies."

"Yeah?"

"Yeah, my mom wasn't home, so I helped deliver them."

"Jesus, really?"

"Yeah. And . . . my sister's gay."

"Heather?"

"I only have one sister. Maybe she's not gay, but she definitely has a girlfriend."

"Huh . . ." Neal narrowed his eyes, then shook his head.

"What?"

"I . . . for a second, just—nothing, déjà vu or something."

Georgie turned completely in his arms, and took his face in her hands. There were snowflakes on his cheeks and nose and eyelashes. She wiped them away. "Neal . . ."

He wrapped his arms tight around her waist again. "Don't, Georgie. We've been through it. Enough. For now."

"It's just—one more thing."

"Okay, one more thing."

"I'm going to be better."

"We both are."

"I'm going to try harder."

"I believe you."

She held his face still and sank her eyes into his as deeply as she could. She tried to pour fire into them. "From this day forward, Neal."

Neal lowered his eyebrows, tenderly, like he was untangling something that might fall apart in his hands.

He opened his mouth to speak, but Georgie leaned in and stopped him. She couldn't help herself, his lips were right there. Neal's lips were always right there—that's one reason it was so frustrating when she felt like she wasn't allowed to kiss him.

She kissed him now. He spread his fingers out against her ribs and let her push his head back.

When Georgie jerked away, he made a noise like it hurt. "Come on, Georgie. No more 'one more thing's.'"

"No, I just remembered—I have to call my mom."

"You do?"

Georgie pushed away from him, but he didn't let go.

"I have to call her. I never told her I was leaving—I just left, I disappeared."

"So call her. Where's your phone?"

"It's dead. For good." Georgie reached her hands under Neal's coat, looking for his pockets. "Where's your phone?"

He squirmed and dropped his arms. "Inside. Dead. I was letting Alice play Tetris—sorry."

Georgie turned to go inside, stomping the snow off her borrowed Ugg boots. "It's okay. I'll just use the landline."

"Just borrow my mom's phone," he said. "She got rid of the landline."

Georgie stopped and looked back at him. "She did?"

"Yeah. Years ago. After my dad died."

"Oh . . ."

Neal pulled his jacket tighter around her. "Come on, let's go inside. You're shivering."

"I'm fine, Neal."

"Good, let's go be fine where it's warm."

"I just . . ." She reached up and touched his face again. "I almost . . ."

He whispered: "Enough, Georgie. You're here now. Be *here* now."